PRAISE FOR JANE R...
NOVEL, *THE LIKELY ...*
OF OLIVER CLOCK:

'A heart-warming, charming tale of love.'

—*Daily Mirror*

'Must Read of the Week'

—*Saturday Express*

'If you're looking for a feel-good read, this is it.'

—*Take a Break*

'A charming and quirky tale.'

—*People's Friend*

'Shy, self-deprecating Oliver is an unlikely hero, but I defy anyone not to warm instantly to his charm.'

—*My Weekly*

'Oliver is a fascinating character and this book is perfect for making you think about pushing yourself out of your comfort zone . . . It's the perfect #UpLit start to 2020.'

—*19 Degrees Magazine*

Geraldine Verne's Red Suitcase

JANE RILEY

Text copyright © 2021 by Jane Riley
All rights reserved.

Published by Lake Union Publishing, Seattle

www.apub.com

Amazon, the Amazon logo, and Lake Union Publishing are trademarks of Amazon.com, Inc., or its affiliates.

ISBN-13: 9781542017350
ISBN-10: 1542017351

Cover design and illustration by Leo Nickolls

Printed in the United States of America

To Will

To my thinking, a great librarian must have a clear head, a strong hand and, above all, a great heart. And when I look into the future, I am inclined to think that most of the men who achieve this greatness will be women.

Melvil Dewey (1851–1931)

Founder of modern librarianship and the Dewey Decimal system of classifying books

PART ONE

306.7 LOVE

Apple-Crumble Days

If much of life is about showing up, I'd say I've been doing okay. Not only have I been putting in an appearance for the past three months, I've established a routine. Now my days are reassuringly the same. Far more so, even, than they were before retiring from the library in 2012, which I always love to say was the same day Sweden won the Eurovision song contest.

Every morning, when daylight jabs at my eyelids, I flip off the covers, sit up and take hold of the suitcase I park next to the bed each night, and give it a twirl. I spin it clockwise, then anti-clockwise. Sometimes I'll hum a tune; sometimes I won't. After about two rounds – give or take – I slide into my pale-pink slippers with matted lining, slip into my blue dressing gown – that's now tea-stained and beltless – and, wheeling the case with me, go to the front door. It takes a few seconds to get outside as I have to take off the chain I've started using again and fiddle around with the key as the door lock has become sticky. I pause for a moment on the porch to survey the street – the double-fronted brick houses on the other side of the road glowing orange in the sunrise, and our now forlorn community nature strip – before walking down to the mildewed letterbox last painted in 1995, to retrieve the newspaper and return inside.

With the paper in one hand and the case in the other, I head down the hallway to the kitchen at the back of the house. I make two mugs of tea using the pre-used bags slouching in a small dish by the kettle – yesterday's bags that are perfectly useable – as well as two slices of toast with bread from the freezer. The only change to my routine at this point is whether I spread strawberry jam or honey on the toast. It depends what tickles my fancy. I'll put the radio on low to keep the fridge company, settle myself at the kitchen table and open the paper. I've always thought it important to keep up with what's going on outside the four walls of your house. I'm constantly astounded by how much happens in twenty-four hours. It's chaos out there, the world a constant flurry of action. At least inside I can guarantee the absence of bickering politicians, minimal climate change (unless I forget to turn off the oven), and no exploding bombs – apart from the occasional odourless insect-control bomb detonated when required.

After reading the news and finishing the toast and the teas, I head for the laundry basket, where I've taken to storing every newspaper in case I want to read it again, then back to the living room to see what's on the television. My preference is for game shows and music competition programs but to be honest, even if what's playing is chat-show drivel or a soap opera, I won't turn it off. It's nice to feel like you have visitors without actually having them. I might also read a book, waft around with a feather duster, have a nap, do some baking, flick through an old photo album, forget to have lunch, then remember at dinner, so have both meals at the same time, watch the telly, twirl the case and head to bed. All in all, my days are as soothing as apple crumble.

Until this morning when I couldn't get further than the porch. It's only a nine-metre walk down the front path to fetch the paper, but the thought of it made my chest tighten and my breath quicken. My heart was sprinting like a thoroughbred on race day and I hadn't even gone anywhere. It was confounding but I told myself not to be so silly and to keep going as it was the most exercise I'd been getting of late.

'Go on, old girl,' I said, as if I really was a horse.

But the vast open space of the outside world was making me feel vulnerable and, paradoxically, claustrophobic. It didn't help that only the day before the delivery boy threw not just the paper over the fence but also a jeer at my bedraggled appearance. Even though I told myself I didn't care what he thought of me, his jibe hurt. It felt like I was being judged, and that no one could possibly understand what I was going through.

'Go on,' I said again.

Yet my mouth felt like the Sahara and my palms were clammy. My body's biosphere was in such a muddle that the only thing I seemed able to control was my legs' forward motion. I hurriedly reversed and went back inside leaving the paper where it was.

'Phew,' I sighed once the front door was shut and locked. 'Phewey, Dewey and Louie,' I said, hoping a reference to Donald Duck's nephews might make me feel better. It used to work on the kids at the library.

It had minimal effect. I felt so discombobulated, I had to bake. Ever since winning the under-fifteens' cake competition at the County Women's Fair in 1960, I've enjoyed baking. Not only do I find it therapeutic, I get immense satisfaction gifting others cakes and biscuits and, of course, savouring my handiwork before it hits my thighs. Birthday cakes are a specialty. At the whiff of anyone's impending birthday – a friend, fellow librarian, the Queen – I get out the mixer and turn our small kitchen into a flurry of flour cloud and machine whirring. I've found other reasons to bake, too: World Baking Day, Cake Decorating Day, the library's thirtieth anniversary. Over the years, I've become skilful at producing light, airy mixtures topped with piped icing. If only I could have put that on a

CV! But skill with a piping bag was never a prerequisite for librarianship. You only need to know its Dewey Decimal Classification and where you might find a book on the subject in the library.

For my husband's birthdays, I always made something new. The first was a lemon cake, the next chocolate, followed by a cream sponge. Then I moved on to more elaborate concoctions like a triple-layer salted caramel apple cake, and a double-layer vanilla buttermilk cake with raspberries and orange cream-cheese frosting. The more words in the title, the bigger the challenge. As each year went by, I upped the complexity, the flavours, the layers. We both knew I'd rather have been baking for children's birthday parties but when things don't work out in life, you have to adapt, don't you? If I couldn't make a farmyard cake with chocolate finger biscuits for a fence or a green caterpillar with gumdrop eyes then I had to find alternatives.

I pulled out my favourite baking book, and after flipping between the recipes for peanut butter cookies and Louise cakes, I decided to make them both. Until I realised I didn't have enough ingredients. I closed my eyes and swallowed the lump in my throat as despondency threatened to overwhelm my resolve. But I couldn't let an absence of flour and sugar drag me further into despair; I just couldn't. I went straight to the computer to place an online grocery order and discovered the therapeutic benefits of pushing the 'submit order' button.

Toilet Paper

The next day I didn't feel any better. My heart giddied up before I'd even finished unlocking the front door. I kept my grip on the suitcase handle as I stepped over the threshold. It still didn't ease, so I remained straddled half inside, half out. I spotted yesterday's newspaper in the letterbox and the current one on the lawn next to it but knew there was no chance of getting to them. If only the delivery person had a decent bowling arm so they could lob the rolled-up paper on to the porch. I made a note to ask my dear friend Len, widower of my best friend Pam, if he could butter up the newsagent to make it happen, before stepping back inside the house and closing the door.

Later, while I was rereading an article on gnome collectors, the doorbell rang. I was excited. Who'd have guessed how much joy I would get from doing a supermarket run from the comfort of my own home? Not me. Tying up my dressing gown with a trouser belt, I went to greet the delivery man. He'd already left two boxes at the front door and was on the footpath loading a removalist's hand trolley with a stack of toilet paper. I waited in the hallway, holding on to the door as he wheeled the trolley up the path and the steps, then on to the porch.

'That's a lot of toilet rolls,' I laughed, assuming the ten ten-packs were not all for me.

'Stocking up, I presume?' he said.

I calculated the total. 'That's a hundred rolls.'

The man looked at the order form taped to one of the boxes. 'Yep.' He nodded.

'I only ordered one pack.'

'Not according to this.'

'But I don't have storage space for that many rolls.'

He shrugged. 'It's good to be prepared. Do you want me to wheel them inside for you?'

I stared at the man with his sweat-stained armpits and hairy knuckles and shook my head. It was kind of him to offer and in the past I may have accepted, but right then I did not care for a stranger in my house.

'You sure? I don't mind,' he continued. 'I could bring it all in. A quick trip to your kitchen won't hold me up.'

'I can manage,' I said. 'A bit of heavy lifting is good for the arms, isn't it?' I tried to joke.

He smiled. I would have reciprocated had I not burst into tears.

'Oh, come now,' the man said reaching an arm out. 'It's okay. Look on the bright side, you won't have to think about toilet paper for months.'

'I'm sorry,' I spluttered, rubbing a hand across my dripping nose.

'Here,' he said, ripping open the top pack and handing me a roll. 'See, now you've got enough paper to handle waterworks from both ends,' he laughed.

I nodded and cried and blew my nose.

'Are you sure you're all right?' He smiled at me, sympathetically.

'Thank you.' I sniffed, so embarrassed I could barely look at him. 'Just one of those . . .'

'Don't worry, we all get them.'

He headed back down the path and I watched his truck disappear, spitting exhaust fumes down the street, then turned to the mountain of toilet rolls I had inadvertently ordered. Three months ago, I would have seen the funny side of a woman living on her own purchasing one hundred rolls of toilet paper. But right then it seemed very unfunny. I blew my nose a few more times, shoved the toilet roll back into its pack and proceeded to take the shopping inside as quickly as I could. My heart was banging around in my chest and it was a relief to finally shut the door. Leaving the toilet paper in the hallway, I took myself back to bed. I needed to start the day all over again.

But I couldn't sleep, so when I thought enough time had elapsed and I wasn't going to start crying again, I began my daily routine by giving the suitcase a twirl. The wheels clattered on the floorboards like miniature teacups rattling on saucers and the frayed ends of the black ribbon on the handle flapped as if in protest. Even though my eyes rolled soggily in their sockets and my hips cricked, it brought a smile to my face, as it always did. You see, I know it looks as if I'm spinning an old and scuffed bright-red, four-wheel, cabin-sized case as if I've got an undiagnosed obsessive suitcase-spinning disorder; or that I am wheeling it around because I need a walking frame and am too thrifty to spend money on one. But it's neither of those.

What I'm really doing is dancing with my husband and it's the most joyous thing in the world. It was when he was alive, and it still is, even though he's passed. We dance and wobble as if we've not a care in the world. When he was alive, he never liked dancing. He thought he was no good. But I told him plenty of times that I never desired a man with Fred Astaire legs. *I love you just how you are, mistimed footwork or not. So, come on*, I'd say, *take my hands and sway your hips and let the music transport you to another place – providing it's with me, of course*. At that, he would laugh and say, 'Yes, with you, silly,' and we'd have a giggle and a shimmy, and all would be fine with the world.

Even though we've been married for more than fifty years, I love Jack Verne as much as I did on our wedding day, and I'm pretty sure he'd say the same about me. When he died three months and three days ago, I wanted to keep him close by me wherever I went, so we could still be a team, like a pair of socks or macaroni with cheese sauce. I don't mean via a photo of him tucked into my purse either, but the whole of him in an urn. In order to practically and easily transport him, I decided to use one of our small suitcases, last employed for travel four years ago so wherever I went, Jack could come too, even though I know that might make me sound bonkers. To be fair, I have been called that before. Once, Jack said I was bonkers when I cartwheeled down our hallway. We'd just moved into this house and when I was younger I was prone to spontaneous cartwheeling at times of supreme happiness. These days all I can physically manage when overjoyed is the cartwheeling of my arms. But it matters little providing Jack is by my side.

And to think, it all started at the library in which I worked fifty years ago.

595.789 Butterflies

It was 1966. I was twenty-one and he, twenty-three. I can remember it like you might recall the best meal you've ever eaten, where every sense feels as alert and alive as it was when it happened. Jack turned up an hour before closing at seven o'clock in a brown suit, rust-coloured striped tie and pocket handkerchief. He was slim but not skinny, tall but not much taller than me, with a hair quiff I wanted to ruffle. I was going through the book-returns bin when he approached and said, 'Butterflies,' as if it was a code word for something else I should have known about, rather than a question as to where he might find information on them in the library. He smelled like cloves and his voice was the soft patter of raindrops.

I leant towards him and said, 'Five ninety,' in a similarly secretive way.

He nodded, tipped his quiff and walked to the aisle classified *590 Animals* in search of books on butterflies. Half an hour later he returned with three, none of which had been on loan for months. Who was this man who wanted books on a topic few others did? I was intrigued. I stamped his books and slipped the return-dated docket inside the hardback on African butterflies.

'Thank you,' he said and left as quietly as he had arrived.

After that, he appeared at the library at the same time for the next four Thursdays. Every time, he tipped his quiff and said only,

'Five nine five point seven eight nine,' the precise Dewey Decimal Classification number for butterflies, and headed to the appropriate aisle. On the sixth Thursday, I discovered 'butterfly man' had a name.

'Jack,' he said, introducing himself. 'I don't suppose you'd be free for a light supper after closing tonight?'

I blushed and looked away. I hadn't been expecting an invitation for a date. I hadn't been looking for a date at all. I'd been so put off men after *the incident* and subsequent break-up from my previous boyfriend that I had been considering the benefits of remaining a spinster like my colleague Margaret, who at thirty-eight didn't seem to care about societal expectations. And why not? We were part of an expanding, modernising post-war boom that enabled us to be financially independent. We didn't need a man. Yet, unlike Margaret, I still found myself wanting one. And the man who stood before me was beguiling with his quiet confidence, politeness and well-dressedness.

'I suppose I might be,' I said when my cheeks had dulled to a dusky rose.

'Wonderful.' He nodded. 'I'll come back in an hour.'

I sensed Margaret watching me watching him leave.

'He seems nice,' she said, sidling over to me.

'He does,' I replied.

'Well, don't lead him on. You know what men are like,' she whispered in her authoritative but hushed library voice.

I laughed and said, 'No, Mum.'

That night Jack spun a cocoon around me with his talk of exotic butterflies and desire for travel. He may have worked in a dimly lit office as an accountant with a disposition for ledgers and numbers, but his dreams lay in the wilds of unknown worlds. He spoke as if he was an early explorer setting sail to faraway lands in search of flora and fauna, even though he had only recently moved a few miles down the road and lived in a flat with four chairs, one table and two bachelor friends. He told me how his fascination with butterflies began when he was a child and he first saw the rows and rows of centuries-old, velvet-winged butterflies from places he had never heard of at the Natural History Museum.

'You can't imagine how I felt seeing them, Geraldine. They were magical, other-worldly with their colours and patterns, and made me wonder at the adventures the insects and their collectors must have been on,' he said, his eyes momentarily elsewhere. 'When I got a butterfly net for my seventh birthday, it felt as if I could go on my own exploits and run free with this flimsy framed net, pretending I was far more important than a small boy in a field. Then, when my father gave me his empty cigar boxes for storing the butterflies I had caught, my collecting really began. It made me want to one day explore new worlds and find living, exotic butterflies in their natural habitat.'

I nodded and smiled, and he lured me in with his cinnamon eyes and ignited a sense of adventure in me that the library books I was surrounded by were unable to do. When he kissed my hand goodbye, I went home that night wondering whether maybe, just maybe, love was lingering around the corner.

Our Friend Len Goodman

I left the bedroom and wheeled Jack to the living room. Sitting on the sofa, I turned on the television. The glossy face of an info-mercial presenter was giving the morning show host a Thermomix demonstration. Despite my disinterest in expensive kitchen gadgets and the woman's disturbing hairstyle that resembled a ball of yellow knitting yarn, I watched for a minute or two until I fancied another round of tea and toast and a read of last weekend's newspaper. That's when the phone rang. I froze, the hand holding the corner of the paper hovering in the air and my teacup poised centimetres from my mouth. It was like playing musical statues with children at the library.

'Don't answer,' I told Jack, which meant I would have been out had we really been playing.

I strained to see the caller's number; it was Len. I relaxed. I didn't mind picking up the phone for him, providing he didn't pressure me to go out yet again.

'Hey, Geri, what's happening?' he said. He was always lively, Len. Like a ball that never lost its bounce.

'Oh, you know. This and that,' I replied. 'Man torches family house,' I read. 'Media profits from fake news—'

'I mean with you,' he interrupted. 'How are you?'

'There's unlimited rides for the over-sixties at Luna Park,' I continued, spotting an ad.

'Geri . . .'

'I thought you liked that sort of thing.' I was trying to sound upbeat because Len was an upbeat kind of a man.

'Are you suggesting we go together?' He sounded keen. I knew he would be. But he'd have to find someone else to go with. His girlfriend, Crystal, would have been my pick.

'I can't, Len,' I muttered.

I heard him sigh. 'I thought you could join us down at the club tonight. You don't need to stay for bingo. Just a quick bite with Crystal and me before the place fills up, then we'd drop you home. It'd be an hour or two, tops.'

I stared out the window above the sink that overlooked the back garden and realised I couldn't see out for all the grime. I wiped it with the dishcloth but only sullied it more. I searched under the sink for window cleaner.

'Geri?'

'That sounds a lovely idea, Len . . .' I squirted liquid on to the pane.

'Great!'

'But not tonight.'

He sighed again. It wasn't as loud, but still. 'The thing is, I'm worried about you, Geri. I want to help. We all want to help.'

'I appreciate it, Len. I really do.'

'It's small steps, Geri.'

I rubbed the glass with a tea towel, yet the stains were stubborn and I suspected there were more on the outside than in. I squirted again and scrubbed.

'Look, you know I know what it's like,' he continued. 'When Pam died . . .' He paused and I wished he hadn't made me think of my oldest, dearest friend's death five years ago. It was bad enough thinking of Jack's and how I used to want to leave the house but no longer did. How the less I ventured outside, the higher my rate of contentment. I rested a hand on the bench and clenched my eyes shut.

Len started up again. 'It's tough, Geri. No one's saying it isn't. But it does help to get out and about every now and then. To get some fresh air, have some company . . .'

I nodded, even though he couldn't see me.

'I know! How about I come by at five?' he suggested eagerly.

I didn't answer. Len may have thought I was nodding again, even though I wasn't. He had a good heart, but I didn't want to be coerced into doing something I didn't feel comfortable with. I knew having a cheap meal at the club with friends wasn't a big deal. I'd done it many times before, yet something was stopping me. Like an invisible laser beam was running around my house keeping me inside.

'What do you say?'

'I don't think I'll be very good company,' I mumbled.

'Don't be silly, you're great company. Anyway, no one expects you to be the life of the party all the time. It'd be nice to have your presence. That's all we're saying.'

I chewed a nail.

'Have a think about it and I'll drop by later.'

I stared at the receiver. My eyes welled up. One receiver became three. I put it down and went over to Jack. I stroked his head and tried to pull myself together.

'Come on, Jackie-boy, let's go and see if that Thermomix woman has finally left the studio.'

Ruby and Benny

Thankfully she had. So Jack and I watched the news, took note of the day's weather, tomorrow's weather and the forecast for the following week, regardless of whether we would be going out or not. Heavy rain could alert you to a leak in the roof, wind could knock over a rangy pot plant sitting unevenly on its feet or a sun-filled sky could wilt the flowers.

'Good news, Jack. We won't need an umbrella today. Only sunscreen.'

I changed channels when the ads came on because no one wants to be shouted at in the comfort of their own home. I kept it on a soap opera but cut the sound. Back when Jack was feeling poorly, we sometimes muted a television drama and made up the script. We put on silly voices and managed, quite successfully I think, to turn a daytime soap opera into a satire about real estate. But it's not much fun doing it on your own.

Eventually, I got off the couch, peeled back the curtains and looked out the front window. There was activity on the footpath across the road – activity I'd not seen before. The two children from the house across the road had set up a lolly-pink wooden table with a tray of muffins, a jug of lemonade and plastic cups. The boy, whom I guessed was about six, sat behind it grinning and holding a sign that said: 'Glass of lemonade = $1, chocolate muffin = $2'. The girl, who looked about nine, was trying to wave down cars and passers-by. A sticky lump formed in my throat, as if I'd swallowed chewing gum and it had got stuck, which was a silly analogy because I don't even like chewing gum. Nevertheless, there it was and something about the lump made me want to hurry over to them, bundle them against my bosom, tell them how wonderful they were, and join them in the enthusiastic selling of their wares. I let the curtain fall and went to unlock the front door. I opened it just enough to hear what the girl was calling out.

'Muffins for two dollars, homemade lemonade for one,' she sang, pigtails sweeping her shoulders, a frilled skirt tickling her knees.

I wondered what the muffins were like. Had they bought cheap ones from the supermarket or made them themselves? If the latter, had they used good quality chocolate? I opened the door a little wider. As I peered out, I felt like a turtle stretching its head out from its shell as if wishing to escape its own home.

'Muffins for two dollars, homemade lemonade for one,' the girl repeated.

'Lemonade for one,' chimed in the boy.

A postie rode past on his bike, stopped, reversed and pulled over next to the table.

'Lemonade, eh?' he said.

The boy jumped up from his seat. 'Do you want one?' He was still grinning. Poor kid was going to have very sore cheeks by the end of the day.

'Sure, why not? It's hot today.'

'I'll do it, Benny,' his sister said, rushing over to pour the man a glass.

He drank it on the spot, reached into his pocket and handed over a coin. 'Thanks kids,' he said and rode off.

The girl high-fived her brother and for a few seconds, joy swelled in their little hearts at their first sale of the day.

I desperately wanted to go over to them, to pretend they were the children I never had, or perhaps the grandchildren I could have had. Or even the children who might have taken part in Jack's free, monthly 'Butterfly Hour' at the library had he still been around to host them. I stayed behind the threshold and waved. 'Yoo-hoo,' I called out.

They didn't hear. I tried again.

The girl shaded her eyes with a hand and looked in my direction. I waved frantically and beckoned them over. The girl glanced at her brother, who shrugged.

'I don't bite,' I shouted.

The girl gestured for the boy to wait, picked up a muffin and paper napkin and went to cross the road. My heart leapt to attention as it always did when I saw little children crossing roads on their own. 'Watch for cars,' I warned.

The girl looked once both ways, then ran. She bounded up my path and up the steps to the porch so quickly I thought she was going to keep running into the house and out the other end. She braked, let out a few hot breaths and shoved the muffin sitting in the napkin at me.

'Do you want one?' she asked.

I peered at the muffin.

'It won't bite,' she said, fiddling with a pigtail.

I smiled and let her drop the cake into my hand. I felt its weight in my palm. It was heavy for a muffin, solid like an avocado and there were white tufts of flour throughout. I looked at the girl and smiled again.

'What's your name?' I asked.

'Ruby. My brother's Ben.' She turned and waved at him.

17

I waved, too, at the fluff of hair and two eyes smiling at us from behind the table.

'Two dollars, did you say?' I asked.

Ruby nodded.

'All right, wait there.' I put up a hand as I've seen people do to dogs when they want them to stay put and went inside to the coin jar on the chest of drawers in our bedroom. I also stopped by the hall table to look in one of the drawers before returning to Ruby. I gave her four dollars and a tube of sunscreen.

'It's going to be sunny all day today,' I told her. 'Your mother won't be happy if you end up as pink as your table out there. You should also be wearing hats. Oh, and you can keep the change.'

Ruby's eyebrows lifted in delight. 'Thank you, Mrs . . .'

'Verne,' I said.

The girl skipped back down the stairs and across the road to where her brother sat waiting for her. She showed him the coins in her hand and his face lit up like a struck match. I swallowed the pesky ball of phlegmy gum that had returned, closed the front door, locked it and took the muffin to Jack.

'I think we know what it's going to be like, don't we?' I said.

I bit into it and chewed. It was, as I suspected, floury and over-mixed but it didn't matter because it was infused with youthful enthusiasm.

'I think we'll give the bakers ten out of ten and the muffin six. But you know what? It's given me an idea.'

306.7 Social Sciences: Love

Once, Jack saved my life. That was when I discovered the true depth of his love for me. I saw it in his eyes, where an enormous amount of matter was packed into a very small area. His heart had squeezed out love, like it was at the end of a toothpaste tube, straight up his optic nerves, through the retinas and into the corneas of his lovely brown eyes. That's when I saw his fear of losing me, his willing me to be all right, the power of his inner strength, the depth of his love.

We were driving in the country on a road so straight it looked like a triangle piercing the horizon. I was behind the wheel and even though we were supposed to be taking turns, Jack had fallen asleep. It took his butterfly recording notebook to slide off his thigh and hit the passenger door for him to wake.

'How long was I asleep?' he asked.

'Hours,' I laughed.

'Oh gosh, I should be driving. Let me take over.'

'It's fine,' I said, patting his leg.

'I just had an amazing dream, Geri. We won the jackpot and you were laughing about the pun. How it was my pot of gold.' He chuckled.

As I flung my head back with laughter, a bird hit the windscreen. There was an explosion of feathers, wings and bird brain.

The car swerved. One minute my hands were on the steering wheel, the next they weren't. One minute my foot was on the accelerator, the next it wasn't. My limbs touched nothing. They were suspended in the air as if we'd lost gravity. Time slowed. Then it sped. A horn boomed. The car filled with panic, began drowning in fright. Through the limbs of the splattered bird, a truck's over-sized silver radiator glinted in the sun. It was travelling at speed towards us. I saw it but could do nothing.

'I've got it,' Jack shouted. He grabbed the steering wheel and spun it away from me. I turned to look at him, my mouth wide in horror. *Help, Jack*, I was saying without saying a word. He caught my eye and his eyes spoke: *I've got this, Geri, I've got it.* He held my gaze for a split second and that's when I saw the love. That's when I disappeared into his pupils and saw how far the love went. It was deep and endless. Did I know, at that moment, we were going to be all right? I couldn't say. But what I did know was that right then I felt saved. I felt whole. I felt loved. And that whatever was going to happen next would not change a thing.

Jack's eyes returned to the steering wheel, his jaw clenched, the veins in his arms thick like rope. I leant back, stiff with fear, and watched him take control. He spun the car to the left. The tyres screamed. The truck thundered past in a vibration of wind, speed and tooting. He spun the car to the right.

'Okay, Geri. Foot on the brake but not too hard. That's it. Slow, slow . . . okay, fine.'

We juddered to a stop, half on the road and half off. Whiplash jolted our necks. The bird slid off the bonnet, leaving a glistening smear of bloody residue on the glass. We looked at each other.

'That was close,' Jack said.

I nodded, my mouth open, dry.

'Are you okay?'

I nodded again. Then he hugged me and we held each other and held each other and held each other . . . Until a knock on my window broke our seal.

'Everything all right?' A man with hair like fern fronds had his face up against the glass.

We smiled and nodded and gave him a thumbs up. He returned the gesture and thumped the car roof before going back to his van.

Love: it can be found in section 306.7 under Social Sciences.

It can also be discovered deep in the aisle of my heart.

Staying In

I spent the early part of the afternoon flicking through recipe books until I remembered I had planned to make Louise cakes. I started on the shortbread base and was about to put it in the oven when there was a knock on the door. More pestering from the outside world! I decided to ignore it until there was a second knock followed by the doorbell, as if it was the start of a tune I hadn't heard before. I sighed. It was probably Len.

'Coming,' I called, even though he wouldn't have heard.

Wheeling the suitcase with me, I opened the front door as far as the security chain would allow. Len looked summery in a sun dress and orthotic sandals. I was taken aback as Len wasn't in the habit of wearing dresses and sandals. I had to check again. My heart sank.

'Hello, I'm from Meals on Wheels,' said the woman who wasn't Len. 'Can you open the door a little more?'

'No.'

'Okay, well, we're doing a pamphlet drop about our services in your area. You might be interested. For yourself or for someone else.'

A leaflet appeared through the opening. The expectation was that I would take it, but I didn't see the point. I could cook perfectly well and didn't need to pay for external help. The paper waggled at me, then dropped to the ground.

'It's a council initiative,' the woman continued. 'They, and we, want to reach out to let people know what services are available to them in the community. And the best thing? It's government-subsidised.'

The woman paused as if expecting me to jump at the idea. 'Is that it?' I asked.

'Um . . .'

'Super. Well, have a nice day,' I said and shut the door.

'Please have a read and pass it on to others,' the woman called out as if I hadn't just slammed the door in her face. I felt sorry for her. No one wants to be a door-to-door salesperson.

I picked up the leaflet, threw a quick glance at the photo of a cheery man receiving a meal from an equally cheery woman, noted their fake smiles and the unnecessary sexism and screwed it up. I watched her leave through the gap in the curtains of the living-room window. Ruby and Benny were still at their stall. Benny looked hot and bored and Ruby was turning her pigtails into plaits. I let the curtain fall back and returned to the kitchen with Jack.

I put the biscuit base in the oven and flicked on the kettle. Waiting for it to boil, I started decanting the new packets of coconut and flour into Tupperware containers. That was when I spotted a dusty unopened bottle of Baileys at the back of the pantry. I'd forgotten it was there.

'That'll help take the edge off things, won't it, Jack?'

I knew he'd agree and would want one with me. I made two teas and threw in a splash of liqueur. It worked a treat, despite making me feel light-headed on account of missing lunch, but it made the prepping of the coconut meringue topping even more enjoyable. Then the doorbell started up again like we were in a belfry. I took a swig of Baileys from the bottle and went to the living room to peek around the curtain. This time it was definitely Len. I considered my options, which weren't extensive. If I didn't answer, I knew he would search for me, looking in all the windows, worried something might have happened to me. If I did answer, I'd have to disappoint him by telling him I wasn't going out. Both were unsatisfactory on multiple counts, primarily the distress they would cause us. I knew I'd have to settle on option two, because I think I was better at handling stress than Len and knew the Baileys would be waiting for me when it was over.

I opened the front door as far as the security chain would allow.

'Oh, hi, Geri. Is that all I get? A fifteen-centimetre slot?'

'Yes, don't be greedy,' I said, aiming for a light-hearted tone even though I slurred the 'yes'.

'Come on, Geri . . .'

He was a plaster cast of polyester in a white jacket with vanilla trousers. I wasn't sure if it suited him or not. They may have complemented his olive skin but they made his eyes appear to bulge.

Even so, I said jovially, 'You're looking sharp, Len. Like a block of Parmesan cheese.' He didn't react. I'd have thought a compliment would have cheered him up.

'Are you still in your pyjamas?'

'Nightdress. Jack bought it for me,' I added, looking down at my white cotton nightie sprinkled with small pink flowers, and summer dressing gown, which sometime during the day had lost the trouser belt that had tied it up.

'It's four in the afternoon.'

I shrugged. He frowned.

'Can I come in?'

'Not today.'

'Why not?'

'I'm busy.'

'Not even for a quick cuppa?'

I tried to think of something to say that would make him feel better without regurgitating the cliché 'it's not you, it's me'.

'I'm not going to force you to come out with us, you know.' He paused. I didn't respond. 'It's just . . . well . . . you're scaring me.'

I was? I know my interest in grooming had diminished and my possum-coloured hair was now so frizzy and wild I'd have gotten rid of the hairbrush altogether if it wasn't also useful as a back scratcher. But scary?

'I don't want to lose you, Geri.'

'I don't want to lose you, either,' I replied, extending a hand through the door opening.

'You know Jack wouldn't want to see you like this,' he whispered, squeezing my hand.

I wanted to say, Jack sees me like this every day and doesn't seem bothered. *You don't care, do you, Jackie-boy?* I looked around for him but realised I'd left him in the kitchen. I squeezed Len's hand instead.

'Look, you don't have to come out tonight,' Len continued. 'But think about it. For another time.'

My palms started to sweat and my throat tightened. Maybe I was becoming allergic to the mere thought of going out. I retracted my hand.

'Geoff and Linda, and Joyce and Barry have been asking after you, too. They've tried visiting and calling but you don't answer.'

'Fifty-eight make them wait,' I quipped, remembering some bingo lingo.

'You see, I know you've been missing bingo. Hey, how about we resurrect our weekly curry nights? I really enjoyed those. I could come to you and maybe Crystal, as well, if you didn't mind. We could even throw in a game of charades.'

I gritted my teeth to stop the tears coming. The curry nights had been fun. They were a Len suggestion after Jack got sick. I can't remember why they stopped. Probably when Len's social life took off after he joined a dating site.

'Geri?'

'Yes?' A tear trickled down my cheek.

'I'm not suggesting we start the curry nights tonight,' he said softly. 'It's an idea, that's all.'

'Uh huh,' I mumbled as more tears fell. I had to close the door so he wouldn't see. I did it gently, though. I didn't want him to think I was being rude.

'Geri?'

I didn't say anything. I wanted him to go, yet I didn't want him to go.

'I know you're still finding it tough . . .' He sounded close to the door, like his cheek was pressed against the wood. 'Geri?'

'Sorry, Len,' I whispered.

'Pardon? I can't hear you.'

I bit my lip and leant against the door. He called my name again, but I didn't respond. Finally, I heard his footsteps retreating down the steps to the path. I stepped away from the door and walked as fast as I could back to my husband in the kitchen, taking care not to trip over all the toilet paper. The thing was, when it was only Jack and me in the house, it felt like he was still with me, but in the presence of others, it was disturbingly clear that he was very much gone.

Louise Cakes

I managed to rescue the biscuit base from the oven before it charred and then start on the rest of the mixture – spreading a layer of jam over the base and making the meringue topping. After putting the completed Louise cakes back into the oven, I returned to the front of the house to check whether Ruby and Benny were still at their stall. They weren't. But it wasn't a bother as the cakes would need cooling before they could be sliced and stored. I spent the evening sipping Baileys neat and shoving toilet rolls in spare cupboards. When I got to the last eight rolls, I had to resort to the chest of drawers in our bedroom. Although I'd not yet disposed of any of Jack's clothes, I thought I could easily move his jumpers out of the bottom drawer to the shelf at the top of the wardrobe. What I wasn't expecting was a sheet of champagne-cream notepaper to slip out like a falling feather from between two of his jumpers. It was handwritten in Jack's distinctive style and addressed to me.

> *Darling Geri-pie,*
> *I've no idea when you'll find this – whether a week after I've gone or months later – but it doesn't matter. What matters is that you find it at all. Now that you have, let the fun begin! I know what you're thinking: what is he on about, the silly man? But you know*

me, I can't pass over an opportunity for a cryptic conundrum. It's my last chance, after all. I also don't want you feeling sad, even though I'm sure you will be. I thought a little game might help take your mind off things. So without further ado, let's get started. Below is a clue which will lead you to the next clue and the next. Solve them all and, well . . . you'll see!

Clue Number One: 'Naturalist author doctors a line of heart' (4, 2, 5).

All my love, Jackie-boy xx

I closed my eyes and pressed the letter to my chest as if it were possible to be recharged by words on a page. Tears spluttered out of me like a geyser and for the second time that week I made use of my excess toilet paper to blow my nose. I read the note again but felt in such a muddle of happy-sadness that I couldn't even begin to solve the clue. I didn't even care to. It was enough to know that not only had Jack thought to invent a game but had also made it happen during his last days. His love filled me up and warmed my heart far better than the shepherd's pie freezer-meal I had for dinner would ever do.

I went to bed early, Jack's words swirling dreamily around my mind. I must have slept in because when I awoke, I heard Ruby shouting, 'Glass of lemonade, one dollar. Chocolate muffin, two dollars.' I looked out the window. There they were again, the darlings. Ruby's hair was still in plaits and Benny now wore a cap. The lemonade jug was full and sat next to what looked like the chocolate muffins from the day before. I slipped on my dressing gown, grabbed Jack and hurried to the kitchen. I filled a round pictorial biscuit tin I've had for about forty years with the Louise cakes and went to the front door.

'Ruby,' I called out. 'Hello, Ruby . . .'

A van trundled past, obscuring my view and drowning me out. After they finished serving a dog walker, I tried again, using my loudest voice. Ruby shaded her eyes and looked in my direction. I beckoned her over. She grabbed a muffin and ran over with as much enthusiasm as she had the last time.

'Do you want another muffin?' she asked excitedly.

'Not really,' I said. 'I have a proposition for you.'

'What's that?'

'Would you like something new to sell?' I lifted the lid and showed her the contents of the tin. 'They're Louise cakes. Have you had them before?'

She shook her head.

'They're very yummy. A mix of shortbread, jam and meringue. I thought your customers might like to try them. I've made a sign, too, so people in passing cars will know what they are.'

She chewed a lip. 'Mum says we're not allowed to take anything from strangers.'

'Am I a stranger? Strange, maybe, but . . .' I gave a smile.

Ruby looked at me as if working out just how crazy I was. I realised I should have brushed my hair and tied up my dressing gown.

'Do you want money for them?' she asked.

'Oh no, not all,' I laughed. 'They're a gift for you to sell. Or you can eat them all yourselves if you really want. I won't tell your mother.'

She looked a little shocked at my last comment.

'Well, anyway, *I'm* not going to eat them and my husband needs to lose weight so you may as well take them.' I don't know why I made up the last bit or even mentioned Jack at all.

'I didn't think you had a husband anymore,' Ruby said.

I stared at her. I think my mouth fell open in shock.

'What are they called again?' she asked peering in the tin.

'Louise cakes. Would you like them?'

'Thanks, Mrs Verne.'

I'd forgotten how children could brighten your day and since I'd recently read that boredom could be as dangerous as a life-threatening illness, it gave me an idea to jazz up my routine. I moved a chair to the front living-room window and parked Jack next to me so we could watch the children and find out if my baking would help lift sales. Ruby pushed their muffins to one side and placed my tin on its lid in the middle of the table. She wedged the sign I'd written under the lemonade jug and folded it down so it faced the road. Had I been with them, I would have told her that was a silly idea because as soon as they sold some lemonade, they'd have to lift the jug and the sign might fly away.

'Oh well, they'll learn, won't they, Jack?' I said and patted the case to make sure my husband wasn't feeling left out.

As we waited for a customer to come along, Benny rearranged the plastic cups and Ruby publicised their wares to anyone who passed. She was so loud, I could hear her through the window.

'Loo-wheeeze cakes,' she cried. 'Two dollars for Loo-wheeeze cakes.'

Two red-faced joggers carrying takeaway coffees paused at the table. Ruby, chatting non-stop, angled the tin in their direction and Benny, with more energy than a lithium battery, burst into a breakdance. The couple laughed and the man pulled out some money from his shorts pocket. They bought two Louise cakes and two glasses of lemonade and the sign didn't fly away. Then Roberta, who lived a few doors down and worked in cabin crew for the national airline, wandered over. I didn't know her but wished I did as I always thought it would be nice to have a friend who might supply you with free hotel shower caps and airline eye masks. She bought three Louise cakes. After that, a man with hair the colour of my stainless-steel kettle peeled out of a car, and a woman with a toddler in a pushchair approached the stall. The children made two more Louise cake sales. I clapped and said to Jack, 'This is better than daytime television, isn't it?'

It made me wonder if I should make something more for them. The peanut butter cookies, perhaps? As I pondered the options, sales activity came to a halt. Benny started drawing hopscotch squares with yellow chalk on the pavement and Ruby looked over in my direction. I waved but she couldn't see me. I think my eyes closed because sometime later I woke to find nails tapping the glass and a face peering at me through the window. I screamed. I couldn't help it; I thought I was having an Alfred Hitchcock-inspired nightmare, even though it was only Sue from number twenty-eight.

'Geri, it's only me!' she laughed, her straight hair now so long she reminded me of a greying Afghan hound.

I laughed and gave her a thumbs up.

'I bumped into Len the other day,' she said loudly, not realising I didn't have double-glazing. 'Isn't he a sweetheart? We got talking about you and I thought I must drop by to see if you're okay.'

Sue – now divorced – had always fancied Len but had yet to accept that Len didn't fancy her.

'I'm okay, thanks, Sue,' I shouted back.

'Do you need any help? Groceries? Gardening?'

She was quite close to the window now and I thought it would be funny to press my nose to the glass and pull a face, until Jack told me off for thinking such a thing. Even though I've naughtily given her two nicknames – Mao Sue Tung and Mussuelini – it's not because I dislike her. It's just that she has a tendency to be interfering,

31

and when you're a private person as I am, the two tend to clash. After her marriage break-up a few years ago, she got obsessed with knitting, primarily of cacti in pots with pins for prickles, which she loved gifting to others for no explicable reason.

'All good, thanks, Sue.'

'What about some company?'

'If you don't mind chatting behind the glass . . .'

'Not at all.'

'You'll have to stand, though. We had a cane seater on the porch once . . .' I said, thinking of the three-seater Jack and I used to perch on while we watched the world go by on summer evenings. Two days after Jack's death, I asked the Kanesh boys next door to remove it for me because I didn't care to sit on it anymore. I told them they could keep it for their games room or leave it on the footpath for someone else to take away.

'Yes, I remember.' Sue nodded. 'You've got such a good view of the street from this spot. You should get something else to sit on.'

'I'm happy here for now,' I said.

She looked at me for a minute as if about to say something I feared would make me cry. But thankfully, she changed her mind and said instead, 'Actually, I wanted to tell you about my new initiative. I've decided to start a community Neighbourhood Watch Program and I'm visiting everyone in the area to see who wants to be involved. You see, there's been a spate of burglaries in the area. At one hundred Brown Street, thirty-two Dixon Avenue, sixty-six Renegade Parade, four Fern Road. So far, I've got the Kaneshes next door to you, the couple who live next to me and my friend Bev in Dixon Avenue. Once I've got enough interest, I'll register the group and we can have our first meeting to discuss crime prevention strategies and home security. It's a win–win for all concerned. Apart from the burglars, of course.' She chortled. 'I'd love you to be at the meeting but if not, you must have a sticker for your front door telling burglars you're part of the scheme.' She reached into her bag and pulled out a sheet of stickers. She peeled one off and stuck it on to the window, before wedging the sheet into the window frame. 'You can put them anywhere you like!' she trilled.

'What about a brooch?'

'Ooh, yes, that would be a good idea, wouldn't it?'

'Actually, I don't think it would . . .' I muttered but Sue had started talking again.

'The other thing I wanted to mention was home security. You may already have systems in place . . .'

Two locks on the front door, thank you, Sue. I stifled a yawn.

'Well, thanks for the chat. You've got my number in case of emergency, haven't you? Perhaps I'll write it on here, just in case,' she added, pulling a leaflet from her bag.

I watched her scribble her telephone number and then head down the path. She waved and blew kisses at the gate. I raised a hand and watched her disappear. I waited by the window a little longer, hoping for more entertainment, but Ruby and Benny had packed up. The only evidence of their presence was the chalky lemon hopscotch design on the pavement and my sign in the gutter.

914.4 France

Jack's passion for butterflies proved catching and I couldn't help but get hooked on them, too. I loved being outdoors as much as he did, and the anticipation of wondering what we'd discover. In the early days, whenever we took a weekend break or went camping, we'd see how many butterflies we could spot. Then, when we could afford it, we'd go on an overseas holiday and do the same. It wasn't until Jack retired that we started going on specialty butterfly-spotting tours – usually overseas – with other hobby lepidopterists. Sometimes we'd go as often as twice a year and tag on a general sightseeing trip at either end. Our last such holiday was four years ago on an organised butterfly-spotting trip in the eastern French Pyrenees, bordering Spain and Andorra. It was an all-inclusive week involving gentle walks across meadows and mountain terrain in a small group with an expert lepidopterist and accommodation in a village hotel at the foothills of Mount Canigou. It was also the last time we used our two red suitcases.

When we decided to go, Jack announced he was going to buy an extra lottery ticket on top of his usual weekly purchase, hoping that a win could help fund the trip.

'Extra mosquito repellent would be more useful.' I laughed, even though I was being serious.

'I wouldn't mock if I were you,' Jack said. 'You might be pleasantly surprised.'

'But we're going whether you win or not, aren't we?'

'Of course. But how much sweeter would it be if the trip ended up being free?' Jack grinned. The thrill of a bargain excited him as much as the thought of sighting more than seventy-five spring butterflies in the mountains of France.

'After all these years, I still don't understand how an accountant could have such disregard for the inherent false economy of weekly lottery ticket purchasing,' I said, which I had done before, even though it didn't make any difference.

'I suppose it's just one of life's little mysteries,' he chuckled.

As it turned out I *was* surprised. But only mildly, for the first ticket won nothing and the second only enough for a cappuccino and croissant for us to share. Contrary to what Jack had hoped, our retirement savings would not be eased by a windfall. Nevertheless, Jack was ecstatic. He skipped around our kitchen table in delight, waving the ticket as if it were dripping in gold. So the trip started with a lottery-winning bang and proved to be a good omen for the rest of it.

By the end of the week, we had sighted sixty-one butterflies including the Clouded Apollo, False Heath Fritillary and Olive Skipper, and through the binoculars, the tip of the rare and beautiful Violet Copper as it darted to a distant flower. Our red suitcases returned home with a near-empty bottle of mosquito spray in mine and, in Jack's, a camera film loaded with exquisite European butterflies, mountain-rimmed meadows and the occasional shot of us.

The Butterfly Room

The following morning, I returned to my spot by the window. The children weren't there yet. Perhaps they'd overslept. Or maybe they were baking. Jack and I waited for a bit but then I got bored so decided to make them a batch of jam drops. Except there was no jam left. They would have to be just 'drops'.

Two hours later, they still hadn't set up shop. It was disappointing and I felt strangely empty inside. I made a Baileys on ice with a dash of milk to fill the hole and wandered back to the living room. I turned on the television but couldn't concentrate. I got up to blow dust off my metre-high tinsel Christmas tree on the coffee table that had long ago lost its sparkle. I loved that tree, having originally bought it after feeling sorry for fir trees being cut down for short-term festive use. At the time, I told Jack we should be more environmentally friendly and that the made-in-China artificial tree could be used for all sorts of occasions, not just Christmas. I made it a permanent fixture in the living room and kept small boxes of decorations in the hall cupboard, categorised according to seasons and festivities: Easter, Halloween, spring, summer, winter, autumn. For the off-seasons, I had a selection of butterflies that looked pretty when back-lit at night by the streetlights, providing we didn't close the curtains. Unsurprisingly, they were Jack's favourite decorations. When he died, I stopped decorating it. Instead of wearing black to honour his passing, I plucked the tree of all ornamentation and it has been bare ever since. Even though it looks better jazzed up, I was yet to feel festive. I gave another blow for good measure and adjusted some of the branches, which were kinked like arthritic fingers.

Still feeling restless, I finished the Baileys and decided to go to the one room in the house that usually never failed to please: our butterfly room. When we first bought the house, we'd envisaged it as a child's bedroom. But when we ended up childless, it officially became the Butterfly Room. Under the window is a workbench that was originally a large desk bought in an office clear-out thirty-five years ago. To its left, a vintage library-card catalogue set of drawers I saved from the library, which houses tools – tracing paper, mounting needles, tweezers and spreading boards – as well as the works-in-progress of butterflies in various stages of the preserving process. Hanging on the sky-blue walls are black display cases featuring butterflies we have either collected or caught, which Jack prepared and mounted with such care you would be forgiven for thinking they were still alive.

Jack's interest in butterflies was such that he knew everything about every butterfly we had – their Latin, common and zoological names, their origin, habitat, habits, physical characteristics and peculiarities. And because he did, so did I. I could rattle off titbits of info with little prompting. For instance, on one wall, middle case, second in on the third row was the Blue Tiger butterfly, *Tirumala hamata*, which I had found teetering on a cluster of purple flowers during a day trip up the coast with a picnic lunch of ham sandwiches and homemade flapjacks. On the case nearest the door, top row in the middle, was the orange and black Lurcher butterfly, *Yoma sabina*, that likes to pretend it is a dead leaf. And on the left wall, closest to the window on the fourth row, was the Diadem, *Hypolimnas misippus*, which Jack had spotted on a red hibiscus flower on one of our first dates on 14 March 1966, a year to the day that my life turned topsy-turvy. The butterflies became markers for events in our lives, each one bullet-pointing a particular moment in time.

Sometimes I'd come in here, sit in the swivel chair and reminisce. It's occasionally painful, but more often comforting. Either way, after Jack died, I cleaned it fastidiously every week on a Friday morning. I'd work my way around the room, dusting, polishing, glass-cleaning until the place had the gold-leaf lustre of a Common Crow butterfly's chrysalis, and the display cases were so clear it looked as if there were no glass at all. When I'd finished, I would doodle a love heart on the corner of Jack's notepad and flip the desktop calendar to the correct date. Except a few weeks ago I started getting lax. I'd fiddle around with a duster and that was about it. It wasn't that I no longer cared, rather I felt less bothered, as if I was hooked up to an IV drip of apathy, a slow transfusion of listlessness. What's more, as with my attitude to the cleaning of the rest of the house, I figured if I wasn't accepting visitors, what did it matter if my standards dropped?

I wheeled Jack inside. The hinges squealed with displeasure. I'd have squirted them with WD40 if I'd been comfortable going to the shed at the end of the back garden to fetch it. The display cases sparkled, not with glass cleaner, but with my tears. I had to steady myself on Jack's handles. Instead of feeling reassured by the room and its nostalgia, I felt trapped and vulnerable like I never had before. I'd kept the room as a shrine but like most shrines, it was frozen in time, and now, so was I. All I wanted was for Jack to emerge from the shadows as if he'd never left. He could have jumped out from underneath the desk, shouting, 'Surprise!' Or walked in behind me with a bunch of poppies from the nature strip. Or taken my hands and started dancing. I wouldn't have minded which. But he was never going to. He was now only a figment of my imagination and I was like the butterflies pinned behind glass with nowhere to go and no one to fly with. I felt cornered, captured, and couldn't stay in here any longer. With shaking hands and a jumpy heart, I wheeled Jack behind me and slammed the door shut.

'What the hell happened just then, Jack?' I asked him. 'How can a room make one feel so bad?'

After that, I needed a distraction. I lay on the bed, pulled out Jack's note from the book on the side table and reread the clue: 'Naturalist author doctors a line of heart (4, 2, 5)'. What was he talking about? I hadn't deciphered a cryptic clue in such a long time that I'd forgotten what to do. It would have been helpful to be in section 398.6 Riddles. I read it again and a third time for good measure. What word game was he using? Were there hidden words, synonyms, or was it some sort of anagram? The only thing I knew for sure was that the answer comprised three words of four, two and five letters. But the more I stared at the clue, the more confused I felt. While his code-cracking game was a sweet idea, it was no fun without him to help me. It merely heightened the extent of my longing. I closed my eyes and fell asleep as the unsolved clue dropped on to the floor and slipped under the bed.

Frozen in Time

The next day, I was still out of sorts and had to have Baileys in my tea for breakfast. It was while I was leaning against the kitchen bench eating a jamless jam drop that I heard a knock at the door. I ignored it. Then a face appeared at the kitchen window. I rushed to the fridge, opened the door and hid behind it.

'Geri? Are you there?' Len called.

I sighed.

'This is getting ridiculous, Geri. I don't understand why you won't see me.'

I chewed my lip. He was missing the point. Of course I was happy to see him. I just didn't want *him* to see *me*. To see the state I was in. How I no longer felt like the person I was before. How I didn't know who I was anymore.

'You know, your windows could do with a clean. I don't mind coming over and doing them sometime.' He paused, waiting for a response. 'Anyway, I'm here to see if you need groceries.'

I felt that if I said one word I would break down. I nibbled on the last carrot to distract me.

'We had a good night on Saturday, by the way. Crystal won the bingo.'

I shivered from the fridge's icy temperature, wondering how long I could last, but inadvertently coughed on a carrot crumb.

'Geri? Is that you?'

I couldn't stop coughing. A shard of carrot was stuck in my throat. On and on I went, my eyes watering, cheeks getting hotter. I opened the milk but what was left had gone off and there were no other liquids in the fridge. I needed a drink so badly, I had no option but to come out from my hiding place and pour a glass of water at the sink.

'There you are!' he cried. 'Thank goodness for that. Are you all right? Can you let me in?'

I gulped down water, got my breath back and opened the window.

'I meant the door,' he said.

I looked into the sink. I didn't want to see my shame reflecting off his face.

'Oh, Geri,' he sighed.

He extended an arm through the window and tried to touch my hand. I moved away.

'It would be so much better if I could come inside,' he said.

A tear plopped on to the dish brush.

'Okay, look, I really don't want to have to discuss this through a window. I was wanting to tell you on Saturday night . . .' He paused as if to gauge my reaction, but I didn't care what he had to say. I peeked at him through my lank hair. He ran a hand over his head. 'So, here goes. I don't know if you remember that Cryssie and I booked a cruise way back when?' He paused again to allow me time to take in what he had said. 'Well, we're going in less than a week. It's a four-week trip cruising the Nile – Egypt and Jordan.'

I did remember now that he mentioned it.

'The thing is, I'm worried about leaving you, but we booked this thing ages ago.'

'It sounds nice, Len. You deserve a holiday.'

41

'It means we will have to put some things in place for you. Make sure you've got enough supplies, perhaps clean the house. Then I got this in the letterbox.' He pulled out a leaflet from his back pocket and held it up to show me. 'Meals on Wheels. How good would that be?'

'So you met the salesperson, too?'

'Wouldn't it be ideal? Here, look' – he pointed – 'you're guaranteed fresh, hot food every day and have total control over the choice and time of delivery.'

'But I don't need it. I shop online.'

'Yeah, but this way, meals would be prepared for you. You wouldn't have to worry about any of it.'

'I'm not worried.'

'That's because you haven't been looking after yourself properly. You can't live on cake alone.'

I shrugged.

'I mean, listen . . .' He started reading, 'The food provided by Meals on Wheels is nutritionally balanced and tasty. It caters to specific dietary needs, cultural preferences and tastes. The menus are designed to be healthy and varied and our team of chefs and catering companies go out of their way to keep our clients happy.' He sounded like he was on commission.

'I appreciate your concern, Len, but I really don't want it.'

'Have a think about it at least.' He dropped the leaflet and it fell into the sink. 'Can I get you anything in the meantime?'

'Milk,' I said.

'And?'

'Carrots?' I shrugged.

'Is that it?'

'Actually, I'd love the newspaper to be delivered to the porch. Do you think they'll do that?'

'No harm in asking.'

'Thank you, Len.'

'By the way, I hope you don't mind me saying, but when did you last wash?'

The cheek of it!

'Sorry, Geri, just making sure you're okay.'

I closed the window and listened to Len's footsteps on the gravel growing fainter and fainter. When I could no longer hear them, I took Jack to the living room and slumped in an armchair. I felt bad, metaphorically and literally, for shutting Len out when he was being nothing but kind and patient with me. I felt like I had lost the ability to conduct a proper conversation with a friend. How could I no longer find the words to express myself? Yet I couldn't seem to change. I felt stuck in a loop of self-isolation and brain fog, and no good to anyone. I knew the outside world didn't mean to badger, but I wanted to hide from it. I wanted Len to enjoy his holiday yet didn't want him to go. I didn't want him worrying about me but was too proud to accept help. I was a confusing conundrum myself, a puzzle even I didn't know how to solve. I stared at the clock on the wall. It said one thirty, but surely it wasn't the afternoon already?

I sank further into the sagging back of the chair. I felt small and sad and very sorry for myself. Things that had previously consoled or even gladdened me were no longer doing the trick. I felt out of kilter, like a crooked painting on the wall, or a cheese straw without paprika. A house with no windows. A dog with one ear. I could go on. I could go to the library and look up section 400–499 English Language to find the perfect metaphor but would it actually fix anything? I glanced at the clock again. It was still one thirty. Had the clock stopped? Who knew? All I did know was that I was frozen in time, shackled to my self-pity, my grief, my fears. I was like the 'L' in the middle of my name, trapped between other letters, unable to break free. I wanted to be alone, yet I was lonely. I wanted to stay home, yet I felt isolated. I wanted to be with my husband, but he was dead. Tears sprang forth as if I was chopping onions and my heart flapped so vigorously that, had it been windy outside with no roof over the house, I may have taken off. I couldn't bear the sight of the clock looming over me, reminding me of my fate, any longer.

With a surge of adrenalin and rage, I exploded from the armchair, my focus solely on pulling the wooden-framed clock with its black numbers and unmoving hands off the wall. I saw nothing else, not even Jack. I should have, for there he was, in the way. My foot clipped the underside of the suitcase and got stuck. I upended the wheels, lost my balance and floundered. A flailing arm knocked the Christmas tree, the suitcase handle right-jabbed my chin and I fell as if in slow motion, landing with a thud on the living room floor, two suitcase wheels and five Christmas tree branches needling me in the back. My right ankle was at a wrong angle and my left wrist in pain. And it was still one thirty.

Help!

But there was no one to hear me. No one.

Carpet pile scratched my left cheek. Dust and the faint aroma of weeks-old spilt coffee irritated my nostrils. I sneezed. Everything hurt. I felt broken, my spirit shattered, my heart split in two and the only things there for me were an artificial Christmas tree and my husband in a suitcase.

'You're no bloody help, are you, Jack? You're just making it worse.'

What was the point anymore? I was living but not living. Dying but not dying. I wasn't enjoying the present and didn't like the look of the future. I felt weighed down by grief, surrounded by gloom and yearned for an escape. I came to the conclusion that the sensible and most obvious course of action was to give up, and even better, try to join Jack. If I couldn't physically get up, I could lie there peacefully until it happened. It needn't be dramatic or violent.

It would be a simple disappearing act. I closed my teary eyes and imagined I was dissolving slowly and silently into the floor. I would melt away into nothing. I heard the neighbours' garage door clatter open and the dulled voices of the Kaneshes as they went inside. I smelt damp carpet and plastic suitcase wheels, felt pain in my wrist and ankle, pulsating like my heart, and tasted the bitterness of misery. I knew it wouldn't be quick. A person could last a few days without water, but I was prepared to wait. I would eventually drift off to sleep and never wake up.

Ward Twenty-Three

I did wake up. I had a sore head, aching wrist and swollen ankle. Len sat on a chair next to me. Curved teal drapes enclosed us and there was a hum of machinery and trolley wheels.

'Len?' I said.

He looked up from his phone and his face cracked into a smile. 'Hey, Geri, you're awake!'

'What's going on?'

'Well, you executed a very elaborate way to leave the house. I wouldn't recommend you do it again.' He smiled.

I rubbed my temple.

'I'm afraid you had an accident and we had to get an ambulance. You're in emergency and are waiting to be checked out.'

I tried to ease myself to sitting but my head spun and it seemed simpler to lie back down again.

'Yeah, I'd stay there if I were you. Make the most of being waited on, tended to and fed. Okay, so it's not The Ritz but hey-ho.' He laughed.

I pulled the sheet up to my chin and looked around for my husband. It was terrifying to think he wasn't there.

'You see, what happened was, I came back with your groceries . . .'

I closed my eyes and pretended I was lying in my own bed in my own house with the suitcase next to me and Len was on the window seat recounting a story.

'. . . When you didn't answer the door, I looked in the living room window – thankfully you'd opened the curtains – and that's when I saw you on the floor. I had to break a window – sorry – as I couldn't remember where you said the spare key was. But don't worry, I'm getting it fixed. Then Sue turned up because she got a call from the Kaneshes who heard me breaking the window. They thought I was a burglar but were too scared to go over and find out. Sue called local policeman Rog, whom she's working with on her Neighbourhood Watch initiative, and I called an ambulance. It was all go, I tell you. Sue acted like she was a detective on a crime show and any minute I thought a TV crew was going to turn up.' He laughed again, before becoming serious. 'I'd rather you didn't do that again, though, okay?'

'Sorry, Len. It's just . . . it was the clock . . .' I mumbled, memories of the accident coming back to me in dribs and drabs. My lips trembled. I pulled the sheet up higher.

Len leant forward and put his sun-baked hand on my shoulder. 'It's okay, Geri; you're in safe hands now. You might have to stay here for a night or two, though. Crystal's coming with some of your things – nightdress, book, glasses – and Sue's waiting at the house for the glazier.'

I nodded and wanted to ask if Crystal could check on Jack, to make sure he was all right. Perhaps she could throw a rug on him, turn the TV on and leave out a biscuit or two.

'I'd better tell a nurse you've woken,' he said, getting up. 'Don't go anywhere,' he added, chortling his way through the curtains.

Len stayed with me while medical staff prodded and poked and X-rayed. It was a distressing invasion of privacy and called for full eye-closure. When it was over, I was transferred to bed one, room five, ward twenty-three, where, half an hour later, a doctor burst through the drapes as if emulating a comedian opening a theatre show.

'Hello, hello, Mrs Verne. How are you feeling? You're a very lucky lady, you know. You've only got a sprained wrist, twisted ankle and a gash by your left eye. No breaks; no concussion. Maybe next time you exit your armchair with a little more decorum.' She smiled.

Len laughed. I didn't. They didn't realise I'd been hoping for worse, much worse.

She continued, 'You'll need to keep your limbs elevated for the next twenty-four hours to reduce the swelling and take the pain medication every four to six hours. A nurse will come by to check on you and if you need help, press this red button here.'

I nodded.

'Thanks, Doc,' Len said.

I slept little that night because of the racket from neighbouring snorers, nurses and beeping machinery. I was also missing Jack. The more I tried not to think about him, the more I did. I nibbled on a pallid breakfast with lukewarm tea and tried to engage with the magazine Crystal had brought me. But the antics of the guests in the *Big Brother* house and the sight of celebrities in bikinis did little to distract me. Mid-morning, the doctor visited again and told me I had to stay another night. I suspected as much, but it didn't stop me wanting to poke her with her shiny ballpoint pen.

I sulked until a nurse came and told me I had visitors.

'Len?' I asked.

'No,' she said.

Hearing footsteps approach, I ducked under the covers. 'Tell them I'm tired and want to sleep.'

It was too late. I heard the curtain rattle and a high-pitched 'Ahoy, me hearties' decorate the airwaves. Something prodded me in the back. I peeked. A sword was aimed at my face and a miniature pirate stared back at me.

It was Benny. 'Do you want to walk the plank?'

'Sorry, Mrs Verne, Ben gets carried away sometimes.'

I peeled the sheet from my face and saw Benny's mother and Ruby standing behind him.

'We're so sorry you're in hospital,' their mother said. 'Ruby saw an ambulance leave your house and we learnt from one of your friends what had happened. I hope you don't mind us visiting.'

I didn't know what to say because ordinarily I would have minded receiving visitors – whether expected or unexpected. But seeing the beautiful faces of Ruby and Benny proved less troublesome than if they belonged to others.

'We thought you might like some biscuits,' Ruby said, pulling out my tin from behind her back. 'They're melting moments with lemon cream.'

At that point my heart did an about-turn and thawed like it was a slice of cheese I'd taken out of the freezer.

'Open the lid or I'll stab you with my sword,' Benny ordered, pointing his weapon at me.

'Stop it, Benny.' Ruby giggled and took off the lid.

'Mrs Verne might like one now,' their mother suggested.

Ruby came closer and showed me a mound of biscuits. 'Do you want one? Mum helped us.'

'Only if you have one with me,' I said.

'Yay!' Benny exclaimed, dropping his sword and pushing off his eye patch.

'Calm down, Ben. Let Mrs Verne take one first.'

49

I was impressed. They were the perfect creamy yellow of the Swallowtail butterfly and had a firm but buttery consistency that dissolved on the tongue.

'Delicious,' I said.

'Yay,' Benny shouted again.

'It was very kind of you to do some baking for the children,' their mother said.

'It was nothing.' I brushed crumbs off my chest, pretending I wasn't thrilled by their gratitude.

'We sold them all.' Ruby grinned proudly.

'I can do more, if you're having another stall.'

Ruby shrugged. 'We're not allowed on school days. Anyway, I've got another idea. I want to walk people's dogs.'

'Yes, well, we'll see about that,' their mother said. 'I think we should go and let Mrs Verne get some rest.'

Ruby put the tin on the bedside table. 'I hope you get better soon,' she said.

I nodded but felt tears prick my eyes. I had to squeeze my fists to stop more from coming. All I could do was blow them a kiss and watch them leave as Benny's parting words bounced off the vinyl flooring: 'She never said if she wanted to walk the plank . . .'

Our Full-Stop House

When Jack and I first saw number 51 Richmond Road nearly thirty years ago, I called the house the full stop at the end of the sentence because it sat on the corner of two streets as if ending one and beginning another. When we moved in, I joked about getting a name plaque made: 'The Full-Stop House'. Back then, there were two fewer houses, more children and no speed humps to slow down traffic. There were also no community nature strips. Not until Jack created one more than ten years ago. He was ahead of his time then and, thankfully, so was our council, who were unbothered by the couple who replaced roadside turf grass with clusters of native wildflowers. Jack envisaged a street lined with flowering plants and shrubs to *encourage urban wildlife, filter out pollutants and cool the street* as he described it in the council proposal. His enthusiasm for the project won the support of most of our neighbours, some of whom decided, unprompted, to help him out. But with no 'head gardener' anymore, the nature strips were slowly drying up.

In the backseat of Len's car on my way home from the hospital, I saw for the first time in weeks what a dismal state they were in. I had to look away. I was keen to catch sight of our front door, the colour of a dusty moth. I felt even better when a flash of red caught my eye from the bedroom. There was my husband by my bed, looking as good as always if you ignored the scrapes and ratty barcode stickers. A nuggety ball of emotion clumped in my throat. I limped to the case, took the handle, gave it a twirl and smiled, ignoring Len's sideways glance to Crystal.

I let them help me on to the bed and Len plumped two pillows for me to rest against. Crystal fetched a cushion from the window seat to elevate my ankle and gently replaced my Birkenstock slides with the slippers that were sitting by the mahogany wardrobe like two small rabbits hoping to hop inside. Crystal smiled at me again and I couldn't help but think of her eyelash extensions as two rows of centipede legs. With her fake tan and blond highlights, she was an amalgamation of beautification. Yet I knew her heart was genuine. She was the sort of person who treated others like long-lost friends unless, according to Len, her loyalty was tested. Apparently, she went through a painful divorce ten years ago when her husband left her for his cardiac nurse twenty years his junior, and she'd been wishing him a heart attack ever since.

'Remember what the nurse told you,' she said. 'Keep your leg raised as much as possible and wiggle it around to keep the blood circulating, and don't stop wearing the sling.'

'Can we get you anything?' Len asked.

'You've been too kind already,' I said.

'Crystal's brought you some magazines and a face mask and I've replaced the clock batteries in the living room. You're also stocked up with enough food for the next couple of days. Pre-made meals, tubs of yoghurt, fresh fruit, muesli bars, that sort of thing. Crystal's made a meal plan for you.'

She waved a sheet of paper, saying she'd stick it on the fridge, and went to the two large bags she'd brought in with her. 'We were shopping before coming to get you. Do you want to see what we bought?' Before I could answer, she dug into a bag. 'Look,' she said. Out came a straw hat, bejewelled flip-flops, a hot-pink swimsuit with a plunging neckline 'for the aqua-aerobics', and leopard-print active wear 'for the on-board jazzercize'. She put on the hat and flip-flops and held up the swimsuit in front of the mirror. The Nile would not miss Crystal. Len would not miss Crystal if he lost her at the pool complex. 'What do you think?'

I didn't know what to say. I'd not bought a swimsuit for ten years.

'I think it works, don't you?'

'Sure.' I nodded, enjoying the sensation of being back in my own bed in my own home.

'So, Geri . . .' Len sat on the edge of the bed next to me. 'We're going to miss you while we're away.'

'Me too, Len.'

'The thing is . . .' He glanced at Crystal. 'I know you didn't like the idea when I mentioned it before, but you have to remember it's coming from a good place . . .'

He hadn't, had he?

'You see, you've got an excellent reason this time . . .'

'I hope you're not talking about Meals on Wheels.'

'You totally qualify.'

'You know it's a service for the elderly.' I laughed.

'It's for those unable to look after themselves.'

'But I can look after myself.'

'It would only be temporary.'

'How temporary?'

'We can reassess on our return.'

'Reassess?'

'In light of your situation.'

I wasn't sure which particular situation Len was talking about – me in bed with a wonky ankle and an arm in a sling, or the entirety of my widowhood. Len was a dear man and I suspected he was throwing himself into caring for me as he thought Pam would have done had she been alive. But I also think he was having a hard time understanding why my version of grieving was different to his. When Pam died it was a real wrench to both of us – I'd known her fifty-eight years and Len had been married to her for forty. Yet, instead of going out less, he went out more, developing a strong right-arm beer bicep and bar suntan. It took Jack organising a male-bonding fishing trip for Len to ease off the drink and come out the other side. Two years later, he started dating again. Although Pam had been his true love, he found it hard being on his own. At first no one stuck. He bounced haphazardly from one woman to the next like a dented ping-pong ball – until six months ago when he'd met Crystal in the waiting rooms of his podiatrist and her ten-years-younger bounce seduced him into claiming celibacy as only for the impotent. I was relieved. As their relationship strengthened, I had hoped, after Jack died, that Crystal's presence in his life might have distracted him from mine. It didn't. I liked that he cared for me; it was commendable. But it was also exposing, and I did not wish to be exposed.

'I appreciate your concern, Len,' I said. 'But I'm not paying for something I don't need.'

'That's the thing, you don't have to. I am.'

'Shouldn't you be saving your money for future cruises?'

'Don't worry about the money.'

I nodded but what Len didn't realise was that my worries extended further than the contents of his bank account.

'Look, I want to help. I'm here to help,' he explained. 'And it ticks every box.'

'I'm not a box that needs ticking,' I said indignantly.

'No, I know you're not. I didn't mean it like that.'

'He didn't mean it like that,' added Crystal.

'Hate me as much as you want, Geri, but I've already organised it. They're starting Monday.'

'They're what?'

'I promise it won't be forever.' Len reached forward to give me a gentle hug, but I was so annoyed I shrugged it off.

'No, Len. I'm sorry, I don't want it. I'd really like you to cancel it.'

'For god's sake, Geri, I'm only trying to help!' he shouted in a very un-Len-like way, stomping his foot and standing up. I startled. 'Honestly, you've no idea how frustrating you are. I get what you're going through. It's horrible. Grief comes in waves. One minute you're up, the next you're down. But all the while you have to keep inching forward until, eventually, you're able to move on. Okay, so you've had a recent setback but that's why you accept all the support you can get to help with the moving on bit. Why can't you put aside your pride and take it? There's no shame in having Meals on Wheels. But there is in wallowing in self-pity and rebuffing old friends who mean well.' He glared at me, his chest heaving.

I lowered my head. Words banked up in my throat like cars in a pile-up. Crystal quietly occupied herself by putting the new magazines, my glasses and anti-inflammatories on to the bedside table.

'I don't want you to be mad at me, Len,' I said eventually.

'I don't want to be mad with you either,' he mumbled.

I nodded and felt a tear slide down my cheek.

'Look,' he sighed. 'They'll be nice people. They're volunteers; they do this all the time. All they're doing is dropping off a meal and they can probably do that at the front door anyway.'

'Okay,' I accepted.

'Good.' He sighed again. 'Can we get you anything else before we go?'

I felt too contrite to ask for a tea – let alone two – so shook my head.

Crystal patted my leg, then wrote her phone number on a Post-it note in case I needed to contact them and couldn't get hold of Len.

'Okay, so that's it, then,' Len said. 'Sorry we're going away but there it is.'

'I do appreciate all you do for me, Len. And you, too, Crystal,' I said. 'Please don't worry about me. I want you to enjoy your holiday.'

'Sure,' he said, even though I could tell he was still angry with me. 'Just look after yourself, okay?'

Meals on Wheels

I felt sick with shame after they left. It was horrible being shouted at by Len and I hated the thought of jeopardising our friendship. Feeling less amenable to any more visitors, I made a sign for the front door: 'Lady sleeping. Do not disturb'. The Kaneshes did that when their sons were babies and it seemed to work for them. I needed to wallow and then work out how to un-wallow.

I hobbled down to the kitchen to find the Baileys. Someone had moved it to the back of the pantry. I fished it out and took a slug from the bottle, noticing my new, shiny, dish-free sink, the faint smell of lemon cleaner and four recent newspapers on the table. I went to the fridge. Inside were ready-made meals and food packets that were stickered with the letters B, M, L, A or D according to prescribed meal and snack times. It was a Crystal-alphabet version of the Dewey Decimal system. It was a cute idea, but I didn't feel like any of it. I shut the door and took the Baileys to the living room. There, the curtains, which were open wide, showed off the brand-new front window pane, the glass coffee table now sparkled, the sofa cushions were freshly plumped, the Christmas tree restored to its kink-free state, and the wall clock no longer said one thirty. I exited and went back to Jack in the bedroom. Taking an anti-inflammatory with some Baileys, I slid under the covers and wondered why I deserved the kindness of my friends.

Come Monday, I knew I had to try hard to accept the arrival of the Meals on Wheels volunteers, for Len's sake if nothing else. Even so, I dreaded an interaction with strangers inside my home. Having realised I didn't know exactly when they'd be arriving, the uncertainty made me anxious. I put a kitchen chair by the front window again and closed the curtains, leaving enough of a gap so I could still see out. Jack sat with me, as upright as he could, yet he had developed a lean and looked permanently about to fall over. An hour went by and nobody came. I became uncomfortable and my leg ached so I got up and turned on the television. A re-run of *Doctor Who* was playing. It wasn't disagreeable. When the ads started, I went back to the window. Still no sign of any volunteers. I returned to the sofa. I did this a few times until I couldn't be bothered to get up anymore. It was snug lying on the sofa and meant I could keep my leg elevated with ease. The doorbell rang. I won't lie; I jumped. I told myself off for getting a fright, then got up and wheeled Jack to the window. Two women stood at the front door: a younger one with short-cropped hair, her hands shoved into her jeans pockets, and an older one with ash-coloured hair and cigarette-thin lips, who had one finger on the doorbell and held an aluminium tray with half-moon food covers in the other hand. She was reading my sign but, at the same time, disregarding it.

'Come on, Jack, let's get this over with.'

I opened the door, keeping the security chain attached.

'Hello, Mrs Verne, we're from Meals on Wheels,' said the older woman. 'You weren't sleeping, were you?'

'No, but I could have been.'

'Oh good. Can we come in?'

'Perhaps you could leave it on the porch,' I suggested. 'My friend who organised it said that might be possible.'

'I'm afraid we're not allowed. Health and safety, you see.'

'I won't tell anyone,' I added hopefully.

The women looked at each other. I squeezed Jack and realised my palms were sweating.

'I'm really sorry. This is just how it is. It won't take long.'

I closed my eyes, a sicky feeling rising up my oesophagus.

'Did you know these were also here?' The younger sidekick pointed to three cards and a large yellow-and-white flower bouquet leaning against the side of the house. At least someone had read the sign. 'Aren't they beautiful?'

The flowers were pretty and reminded me of how long it had been since I'd had fresh-cut flowers in the house. I unhooked the door chain.

'Thanks, Mrs Verne. We won't be long, honestly.'

I pressed my good hand to my chest in case my heart escaped and opened the door, letting the outside world tiptoe in. As soon as the women were inside, I started counting backwards from two thousand. I'd recently read it helped with insomnia, so thought it might work for anxiety.

'Is it okay if we take the meal to the kitchen?'

I pointed down the hallway, all the while counting in my head. The girl stopped to put the flowers and cards on the hall table, then Jack and I followed them and the smell of hot tomatoes and a perfume I was unable to name into the kitchen. Before I could stop them, they were microwaving the meal and setting the table. But to the women's credit they didn't bombard me with questions and were trying to be speedy. In no time, the meal was ready.

'There we are, Mrs Verne. Lasagne and beans. You've joined at a good time. We have a new supplier and their meals are meant to be tastier and more nutritious. Less salt and all that.'

'I like salt,' I blurted. I don't know why.

'Don't we all,' laughed the woman with the cigarillo mouth. 'Anyhow, I'm Jan and this is Lottie.'

The girl called Lottie was smiling so much her youthful skin cracked as if it was an egg. I smiled back but didn't feel the need to tell them my name as they already knew it. I was also still trying to count.

'Will you be all right with everything else?'

I nodded.

'Good. Well, that's all we have to do.'

'Enjoy your meal, Mrs Verne,' said Lottie, who attempted to seduce me again with her smile that now seemed wider than the width of the hallway. I got a whiff of dog as she passed and tried to guess the breed, which was, I thought, another ingenious attempt at mental distraction. I was still counting, too, as I followed them back down the hall, just in case they pilfered anything on their way out. I watched them all the way to their car and shut the front door on the count of sixty-five whippets.

A Lonely Planet

I took a moment to recalibrate in the living room after they had left.

'See, Len, I did it,' I said proudly, even though the only person around to hear me was Jack leaning against the coffee table. If I could do it once, I could do it again, I decided. I'd prove to my friends that I could accept help. It wouldn't be easy and my knowledge of dog breeds was limited, but I'd give it a go.

Yet even when I'd relaxed, I felt restless. I couldn't concentrate on the television and wasn't bothered to try the meal I'd been left. I decided to take the newspapers that someone had tidied to the laundry. That's when I rediscovered the *Lonely Planet 1000 Ultimate Adventures* travel book that I'd borrowed from the library weeks ago, with several others I had also borrowed neatly stacked underneath. I slumped in an armchair and held my slinged arm as if it, too, was traumatised. I'd forgotten about those books – conveniently forgotten about them because I didn't want to think about Jack's last wish – the request I'd not honoured, nor believed I even could.

It was on his deathbed when he'd uttered the words: 'When I'm reduced to ash, take me somewhere exotic.' Actually, he'd said more than that, but I'd stopped listening properly and hadn't wanted to take them seriously because who wants to dwell on the first five words of a request like that? Even though at the time I knew he didn't have much longer in this world, I did not for one second wish to imagine him as a mound of gritty sand. I couldn't even believe he'd said those words out loud in the first place. I mean, who does that? I remember brushing aside his comment as if he'd merely said, 'When I nod off, can you make sure my face doesn't fall in my food?'

Except once he'd gone, I started thinking about what he'd said. That's what you do, isn't it? You hone in on the last words uttered by both yourself and the one who's passed, hoping you told them you loved them, wondering what their last words may have meant, or if they were drug-induced and had no meaning at all. I regretted not being able to discuss his wish further. For those less travelled, it could simply mean ambling to a neighbouring suburb and tipping the ashes in a flower bed, or going to the zoo and dumping them in the giraffe enclosure when no one was looking. Most people say, 'sprinkle me in the sea' or 'let me loose over a sports ground' or 'plant me in a biodegradable urn with special soil so you can feed me to my favourite tree/flowering shrub/the orchid you gave me'. But I knew Jack had none of those ideas in mind because he mentioned the Mexican Monarch butterfly reserve that he'd always wanted to visit.

So a month after he died, when I started to feel guilty that I'd not entertained the idea of honouring his wish, I decided to look into it further, to show him that I still cared. First, I found out more about the butterfly reserve in Mexico and very quickly discovered it's not the sort of place a seventy-two-year-old widow with no knowledge of Spanish, a dislike for horse riding and limited hiking experience would travel to. Not only that, but there was a warning in place advising travellers not to visit the state of Michoacán where the reserve is located. I was relieved that I could disregard the idea as totally preposterous.

62

Then I went to the library, to section 913–919 Travel, and found several books which featured experiences that could be deemed exotic. The *Lonely Planet* chapter titles offered glimpses into outlandish outdoor experiences: 'The world's best bouldering', 'Most electrifying tribal encounters', 'The planet's freakiest footraces'; whereas the *National Geographic Journeys of a Lifetime* included a page on Madagascar's rainforest, the Parc National de Masaola with its one hundred and thirty species of butterfly that would have tickled Jack's fancy. There was a book on storm-chasing holidays in the American Midwest; one on extreme mountain adventures; and another on cycling the world's hilliest peaks. I took several of the books home with me but the more I read, the more ludicrous each idea seemed.

I shoved the books aside and thought of two other ideas closer to home. At Jack's funeral, Linda's son had told me about the art of tattooing ashes mixed with ink, as if I'd been considering getting Jack's name etched into my buttock. Then there was Sue's friend's husband who had requested his ashes be mixed into concrete and made into paving stones as a metaphor for his marriage. 'Once downtrodden, always downtrodden,' he apparently wrote in his will. Sue had thought he was being serious.

I went online but the internet only unearthed even more outrageous possibilities: shooting the ashes into space via a rocket or smoking them with friends, which a rapper I'd never heard of once requested. The more I searched, the harder it was to come up with anything I thought befitted Jack, suited the criteria, and was easy and safe for me to do. My conclusion: there was nothing. His request was completely untenable. It also prompted the question of why it mattered whether I honoured his wish or not. Surely it wasn't a big deal if Jack stayed with me, I decided, for that's pretty much how it was when we were married. We hardly spent any time apart. Jack went on the odd boys' fishing trip and I had weekends away with girlfriends, but that was it. Certainly, once we retired, we did everything together. Why would I want to break that by, literally, throwing Jack to the wind and never seeing him again? It was, quite frankly, absurd.

As I was being cuddled by the armchair, I revisited my findings and came, yet again, to the conclusion that my initial decision had been the right one. Jack would stay where he was and that was final.

'I don't see the point in dredging up your old desire, Jackie-boy. This is my new normal, whether you like it or not. I'm moving on and so should you.' I said it forcefully, with authority to show who was in charge. I thumped my good fist on the chair arm and told myself I was happy with the idea. That any qualms I had were from the last dribbles of grief I had yet to blot, and that to banish my guilt, all I had to do was return the library books. Easy.

972 Mexico, Central America

The day before Jack died, he appeared more alert, less in pain, his hands slightly warmer than before, as if his heart had remembered it was still pumping and, overjoyed, decided to flood his body with new blood. When I visited, he asked me to sit closer so he could hold my hands, smell the dab of perfume on my neck and feel the vibrant pulse on my wrist.

'Can I ask you something?' he asked.

'Of course.'

'We haven't talked about what will happen when . . .' He closed his eyes as his breathing became laboured.

'Would you like to write it down?' I suggested.

He didn't respond either way. Mild to enthusiastic nodding isn't recommended for the terminally ill.

'The thing is, Geri,' he started up again, 'I don't want you to die with me. I want you to keep on living.'

I squeezed my eyes shut to stop them from leaking.

'So I had a thought. When I'm gone, when I'm reduced to ash, take me somewhere exotic so you can take yourself somewhere exotic too.'

'What are you talking about, "somewhere exotic"?' I said, sitting up. 'I think the drugs are making you delusional.'

'I'm being serious. You know how I've talked about wanting to go to the Monarch Butterfly Biosphere Reserve in Central Mexico, where you can watch the annual migration of millions, if not billions, of Monarch butterflies? Well, I wish I'd made it happen. It was a bucket-list bullet point I never got around to.'

'Now you're being silly. Why would I want to do that without you?'

'But I'd be with you.'

'It's absurd.'

'It doesn't have to be Mexico. You could pick somewhere else. It was just an idea . . .' His voice wheezed and slowly petered out.

I stroked his thinning hair that was so light and downy it would have flown away if not properly attached. I felt bad shunning his idea, but it was disconcerting talking about ash-scattering in places that seemed beyond my reach. I couldn't bear to talk about such things.

'Can you at least promise not to stop living when I do?' he asked. I felt a tear splutter out of an eye and run down the side of my nose. 'I'm sorry, Geri,' he whispered.

'I could have got a pen and paper if you'd asked,' I said.

He didn't reply. Already he had slipped into slumber, the effort of speaking more than twenty-five words in one go proving too much. And that was the last we spoke of it. For the next day, he slid slowly and silently into a coma from which he never recovered.

The Banishment

I felt emboldened after deciding to ask Lottie to return the library books. I went to the hall table to inspect my gifts. There were three get-well cards. The flowers were from 'the bingo gang': Geoff and Linda, Joyce and Barry. I rearranged the cards in a more aesthetically pleasing manner and went to the bathroom to fill a vase with water. I tied the ribbon around the vase, adjusted the fronds so the bouquet was evenly distributed, and sat them in the middle of the table. Feeling my appetite returning, I wheeled Jack to the kitchen to check out the lasagne. It looked enticingly edible and smelled even better within a ten-centimetre nostril range. I got a spoon and scooped a mouthful. It wasn't bad. I took a bite for Jack, followed by another and another . . . Soon the meal was gone.

Not having felt this full in weeks, I had to go and lie on the bed.

The following day, the Meals on Wheels volunteers returned at around midday. I'd started watching a home renovation program about a couple restoring a crumbling French chateau surrounded by a moat. Abandoning it was annoying. I didn't want to be with the women in the kitchen because it's not pleasant feeling redundant in your own home while strangers fuss around like they own it. I waited in the doorway.

'How did you like the lasagne?' Jan asked.

'It could have had more salt.'

Lottie caught my eye and smiled.

'Come, now, Mrs Verne . . .' Jan said. 'Don't try that with us again. Today's meal is fish pie.'

'Ta-da!' Lottie lifted the lid with a flourish. It looked bland and not properly cooked through, without even a pastry fish decorating the top. 'Oh.' She looked at it with disappointment.

'Now, now, Lottie, it's how it tastes that matters, isn't it?' Jan said.

'Yes, of course.' Lottie nodded.

'I'll pop it in the microwave for you, then you're all set.'

I suspected a stint in the microwave would make the pastry even more tasteless, but I wasn't quick enough to stop her. Lottie mouthed *sorry* while Jan's back was turned. I smiled and for a few seconds shared a secret moment with a stranger. It didn't make me want to eat the pie, though. After they left, I tipped it in the bin.

My third meal was delivered by different volunteers, Eve and Doug, who looked as if they could have age-qualified for the service themselves. I started counting backwards when they stepped inside but had to abandon the dog-breed brainstorming I had done with Lottie for they were pleasantly fragrance-free. As with the other two volunteers, I watched their every move as Sue's warnings about burglars in the area had been preying on my mind. What better way to rob someone than by entering another's house under the guise of providing a service? Now it was not only unsettling to have strangers in my home, but I was worrying they could nick off with something while they were there. They delivered a vegetarian rice bowl with an indeterminate food group they claimed was soybeans. It was surprisingly tasty. I ate two thirds. They came on Thursday, too, and brought a stuffed baked potato and salad, plus the smell of car air freshener – the synthetic lavender version, which put me off the dish.

It was as I was flapping the living room window back and forth with my good arm to air the place that the nurse, who Crystal said would visit, dropped by. She was very pleasant, and I ascertained that, with her smoker's teeth and rumpled dress, she may be one of those medical professionals who didn't mind bending the rules. And, indeed, she happily assessed me at the front door and didn't probe me about my eating or toilet habits, the state of my hair or the house. It was most refreshing. Even better, she told me I was 'beautifully on the mend'. For all of that, she got a yellow daisy from the hall bouquet.

Her diagnosis had me buoyed. I was getting better and soon wouldn't need the Meals on Wheels service at all. I waved goodbye to the nurse and then to Ruby and Benny, whom I spotted on the other side of the road walking a pot-scrub of a dog. They didn't see me. It didn't matter. It was enough that I'd seen them.

On Friday, Jan and Lottie made another appearance.

'I thought you'd had enough of me,' I joked. It came out unintentionally because, in fact, I'd thought it was *me* who'd had enough of *them*. Even though having strangers in my house was unnerving, I was beginning to realise that the volunteers' daily arrival was helping break up the day. I wouldn't go so far as to say I looked forward to it – I still had to backwards-count to calm my anxiety – but I did notice a slight upswing in my mood when they greeted me at the front door. It also made me wonder if I was missing Len and Crystal. I thought I hadn't wanted visitors, yet I sort of did. It was confusing.

'You won't always get the same people every time,' Lottie explained. 'Most of us aren't full-time volunteers and sometimes the roster changes if someone gets sick or goes on holiday.'

'We also don't visit on weekends,' Jan added. 'So today, we've brought two extra meals. One for Saturday, one for Sunday. They're frozen so keep them in the fridge to defrost.' She held up an extra bag.

'I hope they're better than that fish pie,' I said.

'Sorry if expectations were set a little high last time,' Jan said, glancing at Lottie. I sensed the girl had been told off by her superior for her overly enthusiastic meal reveal.

Lottie pulled a silly face behind her back. I tried not to giggle.

'There's no harm in a bit of optimism now and then, is there?' I said in support of the girl.

'Well, anyway, can we come in?' Jan said, changing the subject. 'Today, you've got ravioli and for the weekend, beef stew and tandoori coconut chicken.'

I moved Jack to one side and opened the door to let them pass.

Lottie might have asked me a question then, but I was so busy counting that I let slip, 'One thousand, nine hundred and sixty-nine.'

'Sorry?'

If only I'd said a bingo number, I could have made light of it. Instead, I brushed it aside and said, 'You were saying?'

'Your injuries. How are they?'

'Oh, yes, they're improving, thank you.'

'You'll be able to ditch the suitcase soon, then, won't you?'

I looked at Jack and back to Lottie. 'I suppose I will,' I replied and turned to shut the door so she couldn't see how much her comment had unnerved me. I had feared being questioned about the case and now it was happening. I dallied by the door so that when I got to the kitchen, they were already heating up the day's ravioli and putting the frozen meals into the fridge. They were an efficient team, I had to give them that – I only got to nine hundred and ninety-nine in my counting – before we were back at the front door, saying goodbye.

'Have a nice weekend,' Lottie said.

'I will,' I replied.

I locked the door and trundled down the hallway again, wondering what sort of weekend I'd actually have. I made two cups of tea and sat at the kitchen table.

'Here we are again, Jackie-boy,' I said, patting the case.

He didn't answer and I wished that I didn't want him to. It was true what Len had said about grief coming in waves. I was a surfer riding many waves but never reaching the shore. Was accepting Meals on Wheels help as good as it was going to get? Was this my new status quo – spending weekends alone, too scared to venture outside? Was I going to live out the rest of my days making excuses – or worse, lying – about the suitcase?

I looked at Jack again, but this time saw him for what he was: a faded whoopee-cushion-coloured case now retired from overseas travel. When we'd gone suitcase shopping all those years ago, I hadn't been keen on buying red luggage. Jack had insisted for security purposes, which Sue would have rated as ten out of ten had she known. In the end, I didn't care. If he was happy, I was happy. Now, the red was as muted as Jack and as dented as my heart.

'But I don't want to be dented!' I thumped my good fist on the table. The tea sloshed. 'And I don't want to rely on you for company, Jack, because, quite frankly, you're not giving me much at the moment.'

I stood up, downed some tea and thought for a minute. If I was going to show my friends I could move on, I'd have to do something radical. Something so radical, I had never entertained it before. I picked up Jack's tea and tipped it into the sink.

'Enough is enough, Jackie-boy.' I watched the tea swirl down the drain and felt strangely empowered. I stood up straighter and rolled my shoulders. 'No more talking to you, either.' I shook my head and mimed the zipping up of my mouth.

'In fact,' I started, having a light-bulb moment and unintentionally speaking again, 'there should be no more *you*.'

I gasped at the realisation of what I'd said. After taking a moment to digest the thought, I took a deep breath, grabbed the suitcase handle and wheeled my husband out the back door.

It wasn't easy getting him into the garden shed. There was the lip of the back-door frame to get over, the uneven stone path to walk down, and the threshold of the shed to cross. The case was a lot heavier than I realised with the other items also inside and I only had one arm with which to lift it. I wished I'd taken refreshments with me and had to make do with imagining a swig of liqueur at the end of it.

Finally, we arrived. I flicked the switch of the naked light bulb overhead. It flared into life, highlighting a fairy floss of cobwebs and possum poo on the floor. I'd forgotten how much detritus was jam-packed in here. There was a worktable under the window, a lawnmower, strimmer, outdoor broom, two shelves of rusted tools, half-used paint pots, empty terracotta plant pots, fishing rods not used in five years and golf clubs not used in fifteen. I pulled Jack inside and wheeled him to the back of the shed next to his golf clubs where he could reminisce about his 1994 hole-in-one. If I was to properly move on, I needed to do so without him. If I was going to live – to truly live – I needed to do it without wheeling around the dead. I patted the handle and turned to go. Without once looking back, I left the shed and walked with purpose back to the house.

PART TWO

306.88 GRIEF AND DEALING WITH DEATH

PART TWO

616.9 Cancer

Jack was first diagnosed with cancer seven years ago. It was a chocolate-drop mole on his shoulder, like someone had drawn a thick dot with a black felt pen that, with a lick of a finger, could be wiped away. Except it needed surgery, after which we thought that would be the end of it. But four and a half years later he got another one, and this time it was also in his lymph nodes and liver. Jack tried to be positive.

'It's okay, Geri. I'll do the treatment and all will be fine. I told them we had a week booked in the rainforest surrounds of Far North Queensland that we were going on whether they liked it or not.'

'Oh, Jack . . .'

'Don't worry, we'll still be able to go. The dates work perfectly with the treatment schedule they suggested.'

I looked away. I couldn't bear to tell him that I didn't care whether we went away or not.

'Eighty-five staying alive,' he quipped in bingo lexicon.

When he started the treatment, I took my nursing duties seriously. He became my number one priority. I bought a Halloween nurse's costume to wear, a foldable meal tray so he could easily eat in bed and a long-range walkie-talkie set. I gave them to him after his first day of chemotherapy.

'We'll even be able to communicate when I'm out at the shops as long as it's within a ten-kilometre range,' I explained as he unwrapped the walkie-talkie box.

'I thought that's what mobile phones were for,' he said.

'But this is much more fun, don't you think?' I picked up one of the receivers and pressed it to my ear. 'Geri for Jack. Over.'

'Geri,' Jack sighed and rolled his eyes. Still, it brought a smile to his lips.

'Go on, it's your turn,' I said, pointing to the other receiver.

He pressed it to his ear, even though we were only within a one-metre transmission range and the set wasn't charged. 'All present and accounted for,' he said. 'Over.'

'Eighty-three time for tea?' I asked.

'Roger that,' Jack replied. 'Over.'

At the end, I added Jack's walkie-talkie receiver to the coffin but kept mine in the kitchen, just in case we found heaven to be no more than ten kilometres away.

Moving On

Back in the kitchen, I felt good. So good, I had a Baileys to make me feel even better. Instead of having the ravioli for dinner, I decided to defrost the tandoori chicken in honour of Len's curry nights. While it was in the microwave, I went around the house removing all reminders of Jack. On the hall table, I turned each framed photo of him towards the wall, and then I did the same with those in the living room and the one in our bedroom.

Finally, I sat on the bed and pulled at my engagement and wedding rings. My wrist protested. The rings wouldn't budge. I tried separating them and twisting them individually. They were stubborn. I went to the bathroom and under running warm water, soaped my fingers. Slowly, the rings loosened, and I tried very hard to dismiss the thoughts that came rushing to me. How Jack and I had chosen the engagement ring after his promotion when he wanted to honour his promise of buying me a 'proper' one. How I used to love Jack telling me that the sapphire matched my eyes, even though we both knew my eyes had never been a deep indigo blue and were now a dull grey. How I hadn't taken either ring off since the day I put them on. But I couldn't let these memories dismantle my resolve. I gave both rings another twist and a decent pull and they slipped off as if they had never been steadfast. They tinkled prettily when they hit the bottom of the toothbrush holder. I stared at the indented tan mark on my finger and turned off the tap.

That night I had a dream so intense it seemed real. I dreamed of not only banishing Jack to the shed, but ridding myself of everything that was once his as well. His clothes, his shoes, his toiletries, his paperwork, even the contents of the butterfly room. They flew out of the places they lived like a swarm of insects. As if every item was one of the millions of orange-winged Monarch butterflies on their annual migration from the United States to Mexico – a natural phenomenon I did not want to be reminded of. I woke with a racing heart and wished I could take it out completely, give it a little massage, a hot bath and a glass of wine to calm it down. Or maybe an intravenous injection of Baileys.

After Jack died, Len caught me staring at his clothes in the wardrobe, overcome by the sight of them and the thought of ever having to get rid of them. As if reading my thoughts, he said, 'Don't worry about that now, Geri. Only when you're ready. I can help when the time is right.' He gently led me away from the wardrobe and my unsettling thoughts, and I never revisited them again. As I lay in bed, I considered spending the morning sorting through Jack's side of the wardrobe but feared I would get distracted by the smell of his jackets and begin to reminisce about the times he wore his tweed suit or lemon-sherbet jumper. I still wasn't ready for that. Len had said it wasn't going to be easy, after all. Inch by inch was how he had measured it and I reckoned I'd just done a few metres in a single day. I flung off the covers and eased myself into a sitting position. My good arm extended – it did that without me even thinking about it – and my hand reached out. I wasn't properly looking at what I was doing but when it registered that my fingers couldn't find what they were searching for, I turned and stared at the space between the ends of my knees and the bedside table. The space where the suitcase used to be. I gasped.

As hastily as I could, I got into my dressing gown and slippers and out of the bedroom, away from the shocking thought that I may have had my last dance with Jack and hadn't even realised. I scuttled to the kitchen and made a tea with Baileys, no milk. Then I went through the drawers. In my flustered state, I couldn't remember where I'd put it. It was disconcerting that everything I noted as I searched was Jack's: the steak knives, the wine-bottle-shaped wine stopper, the inscribed hipflask a friend gave him for his sixtieth birthday, the pizza cutter, the green plastic fly swat. I took them out and left them on the bench, wondering if a clean-up of his things would be the only way to stop the reminders of him slapping me in the face. It was in the junk drawer – loose batteries, tissue packs, half-used jotter pads, chewed pencils – that I found it. I took out the walkie-talkie and pressed it to my ear.

'Kitchen to shed. Over.'

I didn't expect him to answer. It was understandable for him to be aggrieved by his current situation. I pressed on, even though I knew I wasn't supposed to be talking to him anymore.

'How are your golf clubs? I thought you might enjoy being with them again.' I paused, wondering what else to say. One shouldn't struggle making small talk with your husband, but I suppose there can always be a first time. 'I know they're a bit dusty and I hope a mouse hasn't scurried out and scared you. I had the tandoori chicken last night. It was a bit dry and not as spicy as you like. I couldn't eat it all and threw the rest out. I did answer all the TV game show questions correctly, though. I'd have won us a hundred thousand dollars if I'd been the one in the hot seat. How good is that? Well, anyway, I hope you're okay in there and aren't too mad at me. It would be extremely helpful if you could be sympathetic to my situation and cut me some slack.' I sighed. 'So that is all. As you were. Over.'

I placed the receiver on the bench and stared at it for a minute. I don't know if I was expecting it to crackle into life or not. When nothing happened, I shoved it to the back of the pot cupboard and finished my tea. I did little else other than have a one-handed hair wash in the bath and rearrange the kitchen drawers so that Jack's items could have a drawer of their own. The bottom one at the far end. The one I usually never open.

On Monday, Lottie arrived on her own. She wore ripped jeans and a food-stained baggy T-shirt. If the current fashion was to present scruffy, then I was right on trend.

'It's just me today,' she said. 'Jan's in the car. She's got a cold and doesn't want to pass it on.'

I peered over Lottie's shoulder, through her large hoop earrings, and saw Jan in the passenger seat. 'She's just sneezed violently,' I noted. 'You might want to take the bus home.'

Lottie laughed. Jan waved at me. I waved back.

'Hey, where's the suitcase?' she asked, stepping inside.

'I've ditched it like you said.'

'But you're still limping.'

I looked down at my ankle. 'You've got to start somewhere, haven't you?'

'How have you been otherwise?'

I thought for a minute and decided my honest answer would take too long and reveal too much. 'Fine,' was all I said as we headed towards the kitchen. I suddenly realised I had forgotten to start counting.

'Is someone coming to check on you?' Lottie put the meal in the microwave to 'give it a zap', as she liked to call it.

'A nurse came the other day.'

'Anyone else?'

I shook my head.

She studied me for a minute before resuming her duties. 'I had an accident once when I was going for a job interview. I tripped on a mat as I got out of the lift, bumped into the woman who was going to be interviewing me, although I didn't know that at the time, spilt coffee on her and tore the meniscus in my knee. For the entire interview, all I could concentrate on was the coffee stain on her shirt and the pain in my leg. She pretended she hadn't minded but I didn't get the job, so you decide.' She laughed, pouring a glass of milk and putting it on the table. 'You just never know when something's going to trip you up, do you? I guess what I'm saying is, if you need to use the suitcase again, do so.'

I smiled. I was pleasantly surprised to realise how less intrusive it seemed when there was only one stranger in the house. I was no longer outnumbered. What's more, as I was at a guess about forty years older than her, I felt I had the upper hand. I had more wisdom and experience. I knew things she didn't, like when you get to my age, you don't drink milk on its own anymore. Still, it was sweet of her to throw in added extras when she didn't have to, so I took a sip to show my appreciation.

'Today's meal is lamb and lentil biryani,' she said, getting it out of the microwave. 'I tried making a curry from scratch once. It was a disaster. I don't know what I did but it ended up tasting like detergent. Some things are better left to the experts, don't you think?'

'You could always find another recipe and try again,' I suggested.

'I can't be bothered. I'd rather save curries for takeaways.'

I thought fondly of Len and wished I hadn't because I felt my bottom lip tremble.

'Are you all right?' she asked.

'It's the Indian spices,' I said. 'They make my eyes water.'

'How about I put a paper towel over the meal . . .'

'Don't worry, it's fine.' I don't know whether she believed me or not, but she reciprocated a smile and then it was like we were in a competition to see who could hold a smile the longest.

'Well, if you'd like me to help with anything else,' she said. 'I know I'm only supposed to be delivering meals, but that doesn't mean I can't do other things, like lifting something heavy or hanging out your washing.'

I could have told her it was just as easy doing no washing at all had I not remembered a task that I did need help with.

'Actually . . .' I began, wondering whether she would mind and what I'd do if she did. I didn't have a plan B.

'Yes?' she said.

'It is a bit of an ask . . .' I pulled a face to show I didn't want to put her out.

But the girl appeared to be open to anything. 'Seriously, I don't mind what it is,' she said. 'The other day, a client wanted me to do her hair in some sort of updo. I mean, I'm terrible with long hair, which is why I have short hair, but I tried my best. To be honest, I think she just wanted the company.'

'I wouldn't dream of asking you to try and do anything with my mop.' I laughed, wishing I hadn't highlighted the state of my hair, which really was in a state. 'It involves a trip to the library.'

'Sure,' she agreed.

'Excellent. Follow me.'

In the living room I pointed to the six books on the floor by the coffee table. 'These need returning, you see.'

'I can do that for you.'

'The library's not far from here.'

'You don't want to go yourself?'

'Oh no. Not at the moment.' I shook my head, probably too vigorously as my hair flew wildly around my head.

'We could go together?'

She'd caught me off-guard and I didn't know what to say. 'Perhaps another time . . . ?' I mumbled.

'Okay.' She nodded and went to pick up the books.

'I hope they're not too heavy.'

'Not at all. Anything else?'

I said no and decided her time was up, keen for her to leave before she asked any more probing questions.

Whisky and Cake

With the library books out of the house, it was time to celebrate. I made a carrot cake with the carrots Len had bought. It was as I was eating a slice that the phone rang. I picked up on the proviso I would hang up if the person on the other end wanted to sell me something.

'Is this Geraldine Verne? It's Liza Nut here from the Douglas Street Library. Your wonderful husband once did a children's talk on butterflies for us and he had such a lovely manner with them that we'd love to have him again. Probably in the next school holidays. I've tried calling his mobile but haven't been able to get through. Is he there?'

My heart sank. Her mention of Jack, as if he was still alive, threw me and, for a second, I couldn't speak but I didn't wish to be rude by hanging up on her.

'That's very kind of you to ask, Liza,' I said, composing myself. 'He has been having phone problems. He's also away at the moment but I'll be sure to ask him when he gets back.'

'That would be wonderful, thank you. Can you tell me when that might be?'

'The thirtieth,' I said, plucking a number from nowhere, hoping she couldn't hear my heart thrashing like it was in a breaststroke race.

I put the phone down. 'Good one, Geri,' I muttered, pushing away the serving of carrot cake. I'd lost my appetite for celebration and wasn't much fussed on the biryani either. I decided to give the rest of the cake and the bottle of Jack's whisky I had spotted in the pantry to Lottie when she next visited as a thank-you for returning the library books. I wrapped the whisky in the last piece of gift wrap I had and a pre-loved gold bow and counted the days until I'd see her again.

When it was Friday, I spotted her arriving from the living-room window and got to the front door before she'd reached the steps.

'Oh, hi, Mrs Verne.' She seemed surprised to see me, which was understandable given my unusually sudden appearance. 'Your letterbox was bursting,' she said, holding up a wad of mail.

'Better than my appendix.'

'Well, yes,' she laughed. 'But it's okay, I've got first-aid training. Bursting letterboxes are a cinch.' Her laughter ricocheted off the rafters and bounced on to the floorboards like a ping-pong ball.

'Did you get to the library?' I asked eagerly.

'Yes, don't worry, the books have been returned and I paid your fine, in case you didn't realise you had one. In fact,' she added, 'this is what these might be.' She waggled the bills again. 'You'd better open them.'

'Yes, yes, I'll deal with them later.' I took the mail off her but left them on the hall table.

'I don't mean to pester but you really shouldn't ignore them. There are four letters from your electricity provider. Have you been paying your bills?'

I shrugged. I couldn't remember.

'It would be awful to lose your power because of late payment. Just think, you wouldn't be able to watch your favourite TV shows.'

I scratched my neck. She had a point.

'I'm sorry you had to pay my fine,' I said. 'Come down to the kitchen and I'll write you a cheque.'

'You must have had the books a while. The fine was huge. But the librarian didn't seem to mind. She asked after you, too. Said you used to go in all the time.'

'That was probably Karen.' I sighed at the memory of my ex-colleague. 'I used to work there.'

'Really?' Lottie said enthusiastically. With her bony arms and pixie haircut, she was like a small bird tweeting down the hallway. 'Did you work there long?' We were in the kitchen now and the meal-heating routine began again.

'Forty-five years,' I said, fishing out the chequebook. 'I started when I was twenty and retired at sixty-five but stayed volunteering during school holidays and at children's story time. I used to joke that you could stick me with the dog-eared dictionaries and I wouldn't look out of place.'

'I should be thanking you for getting me back to the library. I've not read a novel for ages and found a couple to get me started again. I also got another book for you.' She pulled out a hardback on Italy from her backpack. 'You seem to love travel books, so I thought I'd continue the theme. It's due back in three weeks, though, so no forgetting.'

'Thank you,' I said, flipping through it. Even though I had no interest in travelling to Italy, I was touched she had thought of me. 'I've got something for you, too,' I said, pointing to the whisky and cake. 'Sorry about the wrapping,' I added, realising how crinkled the navy paper was and how flaccid the bow, as if tired of having to yet again be the pizazz on a present. 'The cake's homemade.'

'That's very nice of you, Mrs Verne, but I'm not allowed to accept gifts.'

'Who's going to know?' I said.

'I just don't think I should.'

'I won't tell anyone.'

She thought for a minute.

'Jan's not here, is she? Or is she hiding in the car again?' I asked.

'No, she's still ill. Tonsillitis, unfortunately.'

'Oh dear, that's not good. But it is useful for clandestine exchanges.' I chuckled.

She giggled. 'Well, okay then, thank you.'

'Don't drink it all at once, though, will you? I only start adding Baileys to my tea mid-morning.'

'Mrs Verne!'

'Only kidding,' I lied.

After that, it felt as if the temperature in the kitchen had gone up a notch and the mood lightened. Lottie served my meal for the day – minestrone with a bread roll – left two frozen meals for the weekend – beef stew and chicken pot pie – and started chatting again as we headed back to the front door.

'Have you got any plans for the weekend?' she asked.

I thought about what I used to do once upon a time on weekends and how I could have fabricated a competitive bingo night that night, a shopping excursion to a neighbouring suburb on Saturday and lunch with friends on Sunday, but I suspected she'd find me out. Instead, I said, 'I might go clothes shopping,' just to make it look as if I had something planned.

'That sounds nice. I've got a load of work to do and training with my guide dog.'

It was pleasing to learn my nose still functioned at optimum capacity and I was about to ask what sort of dog it was when there was a knock at the door.

'Expecting visitors?' Lottie asked.

'No,' I said. Although I didn't wish to answer it, Lottie wished to leave so I had no choice but to open the door. Still, I kept the key chain attached.

'Is that you, Geri?' A woman's face appeared in the opening. She was tall and thin like a drinking straw. 'It's Denise from down the street.' She paused. 'I'm so sorry for your loss and I'm sorry to bother you but I was hoping to have a chat about the community nature strips. Is now a good time?'

'I suppose so,' I said.

'They're dying, as you've probably noticed, and I was thinking we should revive them. I – we – some of us in the street – thought you might like to be a part of it, given . . . you know . . . your husband and all that.'

'Thank you for thinking of me,' I said.

'If you wanted to come out now and have a look at them . . . ? You might be able to give us some tips.'

I gritted my teeth but had to remain composed for both my inside guest and Denise outside. 'I'm frantically busy at the moment so feel free to press on without me.'

'Are you sure? I know you love gardening like Jack did.'

'I'm sure whatever you do, Jack will approve. Or would have if he were here . . .' I fumbled.

'Okay.' Denise nodded. 'But if you change your mind, I'm at number forty.' She remained on the porch a few more seconds, as if about to say something more, then turned and left.

I gently closed the door. Never had I felt more exposed having a visitor – a sort-of-stranger – witness me hiding in my own home, a mad woman with hair like stuffing exploding from a cushion having an encounter she neither wished to have nor to explain. It was like I'd been caught vacuuming in my underwear.

'That was nice,' Lottie said. 'You don't want to take up her offer?'

I shrugged.

'It'd be lovely being outside, planting plants with your neighbours.'

'It's not my thing,' I said. I opened the door again, checked Denise had gone and pulled it wider.

'I don't believe you.' She may have said it jokingly, but I knew what she was trying to do.

'Thank you again for returning the books.'

'Will you promise to think about it? The gardening?'

'Yes,' I said. 'Now off you go.' This time, I pretended to joke.

'Okay,' she laughed. 'Thanks for the gifts, too, and don't forget to pay your bills.'

She tripped down the steps in her sneakers, a bubbly ray of sunshine. I felt like a puddle of rain.

Then it was the weekend. Outside, the weather went from sunny to drizzly to overcast to sunny again. It was occasionally cool and sometimes warm. But I only knew this because I watched the weather forecast at the end of the nightly news. I didn't venture outside or even think about doing so as I had promised Lottie. I spent my time street-watching from the window, counting cars and pedestrians but never saw Ruby and Benny dog walk again. I did open the door to the butterfly room, though. Only a tiny bit – twenty centimetres at most – as I wasn't yet ready to go inside. Instead, I left it ajar in case the time came. The only thing I added to my daily routine was going to the computer in our second bedroom-turned-study to peruse the internet shops. I hadn't before considered the notion of refreshing my wardrobe in the interests of moving on. But why not – especially if I couldn't yet bring myself to the leave the house? That way, I could show the world the new Geraldine Verne when I was ready.

But I didn't buy anything. I was unable to 'go to checkout' and 'proceed with the order'. I felt guilty treating myself to clothes I didn't know when I'd wear, or where I'd wear them to. Nor did I wish to spend the money – it seemed extravagant and frivolous and I wasn't that kind of woman. I powered off the computer leaving a toffee-coloured coat and a pair of suede mules still in my cart.

Taxidermy

Come Monday, I was eager for Lottie's visit. She was turning into a breath of fresh air in my otherwise humdrum days. What I wasn't expecting was for her to spot the partially open door to the butterfly room as she was leaving.

'What's in here?' she asked, peering inside.

'Just an old hobby room,' I replied, as if it housed an unusual habit I was embarrassed to reveal, like collecting navel fluff and storing it in jars.

'Are they real butterflies?'

'Yes, but they're dead, of course.'

'Can I go in?'

Although I felt uneasy venturing inside, I liked the thought of delaying Lottie's departure. I pushed the door open to let her in.

She went up to the second display case on the right-hand wall. 'They're amazing. They look unreal, almost make-believe.'

'Thank you.'

'Where did you get them?'

'Here and there,' I said. 'We collected them like stamps.'

'Really?' She looked at me as if she hadn't seen me properly before.

'I had thought about taxidermying my husband until I found out the cost . . .' I said, which in retrospect was a little gruesome, but the words just came out like a rogue burp in polite company.

'What?'

'I could have had him standing in the corner, admiring his handiwork while we admired him.'

She laughed. 'Like Madame Tussaud's?'

'Only the likeness would have been spot on.'

'You're too funny.'

'I am?'

'You are.' She smiled, then moved to the next case, studying each butterfly as if she'd never seen one before. 'This is a fantastic collection, you know.' Her interest was flattering. No one else had been in the room for such a long time that I had forgotten what it must look like to others. She continued, 'I didn't know butterfly collecting was such a thing. Did you buy them all?'

'Some, but many we captured and my husband learnt how to preserve them. You're not allowed to do that anymore, what with species dying out.'

'Of course.' She nodded. 'I love animals and wildlife, too. My dad owned a pet shop when we were growing up and we lived above it. Now I'm a graphic designer and illustrator and specialise in drawing animals. I do a lot of children's book illustrations. One day I'd like to write and illustrate my own book.'

I looked at her then, just as she had looked at me, as one does on finding out something new and unexpected about another person.

'How lovely,' I said.

'Yeah, it's a good job. It means I can work from home and be flexible with my time.'

'So you can spend more time with your fiancé?' I pointed in the direction of the ring on her left hand.

She looked at the ring. 'Oh, that,' she said, as if she'd forgotten it was there and was disappointed by its presence, which I didn't think was very fair to her fiancé, who had probably spent an age choosing just the right ring. Then she was back to inspecting the cases. 'Look at the colour on that one,' she said, her mouth so close to the glass that her breath left a dewy cloud.

'That's the green and gold Cairns Birdwing, *Ornithoptera euphorion*,' I explained. 'The largest butterfly in Australia. The males grow to thirteen centimetres and the females twenty. It feeds off rainforest vines.' I felt proud to still be able to remember interesting facts about each specimen.

'And this one?' She pointed.

'The orange and brown Duke of Burgundy, *Hamearis lucina*. Lives in small colonies on grassland or woodland clearings. It's only found in England.'

'What about this one?'

'The Blue Triangle, *Graphium sarpedon choredon*, which has black-edged wings with turquoise centres. It's found in urban areas, forests and woodlands. It was the first one I ever caught. It was teetering on long grass.'

She turned to me. 'You're very knowledgeable.'

'I'm practising for *Mastermind*.'

'Really?'

'No, but I don't mind a TV quiz show every now and then.'

She laughed, then looked at her watch. 'Gosh, I'm sorry, your meal is getting cold.'

'Don't worry. I'll probably have it for dinner.'

'Oh, okay.'

'Do you have more people to visit?'

'Only one, but he's pretty relaxed. Half the time, he's only just eaten breakfast when we arrive. He probably has his meals for dinner, too. Thanks for letting me see these.'

'No problem,' I said, because in fact, sharing the butterflies with Lottie had been a pleasure and helped distract me from thinking of Jack.

As she drove away, heavy drops of rain bounced off the pavement, the weeds, the path. Rain drummed on the roof, giving a standing ovation for a good ten minutes. It was like being in a suburban rainforest in the rainy season, a forest of bricks and lawns getting drenched. I held the front door and watched and listened. Yet despite the noise, it seemed dreadfully quiet all of a sudden and I felt very alone.

The Phone Call

When Lottie returned on Wednesday, she came with a dog. I could hear it panting and slobbering from inside the house. At least it didn't bark at me when I opened the door but was more interested in sniffing my slippers where all sorts of food smells were lurking amongst the fluff.

'This is my guide dog puppy, Oscar,' Lottie said. 'I hope you don't mind me bringing him, but I need to get him used to cars. Is it okay to leave him on the porch?'

'Labrador?' I asked. She nodded. 'Excellent,' I said, pleased to have guessed correctly.

She tied Oscar's lead around a post and patted his head. 'He should be fine there while I sort out your meal.'

He didn't look remotely fine as he couldn't sit still. 'Are you sure he'll be all right?'

'He's only twelve weeks old but needs to learn. This is part of the pre-guide-dog training that starts at fourteen months. If they qualify, that is.'

'Are you looking after him until then?' I asked. 'Sounds like a lot of work.'

'It's a responsibility, of course, but it doesn't feel like work. I love the company.'

'Goldfish provide company.'

She laughed. 'You can't take a goldfish for a walk.'

'Isn't that a bonus?'

I stared at Oscar with his floppy ears and sliver of drool, unsure what exactly I thought of him. In one respect, he embodied everything that was attractive in a dog: large brown eyes, soft fur, child-like enthusiasm. Yet in another respect, he was everything you didn't want: dribble, dog poo, dog breath, the need to be exercised, entertained and trained. Then he started whimpering as we disappeared inside, which highlighted another reason why goldfish were the ideal pet. You could even hear him in the kitchen.

I turned on our radio to help drown his whining and welcomed Rod Stewart into the kitchen.

'Have you ever had a pet?' Lottie asked, presenting me with the day's meal of risotto.

'A few months ago, I had a cockroach living in my recipe books. But then it got trapped between a Gordon Ramsay and a Jamie Oliver.'

She gave me a sideways glance and shook her head. I think she meant it in a nice way. 'I suppose any pet is good company, isn't it?'

For some reason, that made me think of Jack in the suitcase and I had to quickly try and focus on something else. 'What about you, have you had any other pets – one you didn't have to give back?'

She didn't get to answer because my phone rang. I was happy to let it go. But Lottie wouldn't have it.

'There's the phone,' she said, as if I needed hearing aids.

'They can leave a message.'

'It might be important.'

I shrugged and, deciding I'd had enough of Rod, changed the station.

'What if it's one of your children or something?'

'I don't have any.'

'Oh, sorry, I didn't mean . . .'

The phone was still ringing and was annoyingly out of sync with the choral music now playing. With Lottie looking embarrassed by her faux pas and the racket going on, the reasons for answering the phone outweighed those against. I went to the hall table and picked up.

'Hello?'

'Geri? How are you? We've been worried as you've not been in for so long and then that girl came in to return your books and said you'd had an accident.'

'Oh, that's old news, Karen,' I said, surprised at how lovely it was to hear my ex-colleague's voice. I pictured her in her comfortable loafers and berry-coloured lipstick.

'But are you all right? What happened?'

'I tripped, that was all. Things got in the way – you know how it is. You don't need to worry. How is it down at the library?'

'Same as usual. We could have done with your help over the past couple of weeks, though. It's been the school holidays. Little ratbags the lot of them.' She laughed.

That would explain Ruby and Benny's absence, I thought.

'How are you otherwise, Geri? I left a message on your mobile a week or so ago, did you get it?'

At that moment, Lottie touched me on the arm and mouthed, 'I'm off.'

'Just a minute, Karen,' I said, and then to Lottie, loudly and for effect, 'Goodbye, darling.' I sounded ridiculous because I never referred to anyone as darling. Understandably, Lottie looked at me quizzically and Karen, said, 'Pardon?' The thing was, I didn't want Karen thinking she really did need to worry about me, nor finding out that I wasn't up for library visits in the foreseeable future.

'I've got friends over,' I said.

'Sorry to interrupt. I'd love to drop by sometime. Let me know what suits.'

I felt a sizzle behind my eyes and tried to fight it by squeezing them shut.

'If there's anything I can bring you, too . . .' Karen went on.

The next minute, Lottie, who was still there, started picking up the photos I had turned around. Oh no, there was Jack, the husband I had banished and didn't wish to be reminded of. Oh no, not that one of our wedding day . . .

'Geri?'

'Yes? Oh, um, okay. I'll let you know,' I stuttered.

Lottie replaced the photos exactly how I had positioned them, facing the wall, and put a hand on my arm, just above the sling. It was a soft, gentle, *are you okay* kind of a touch that did nothing to contain my emotion. A tear skated across a cheek, dangled on my chin and dropped on to Lottie's hand. She neither wiped it away nor moved her hand.

'Say hi to the others at the library from me, won't you?' I said as a final goodbye and put the phone down slowly, carefully.

'Come on, let's go and see Oscar,' Lottie said, leading me away from the table.

Before I could object, I was on the porch, and she had untied and picked up the puppy and he was licking my good wrist. Karen's call had thrown me. Its unexpectedness, its thoughtfulness; the sound of Karen's voice and the library's closeness despite feeling so far away; the chance to talk to someone who knew me and me them, no introductions required.

'He loves being tickled under his chin, like this.'

The silly dog wagged his tail and grinned with an open-mouthed, tongue-lolling smile.

'I don't want to pry, but are you all right?' Lottie asked. I could have made a joke about my hormones but that wasn't plausible given how few I had left. 'I don't want to leave you like this. Is there someone who could come and be with you?'

Oscar wriggled in her arms.

'Do you think he needs a wee?' I asked to divert further questioning.

'Yes, you might be right.' Lottie took him to the front lawn. Sure enough, the silly dog killed some grass and probably some weeds, then pulled Lottie around the lawn as if she was his toy.

'I suppose you'd better be off, then,' I called out.

'I don't mind staying a little longer. We could take Oscar for a short walk.'

'I'm thinking of having a nap,' I said.

'I could pop in on the weekend, if you like?'

'You don't need to waste your weekend on me.'

'I wouldn't be . . .' Lottie started, then noticed Oscar squatting. 'Dogs, huh?' she sighed, and pulled a dog poo bag from her pocket.

'See what I mean about goldfish . . .' I thought it best to lighten things up.

'Ha-ha,' she called back.

'There's a bin around the side,' I said, pointing to the end of the veranda where the bins were kept – perfectly placed so I could get rid of kitchen rubbish without having to go down the steps and on to the lawn. She gave me a thumbs up and went to dispose of the bag. Oscar frolicked at the end of the lead as if pleased with his productivity.

'I guess that's my cue to leave,' Lottie said. 'Take care of yourself, Mrs Verne.'

I raised a hand but something about the thought of her leaving made me want to burst into tears again. I didn't hang around to watch her drive away.

A Load of Rubbish

After years of hunting butterflies with Jack, you'd think I'd be adept at watching and waiting. For that was all you had to do: watch and wait. To be honest, I often got impatient, but Jack never did. He loved the anticipation, the hoping, the excitement. For him, it was like buying a lottery ticket. He got as much of a thrill – if not more – in the lead up to the event than at any other stage, which was handy because, more often than not, you ended up winning nothing or spotting only Common Brown garden butterflies. After Lottie mentioned dropping by to see me on the weekend, I found myself watching and waiting for her, as if she was so much more than a five-dollar lottery prize or a Common Brown butterfly. Her company was all the more welcome because she came without judgement and didn't seem to view me as the grieving widow in need of her pity.

On Sunday afternoon, I ended up on the threshold of the front door, taking in the world beyond my gate. Although my heart was pumping quickly as it always does when I'm outside, it was not as fast as usual and I had no tightness in my chest. It was like who-ever had been sitting on it had gotten bored and left. There was a skateboarder wheel-tripping down the street, the sound of a lawn-mower in the distance, a truck far away, the low purr of a plane, the smell of roses stolen by a breeze and the stale stench of leftover car exhaust. A bird on a telephone wire. Two birds on a wire. No birds on any wires. Wires undulating in the wind. Whispers rippling down the phone wires. Gossip. Chatter. Tears. Laughter. My tears. Someone else's laughter.

Sue rode past on a bicycle with a basket, wearing a pink helmet and a high-vis vest with the words 'Neighbourhood Watch: Preventing Crime' on the back. My spirits lifted. I waved but Sue was concentrating on the speed hump ahead and didn't see me. I waved at a courier stepping out of his van to deliver a box next door, at a white cat fence-hopping on to my lawn and the off-leash dog weeing on the gate with its owner strolling lazily behind. I kept on waving. I hadn't waved so much since the last royal visit. *Hello, world, I'm here.* Hoping someone might notice. Hoping someone would acknowledge me and wave back.

They didn't.

I waited a little longer and surveyed the street one more time, thinking how nice it would have been for Len to have appeared out of the blue, waving a sunburnt arm.

But there was no Len. There was no Lottie, either with or without her cute but silly dog.

I stepped back inside and shut the front door.

Immediately, I opened it again, ripped off the 'Lady sleeping. Do not disturb' sign, screwed it into a ball and threw it on to the porch.

On Monday, there was still no Lottie. Instead, Doug and Eve came by with a serving of spaghetti Bolognese. I asked them if they knew whether Lottie was all right.

'I suppose so,' Eve said. 'Maybe she's busy.'

'Or the roster's been changed. Who knows?' Doug added.

'Who knows?' I repeated light-heartedly, as if I wasn't bothered. I let them in but found myself reverting to the backwards counting until they had left the property. They seemed nice enough people, but I didn't feel as comfortable with them in the house as I did with Lottie.

On Tuesday, the nurse returned to check on me. She caught me by surprise at two in the afternoon still not dressed, wondering if I could be bothered to make the apple and blackberry tart I fancied eating. I'd forgotten she was coming. She happily checked me at the front door and was so pleased with my progress that she said I no longer needed to wear the sling.

'Can I keep it as a memento?' As much as I was pleased to take off the sling, I had also grown attached to it.

'I suppose,' she said. 'You've got to do the exercises I give you, though, okay?'

On Wednesday, two different volunteers turned up, which unnerved me completely. I wasn't happy with the roster changes and wished even harder that Lottie would resume her duties. I stared at the two women and they stared back at me. Not even a smile was exchanged between us.

'Hi, luv, where's your kitchen?' asked one of the women, shorter than me by a good ten centimetres. I noted she hadn't checked the schedule to see if I had a name.

I pointed towards the gloom at the end of the hall.

'Is Lottie not coming anymore?' I asked.

'Sorry, don't know who she is,' the other one said.

'Young, chatty, short hair like Twiggy . . . ?'

They looked at each other and shrugged. Perhaps they didn't know who Twiggy was. I smiled apologetically. It wasn't reciprocated and that's when I saw myself for who I really was: a name on a timetable with thousands of others. Strangers rostered with strangers, none of whom were the slightest bit interested in the other. And yet, there was an intimacy about our interactions. The volunteers didn't just stay outside the house, they went all the way through it, leaving behind their fingerprints, footprints, smells and sounds. Yet with Lottie it had felt like something so much more. Was I getting attached to her in a way I shouldn't? Had Lottie become my living sling?

The women were still looking at me expectantly. I let them in and started my counting routine as I watched them set up my meal. In silence, they departed, leaving a spicy scent of coq au vin and echoes of their heavy tread clinging to the walls.

After that, I moped around the house, unable to concentrate on a thing. I relinquished all expectations of seeing Lottie again and returned the Meals on Wheels service back to its rightful place as an annoyingly invasive food delivery system. Unable to sit still, I tried to distract myself by putting on a wash, as it was no longer possible to ignore the smell following me around, which no amount of Cacharel's Anaïs Anaïs eau de toilette, which I'd been wearing since 1978, was able to hide. I wafted a broom around the kitchen and washed the dishes in the sink. I did the very minimum of what could be found in the library section 648 Housekeeping purely as a way of keeping myself busy.

By the time Friday lumbered around, I may have smelt a little fresher but felt as flat as a hammered chicken schnitzel.

I turned on the television and was relieved to find something that interested me: David Attenborough's *Blue Planet*. I settled into the sofa, looking forward to being transported to a far-off land. Halfway through, something pinged in my brain, like the power had just been turned back on. I rushed to the bedroom. I may not have previously wanted to play Jack's game. In fact, I had purposely avoided it. Yet it's hard to ignore an idea that pops into your head, and almost impossible not to act upon it. I got on my hands and knees, fished out Jack's note from under the bed and reread the clue: *Naturalist author doctors a line of heart.* Could Jack have been talking about the naturalist David Attenborough and a book he once wrote? Was 'line of heart' an anagram, which was what the word 'doctors' indicated? I went to the bookshelf in the computer room but there were no David Attenborough books there, nor any by any naturalist. I went into the living room. On the bottom shelf of the small wooden bookcase that was my mother's, I found *Life on Earth*, by David Attenborough. I closed my eyes and rearranged the letters. Could 'line of heart' be an anagram of 'life on earth'? It was tricky doing it in my head without writing it down, but I had a hunch it was right. I pulled out the book and fanned the pages, but nothing fell out. I looked on the inside cover. Nothing.

But inside the back cover, there was.

Held in place by its jacket was a piece of cream paper and another clue.

> *Well done, my love, you're on your way. Did it take you long? Oh, how I wish I could be there with you, but all fool me for making you do this after I've gone! Before we get to the next clue, I have something to give you: a rose in your name. Overleaf, you will see a picture of a clotted cream perfumed rose I have called 'Geri-pie'. It's ready and waiting to be delivered. All you have to do is call the number on the back of the picture. I thought it could be the first new plant to revive the garden. You must tend to it, my love, spray it with organic lime–sulphur mix and feed it compost. Nurture it like you would yourself!*

I looked at the rose. It was beautiful. The colour of champagne, its petals fluted and fine. I slipped it into my pocket and went back to the letter.

> *Are you ready for the next puzzle?*
> *Clue number two: 'In a drawer in our house, a small*
> *unit of life comes into the longing to be like some'*
> *(10).*
> > *Good luck!*
> > *Jack x*

This clue was even more cryptic than the first. *What are you trying to do to me, Jack?* Death by cryptogram was not how I'd envisaged going. I read it several times over. Still, I was intrigued, and this time less inclined to ignore it. Rather, I was determined and eager to solve it. More than anything, it was a relief to have something to do, and in a strange way, it was like compensation for not having the suitcase around anymore.

But I didn't get very far because Meals on Wheels arrived. And Lottie was back! When I saw her at the door, my heart may have done a little clap, but I was annoyed at having my feelings meddled with. I was a food processor of emotions as it was. I wanted her there yet didn't want her there.

'You haven't come all week,' I snapped. I couldn't help it.

'Yeah . . . sorry.' She didn't seem very sorry. In fact, she wouldn't even look me in the eye. 'Stuff came up,' she mumbled.

'Stuff?'

She didn't explain but stepped inside. 'Have a good week?' she asked.

'You don't need to bother going to the kitchen. I can carry the meal bag now.' I waggled my left arm.

'Oh yes, the sling's off! How good is that?' she said but didn't stop.

'Lottie, please, I'd like to take it,' I said, quickly following.

'It's okay. This is all part of the service.' Suddenly she was perky. 'You didn't tell me about your week?'

'What if I'd *like* to take it?' I insisted. 'To practise with two useable arms.'

'I know it's hard feeling like you've lost your independence, but I'd make the most of this service while you can. You had a good reason to get it in the first place.'

'I didn't get it, as it happens,' I said. 'A friend organised it behind my back. Technically, you're here against my will.' We were in the kitchen now. I leant back against the door frame and crossed my arms.

'Oh . . .' She looked put out. 'I'm sure they did it to help.'

'He's gone on a cruise with his girlfriend.'

She nodded as if unsure what to say to that. Instead, she took out a meal from the bag for today. 'Macaroni cheese,' she announced with attempted enthusiasm. 'And you've got frozen pork hotpot and vegetable barley soup for the weekend.' She went to put the weekend meals in the fridge. That's when she saw my last two meals on plates, uneaten. 'Hey, what's this? You haven't touched them.'

I made a non-committal noise, which could have been a cat mewling or a squeaky door hinge depending on your point of view. I didn't wish to explain how lacking in appetite I'd been. How all I'd had for lunch yesterday was an apple with defrosted cheddar, after which I fell asleep on the sofa, then woke up with an ear resting on an apple core on the sofa arm. 'I'm saving them,' I said.

'The meals are designed to be eaten fresh.'

I shrugged.

'Look, Mrs Verne, it's not a good idea to skip meals.'

'Who says I'm skipping meals?'

'I saw some in your outdoor bin.'

'So you *were* prying.'

'No, I was throwing away Oscar's poo.'

I looked away. Lottie's visit was disintegrating rapidly and proof I should never have started thinking that her visits were something worth looking forward to.

'I know we can't make you eat what we bring . . .' she started.

'No, you can't,' I cut her off.

'I didn't mean to upset you.'

'Well, you have.' I was in a huff and had no inclination to pretend I wasn't. 'What does it matter to you, anyway? I'm just another client on your list and in a few weeks – when my friend's funds run out – the service will end and we'll never see each other again.'

I wasn't expecting Lottie to look so shocked. Not just that, but only then did I notice the dark rings around her eyes, the frown lines between her brows, and she appeared even more dishevelled than usual.

'Wow, okay, if that's what you think this is . . .' she said.

'Of course it is. It's a business transaction under the guise of care.'

'*Genuine* care, thank you very much.'

'Pfft,' I said, which was a nothing word to mean I had nothing more to say.

'We do care, Mrs Verne. I, especially, care.'

'That's what you've been trained to say.'

'No, it isn't!' She was indignant. But then, so was I.

'I think it's best you finish up and go,' I said as nicely as possible, because while I didn't truly want her to go, I couldn't let myself become attached, knowing I was only going to lose her at a later date.

She lowered her head and sealed her lips, which may have been quivering, I couldn't be sure. She made room for the new meals amongst the old in the fridge and left the macaroni cheese on the table. The atmosphere in the kitchen had become as taut as a rubber band on a homemade slingshot and I told myself the sooner she was gone, the better. Nothing more was said until she slipped past me at the front door.

'Sorry,' she whispered and walked out.

Cryptic Conundrums

Well, that was a disagreeable interaction and necessitated an immediate distraction. I pulled out the photo of the rose from my pocket and stuck it to the fridge door. I admired it for a minute, then returned to Jack's second clue and took it to the living room. I plopped into an armchair and my bottom plunged into the sagging cushion as if, after thirty years of keeping me propped, it had had enough. I reread the clue: *In a drawer in our house, a small unit of life comes into the longing to be like some* (10). It seemed like one of those brain teasers that could keep you occupied for days, weeks even. Yet I didn't want it to get the better of me. I had to solve it for Jack. If for no other reason than because my husband had bothered to spend the last few ounces of energy he had on concocting a game for me to play. If he'd been able to do this for me, surely I could work it out for him.

But how? All I knew was that the answer was one word of ten letters and that I had to break down the clue into parts to find a 'straight' clue – the answer that is hidden somewhere – and a word or words to indicate how it is hidden. The question was, which was what? Was the 'drawer' the straight answer? And why was Jack referring yet again to 'life'? Was it an anagram of 'be like some' or 'unit of life', both of which had ten letters? I wandered around the house mulling it over. I took a pen and paper to the kitchen to play around with the letters and words as I ate the macaroni, but only became more confused. I decided to sleep on it and start again the next day. Yet, even then, I didn't feel any closer to getting the answer. I needed help. Ruling out the 'phone a friend' option, I went to the computer and searched for *how to solve cryptic clues*, finding an extensive ten-page document that was easy to read and understand. I fiddled and scribbled, ate some chocolate, had an instant coffee, drank some Baileys, and squeezed as much out of my brain cells as I could. But all that resulted was me getting irritable. I decided to sleep on it one more time.

It was during my Sunday-morning cup of tea at the kitchen table that something clicked. I fished out the clue from underneath the newspaper and read it again. Could it be that, perhaps, there was a word around a word around a word? I broke the clue down into simple terms. *A small unit of life* is a cell. *Longing* is like missing. *Some* might be any. And if I rearranged those words . . . well . . . could that make 'miscellany'?

Did he mean the junk drawer in the kitchen?

I raced to the kitchen and pulled it open. Although I hadn't long ago been in this drawer and hadn't noticed a note, it didn't mean there wasn't one. I flung everything out but there was no note from Jack. I thought again. The filing cabinet? I went to the butterfly room but there were no files called miscellany or miscellaneous. What about the desk in the computer room? I opened every drawer and rifled around. It wasn't until the last one that I found a manila folder labelled 'Miscellany'. My heart did a fast tempo jig similar to a cha-cha-cha, and this time it felt great.

I held my breath and opened it. There, folded neatly on top, was another handwritten letter from my husband and beneath it was a wooden plaque engraved with the words 'The Ellipsis House'.

Hip hip hooray! You've come to the last clue . . .

The last clue? I was just beginning to enjoy this.

> *But first, your gift. I know you like to call our house*
> *The Full-Stop House, but I've decided to rename it.*
> *A full stop is so final, don't you think? I prefer the*
> *open-endedness of ellipses. Hang it by the front door*
> *as a symbol of hope for the future.*
>
> *Now, to the clue. This one, my dear, is a poem:*
> *Madame,*
> *There's a comma in your midst,*
> *Do you get my gist?*
> *Or perhaps you need another clue.*
> *It is neither a tiger nor a cabbage,*
> *Or even a blue.*
> *Think diamonds and tiaras,*
> *Princesses and queens*
> *Where all is not as it seems.*
> *Have fun!*
> *Love Jack x*

I started to laugh, then cry, then laugh again. How clever was my husband? I needed another round of chocolate and coffee, plus a circuit of the house to get my brain working again. I even picked up the remote control and pretended to turn myself on, which gave me the giggles. Power up, Geri, I laughed, but of course nothing happened. *What are you on about this time, Jackie-boy?*

Perhaps the poem was cryptic and included anagrams and puzzles on each line, I thought. Yet I couldn't seem to make any new words that had any meaning at all. Was he being literal about the comma as a punctuation mark or was he hinting at its historical usage as a placement for orators to know when to take a breath?

Was Jack again referring to life and living as he had done in the previous two clues? Or was it something else? Then there was the tiger and the cabbage – an animal and a plant. But what was the blue? Did it refer to David Attenborough's *Blue Planet* series I was watching on Friday? And when did Jack ever call me madame?

I decided a stint of mindless and menial tasks would help me think. I propped the plaque against the wall on the hall table – I would hang it later – and went into the butterfly room to clean the display cases. I opened the blind above the desk to let in some light, had a swivel in the chair, did a doodle on the notepad, before setting to work on the glass. How much better the frames looked, clear and sparkling and dust-free. I moved around the room from left to right, taking my time.

That's when it hit me. Was Jack's poem about butterflies? A Comma, a Tiger, a Cabbage and a Blue were all species of butterfly. Of course they were! How could I have been so silly not to twig? I went back to the kitchen to read the clue over and over again, before returning to the butterfly room. I worked my way around each display case checking the names of every species. I found the Tiger, the Cabbage and the Blue butterflies, but noted that the poem said that they weren't the answers. When I got to the Comma, with its scalloped orange edge and dark spots, I inspected the case. There was no obvious note. Then again, the poem did say that it was in my 'midst', rather than the answer itself. Was it something to do with the last part which talked about diamonds and tiaras? I went to the next case, and the next. On the fourth row, in the middle, was the butterfly Jack spotted on one of our first dates: the Diadem. Not a crown with jewels, but a butterfly whose colouring and markings are 'not as they seem' because they mimic the toxic African Monarch as a way to ward off prey. Bingo!

I carefully took the case off the wall and turned it over.

There was an envelope taped to the back.

I prised it off and took it to the desk. With my own personal migration of butterflies in my belly, I had to sit down. I ripped open the envelope and unfolded a letter. It began with a quote and explained why Jack had opened the poem with 'Madame'.

'But as she glides past him, beautiful, laughing softly behind her fan, don't we who are men sigh with hope? We, who are not handsome, not brave, nor powerful, yet somehow believe, like Pinkerton, that we deserve a Butterfly.' From Madame Butterfly *by Giacomo Puccini, Act 1, Scene 5.*

Dearest Geri,
Thank you for indulging me in my fun and games. It was, as always, a pleasure to play with you.

You may be wondering why I didn't hand you this note on my deathbed, or leave it with my will, or even just tell you in person. I didn't because how boring would that have been? I also wanted to put words on paper because I think, when spoken aloud, they can get carried away by the breeze and blurred and fuzzied with time – forgotten about even. But the written word does not. It is concrete, final, it lasts – unless it's thrown away, of course!

The thing is, Geri, I want you to know that you have always been and always will be my one and only butterfly. You were the most wonderful wife, gliding into my life when I least expected it and sticking with me and by me for fifty years. You showed me how to love during times of heartache and cry during times of joy. You indulged my silly love of buying lottery tickets, hitting a small ball around a field and cheekily asking strangers for plant cuttings from their gardens. You lifted me up when I didn't get the job I wanted all those years ago, and sang my praises to the ladies at the library so I became the 'Butterfly Man' in the school holidays. You managed to turn a savoury tooth into a sweet one and raise my cholesterol in a gloriously decadent way. How much fun was it when you tried teaching me to cartwheel, as if a man of uncoordinated means had some hope of getting even halfway there? How bland and boring my life would have been without you in it. It would have been like the Cabbage White instead of the colourful Madagascan Sunset Moth.

I cherish every second we had together and dearly wish I didn't have to leave you. I will miss you terribly. I miss you already! Yet however low you may get and however sad you may feel, please promise me you won't stop living. Life is to be treasured and I want you to treasure yours. Live life now for the both of us.

All my love,
Jack x

P.S. There's one more thing to find. This time, no riddle. All you have to do is go to the pots and pans corner cupboard in the kitchen. At the very back, in the far corner is a container. Open it.

I couldn't get to the kitchen fast enough and nearly tripped on a chair leg reaching for the cupboard. I shoved it out of the way, opened the door and pulled out every pot and pan. I had to get on my knees to reach the less accessible items, discovering a pasta maker I'd not used for years and rusty muffin pans I'd forgotten about. There, at the very back in the corner, as Jack had indicated, was a square plastic container holding something round and fat. I pulled it out and took off the lid. There was another letter sitting on top.

Surprise! I've made you a cake! Not just any cake, but your grandmother's fruit cake. I know how much you love it – you made it for our wedding, after all. Plus, fruit cakes are meant to last (although I do hope you don't take years to find it!). But more importantly, I made it so you had something to help mark the start of something new. Think of it as a celebratory christening cake. Serve it with champagne to toast your new beginnings. And whatever you do, don't eat it alone. Enjoy it with others. I give you my blessing to look forward to the future even if I'm no longer physically in it. Hopefully, I'll still be in your heart, as you are in mine, because that's all that truly matters.

It wasn't easy – you know me, fumble-fingers in the kitchen! But I followed the recipe to the letter and also borrowed a cookbook from the library which gave me extra tips on how to age and store fruit cakes. You've been so generous over the years with your endless supply of baking and trying to make me proficient in the kitchen that I wanted to return the favour. I hope, this time, I've done a better job of it and that the cake is, at the very least, edible, if not actually delicious. Next to the cake, you should also find the bottle of brandy I've been using to help keep it moist and fresh, wrapped in a tea towel, so you may now want to add some more.

All I can hope now is that you don't do a kitchen clear-out before finding the first clue. I'm banking on the fact that as you aren't usually a cupboard cleaner, my ruse should work. From my perspective, the plan has gone without a hitch, which makes me feel pretty chuffed. So chuffed that the other day I very nearly blurted it out to you!

Please promise you'll make an occasion of the cake and, as I've said before, don't, whatever you do, give up on life.

Fondest love,

Jack x

P.S. You will also note, another gift – something longer-lasting than cake. I would have buried it in the mixture like a Christmas coin if I hadn't been worried someone might choke on it!

I unwrapped the cake and inspected it. It smelt rich with cinnamon, cloves and brandy, and seemed literally and figuratively too good to eat. There was a small velvet drawstring bag encased in clingfilm on the top. I opened that, too. Inside was a silver cockleshell on a chain. Plus a note: *Do you recognise this, Geri-pie? It's the shell you collected on our visit to the seaside all those years ago – the first time you told me you loved me. I found it in your jewellery box and had it cast in silver.*

I put the chain around my neck and pressed the shell to my skin. I also retrieved the brandy and took a swig from the bottle. I sat with the cake at the kitchen table. I couldn't take my eyes off it and couldn't stop touching the necklace. They were two of the best presents Jack had ever given me.

392.5 Wedding and Marriage Customs

Jack was a gentleman the day I met him and stayed a gentleman until he died. He used to pop foil-covered chocolate into my handbag when I wasn't looking, serenade me outside my house with a pretend guitar and write me letters even when he wasn't going away. When we were first courting, he'd invite me on dates leaving handwritten notes in the letterbox, often teasing me with something cryptic so I was never entirely sure what we were doing. Once, he wrote: *I love 'er. Or should I say, I love you! Be ready for pickup at 7 p.m.*, which was code for going to the cinema to watch the hit movie of 1968, *Oliver!* I loved the suspense so much I forced myself not to work them out. He loved that I loved being surprised.

When Jack proposed, we'd only been going out for six months. His invitation read: *Join me for a starry, starry night and* un petit pique-nique. *Bring nothing but yourself.* So I did. It was a Friday night and he picked me up at dusk, his car laden with quiche, bread, salad, champagne, plastic glasses, corkscrew, picnic rug, utensils. Had I suspected? I liked to think I hadn't noticed Jack's excited agitation – at a level not normally associated with picnics under the stars – the extra attention to detail – the love-heart paper serviettes and strawberries for the champagne, and the worry about the weather.

'It might rain, Geri,' he said the day before. 'We'd better have a back-up plan.'

'A bit of rain might make it more fun,' I said. 'Soggy quiche never killed anyone, did it?' I laughed. 'Anyway, there's always the car.'

Jack pulled a face. Sharing quiche over a gear stick was clearly not what he had in mind. But in the end, it didn't rain and the quiche was tasty. When the sky turned to soot and the moon lit up the stars, Jack poured the last of the champagne and produced a box. A tiny red square that held its very own star inside. It was like a dolls' house chandelier.

'Would you, Geri-pie?' he asked.

A tingle shimmied through me, a full-bodied shiver of joy. I thought about how caring he was, how gentle, funny and kind. 'Would I what, Jackie-boy?' I replied.

'Would you . . . ?' he began, resting on two knees and looking me in the eye as the moon was our witness and the stars our guiding lights.

Before he had time to finish, I answered, 'Would I ever.'

Baked Beans

After what seemed like an age, I dried my eyes, sloshed some brandy over the cake and rewrapped it. I took another nip of brandy and placed the bottle and the cake centre stage in the pantry. What a morning it had been. I felt like a can of drained chickpeas. I went to the bedroom and put my feet up at the window seat and stared at the white flowers of the crab apple tree on the front lawn as they flickered in the wind. A high-waisted cloud cinched in around the sky. A low-flying bird swooped and disappeared. It was while gazing at this view and wallowing in the overwhelming kindness of my husband that I got the urge to talk to someone. Not to myself. Not even to Jack. But to someone living. To make me feel as if I was still part of the world. That I could get to a place of living fully like Jack wanted me to. But Len and Crystal weren't around, I didn't have Lottie's number and other friends I'd not spoken to for a while. Perhaps I could listen to the message my ex-colleague Karen left on my mobile? It would be lovely to hear her voice. Maybe I could call her back and invite her over for a cup of tea.

Years ago, I programmed my mobile phone's ringtone to be that of an old car horn. I loved its burly old-fashioned sound that made others start – but only because I'd set the volume to high so I could hear it from the bottom of my handbag. Jack preferred the demure chime of a crackle of crickets, so that if his phone was in a pocket, it sounded like he'd captured the outdoors and bottled it in his trousers. When he died, I added his mobile to the coffin because I was tired of having to answer it and explain what had happened to those unaware of his death, like the telemarketer, the dry cleaner's, or an acquaintance at the golf club who never checks his emails.

I found my phone lying dormant in my handbag in the wardrobe between my Hush Puppies sandals and walking shoes with orthotic insoles. I pulled it out of the bag and emptied the rest of the contents on to my bed. I found notes, coins, receipts from the chemist and the funeral home, a half-used packet of travel tissues, some foil toffee wrappers, the car keys, and my sunglasses. When would I wear them again? Then I picked up my phone and powered it on. Karen's was the first message to come through.

'Hi, Geri, it's me, Karen, in case you've forgotten what my voice sounds like. Ha-ha! But seriously, we miss you. I heard you had a fall and I hope you're all right. Anyway, give me a call. I'd love a chat.'

I smiled and replayed the message. I was going to replay it for a third time when I noticed there was another from her recorded thirty seconds after the first.

'Me again. I forgot to mention I have a new number so don't call me on the one you have stored. Long story short, I changed phone providers but had to get a new number as I dropped the phone in the toilet. Nincompoop, ha-ha! I couldn't let that pun go to waste, could I? Oops, there I go again . . .' Her laughter echoed long after the call ended. Karen was one of those people who could make a sunflower grow in the middle of winter. She was so crazy-happy that she could make you laugh even if, sometimes, you weren't sure what you were laughing about.

I was about to call her back when an incoming text made me jump. It was from Len.

Hi Geri, how are you going? Did you get my other texts? What a place Egypt is! We're sweating like cheese left out in the midday sun but hey-ho. Here's a photo of us at the Edfu Temple and one of Crystal by the pool on the ship.

There they were, the two of them standing before a gigantic sand-coloured temple. Len was laughing and red-faced and Crystal was hugging his waist, one leg kicked backwards as if caught mid-dance. Then there was Crystal on a sunlounger in her bathers and sun hat with an orange cocktail, the sky hazy, as if too lazy to brighten up. Gosh, I thought, what fun. I realised I felt envious of them sweating like two lumps of cheddar in the midday sun.

Then a new text came through. Len again:

News break! We have a slight problem. There's been a hitch with our flight. Looks like we'll be delayed a day or two. But don't worry, I'll keep you posted. And another thing, if you're getting these, can you please reply? A 'hi' will do. It would be great to hear from you.

Hi, I replied, *nice to hear from you too.*

There were other messages – more from Len, two from unknown numbers, and a few from friends. But there was one name that stood out from all the others: Jack's. I closed my eyes and breathed in and out, long and slow. They were the breaths of a woman who never realised the longing she felt to hear the voice of her dead husband, the husband she was missing so very, very much. I took another deep breath, pressed the message and listened.

'Hi, Geri-pie . . .' His voice sounded lively but weak. It was the voice of a man about to die. 'I've just woken up and fancied baked beans. Any chance of getting a tin?'

I listened to it again.

It was that day in the hospital when Len arrived as I was leaving to do some errands. Jack must have fallen asleep either during or after Len's visit and, on waking, called me as I was in the grocery store. I replayed it. There he was, cocooned in the hospital bed, wrapped in starched sheets, a sliver of the man he once was, his skin the colour of pale mustard, death tickling his funny bone, weariness dragging him under. *Hi, Geri-pie.* The name he loved to call me. *Hi, Jackie-boy.* The name I loved to call him.

Oh, Jack, of all the things you could have asked for.

Yet I bought him a tin of baked beans that day, wrapped it in recycled red cellophane and tied the fluted top with a strip of white curling ribbon. Never had a baked bean tin looked so good. When I gave it to him, he grinned as best he could with a mouth that wanted to droop more than smile, then unwrapped it with his frail hands, savoured the label and the thought of eating its contents before placing it on the table next to him by a glass of water and his packet of pills.

'Thanks, Geri-pie,' he said.

I took his hands and held the bones and we had a moment, just the two of us and a tin of baked beans.

The Shed

How I ended up on the floor at the back of the shed with my head resting on the suitcase, I do not know. I came around to the smell of damp wood and dusty earth. The zippered corner of the canvas dug into my neck and my phone lay in the curl of my lap. My slippers had fallen off and the sleeve of my dressing gown was sodden. I remembered thinking – somewhere between leaving the bedroom and arriving in the shed – that Jack did not deserve to be banished. The man who had secretly made me fruit cake deserved so much more. Not only that, I realised that taking him out of my life had not made living easier. There had to be a better way for me to move on and a nobler way to immortalise my husband. I put an arm around the case and squeezed. It was good to be back with my husband. I felt the fingers on my left hand, at the spot where the rings should have been. The indentations were less pronounced, but my skin was still pale where the rings had once sat. Their absence made my eyes start watering; I couldn't make them stop. I wiped my nose with the back of a hand and inadvertently rubbed a cobweb across my cheek.

'I'm sorry, Jackie-boy,' I spluttered. 'Sorry for banishing you. Sorry for not honouring your last wish. Sorry for lying all those years ago. Sorry I let you down.' Every sorry I could think of tumbled out. 'I will move on. I just haven't figured out how to do it yet.'

Jack may have muttered something back, but my sniffs were banging around the shed like a jar containing a single gumball and I was so engrossed in my own thoughts that I didn't catch it. Then I heard my name.

'Mrs Verne?' a voice called, which was weird because Jack never called me that. 'Mrs Verne?'

I sniffed again and wiped my eyes, only to see a blurred face appear at the door. It was Lottie. 'What are you doing here? Are you all right?'

'Pretty good, thanks.'

'But . . .' She stepped inside and looked around. 'Did you have another fall?'

'I don't think so. I can't remember. Watch your step,' I cautioned as she nearly tripped over the strimmer.

She skipped deftly over the end of it and came towards me. 'Are you hurt?'

I contemplated how sore I was. There was no doubt I was riddled with internal dents and dings that I was only just beginning to recognise – like how loneliness was giving me tummy ache and grief had sprained my soul. If I could have nipped down to the library to section 150 Psychology or 306.88 Grief or 616.85 Depression, I might have been able to provide a clearer diagnosis. But externally, now that my leg and arm had healed, all I had was a small bruise on my thigh from walking into the bed frame in the middle of the night.

'Not really,' I said.

'Okay, good. You gave me a scare, you know. When you didn't answer the door, I went down the side of the house, spotted the back door open, then the shed. How long have you been in here?'

'Honestly, I'm fine. Sit down, if you like.'

She looked at her only seat option – a dirty floor – but sat down anyway, leant against the wall and stretched out her legs.

'I've got you another book, on nature walks around the world,' she said. 'And today's meal of chicken cacciatore.' She took in her surroundings as if considering the merits of lying on the floor of an abandoned shed containing projects once thought about but never started, half-jobs and endless jobs, smelling of soil, sweat and rusted metal. 'Is this your little hidey hole away from the world?' she asked. 'Sometimes I like to escape, too. Although I think there are nicer places, if you don't mind me saying.'

'Probably,' I said.

She smiled.

'I'm sorry about the other day.'

'Me too.'

'I don't want you to be mad at me.'

'I don't either. Anyway, why would *you* want to escape the world? You're young and carefree with a life ahead of you.'

She shrugged. 'A life of sorts.'

'Meaning?'

'Meaning, once upon a time I was engaged and now, it seems, I'm not.'

'Oh, Lottie . . .'

'That's why I didn't visit for a week.'

I placed a hand on her leg.

'We'd been engaged for two years, you know.'

I nodded.

'Well, we'd been having a bit of a break. I thought Josh needed some "time out" because I was "putting the heat on to get married" – his words not mine – but didn't think it meant we'd actually split up, or that he'd start seeing someone else. Last week was the worst. Not only did he tell me it was over, he came to pick up the rest of his things and brought his girlfriend, too. I saw her sitting in his car admiring her nails.'

Lottie looked at her own nails, as if wondering whether, had she bothered to keep them clean and painted, her fiancé may have hung around. 'Sorry to go on. But thanks for listening. You know you can talk to me, too, if there's anything you want to get off your chest.' She looked at me expectantly.

'My friend Bailey lends me his ear from time to time,' I said seriously so that she believed I really did have a friend called Bailey.

'That's nice.'

'It is.' I smiled fondly at the thought of my pantry mate, which was, I remembered, running dangerously low.

'Okay, so do you think it's time to get out of here?'

'Must we? Why don't you tell me more about yourself?'

'I'm not really that interesting.'

'What about your family?'

'Only if you promise to tell me something about you?'

I nodded.

'Okay, well, I have a dad and a younger sister. Technically, I have a mother, but I don't really know her. She walked out on us when I was seven.'

'Oh, Lottie, that's terrible.' Reluctantly childless, I couldn't imagine doing such a thing. 'Did you ever see her again?'

'I tried reconciling with her when I was twenty, but it didn't work out. We'd agree to meet and sometimes she'd turn up and sometimes she wouldn't. She was flaky like that – a taker not a giver, as well as untrustworthy. She stole money off Dad when she left, and although she got in contact a few times, she lied about all sorts of things. Poor Dad didn't deserve to be treated like that. As awful as it sounds, we were probably better off without her. The one positive, because you have to look for them, is that me, my sister and Dad are really close.'

'It's good to look at the positives.'

Lottie giggled. 'Sorry, that made me think of Darryl.'

'Darryl?'

'My pet parrot, who's a very good impersonator and always manages to cheer me up. He only needs to hear something a few times and he'll say it on a regular basis. When Josh came last week, Darryl swore at him every time he walked past. You should have seen the look on Josh's face,' she laughed.

I contemplated the benefits or not of having a bird that mimicked you. I could appreciate the novelty but unlike the TV, there was no mute button.

'Right, now it's your turn.'

With the spotlight on me, I didn't know what to say. There was, of course, so much I could divulge, yet so little I wanted to.

'What about your husband, why don't you tell me about him?' Lottie suggested.

I became aware of the suitcase that was acting as my pillow and felt self-conscious on Jack's behalf. I thought for a minute. 'We were married for fifty years,' I said proudly.

'Wow! So what's the secret? There must be something?'

'You have to be a team, I suppose. Two halves in sync. Jack and I complemented each other like a pair of shoes. A right shoe can never become a left and a left shoe can never become a right, but together they bring out the best in each other.'

'That's good.' Lottie nodded. 'I like that.'

I patted Jack and thanked him for the spur-of-the-moment analogy.

'What else?'

'His middle name was Geoffrey.'

'And?'

'And . . .'

And then I started crying.

'Oh, Mrs Verne, are you okay?'

I flapped a hand as if my tears were a couple of pesky flies and there was nothing to worry about. It was ridiculous that a reminder of my husband's middle name could make me cry.

'I'll get tissues,' she said, getting to her feet and running into the house before I had time to tell her that my dressing gown worked well as a sponge. She was back quickly. 'I couldn't find any unused tissues, so I got a toilet roll.' She tore off six squares. I blew into the paper and regretted not splashing out on the softer, more expensive brand. She tore off some more, then ripped off some for herself and blew loudly. Now she was crying!

'Sorry about the toilet paper,' I said.

'We'll have to get you some more tissues, then. I know, why don't we go on an outing?' Her wet eyes widened. 'You must be in need of some fresh air after being in here.'

'To buy tissues?'

'Why not? An outing would be fun.'

'I wouldn't put tissues and fun in the same sentence.'

'We can put them in two different sentences and make two different outings.' She laughed.

I considered her suggestion. If I was to live up to Jack's expectations, something had to change. I had to start somewhere.

'What I also think we should do is exchange phone numbers,' she added. 'Just in case there's an emergency and friends aren't around to help. Is that your phone? Let's do it now.'

I didn't disagree.

Then she said it was time to get off the floor.

I used Jack for support, got myself halfway, then used Lottie's arms to help get me the rest of the way. Things spun for a minute before settling back into themselves. But now I was up standing and Jack was still lying. 'Can you help me with the case?' I said.

'Let's get you inside first. I can come back for it.'

Lottie instructed me to sit at the kitchen table while she put the kettle on and found a half-eaten packet of ginger biscuits I'd forgotten about, which were so old they didn't need dunking in tea to soften them up.

'Could you get the suitcase now?' I asked.

'I will. But have a biscuit. I'm worried about your blood sugar levels.'

I sipped some tea but abandoned the biscuit and waited for Lottie to return.

'What have you got in this thing?' she asked, heaving it inside.

'Over here,' I said, patting the side of my chair.

She studied me for a second, before wheeling Jack closer, then stared at my hand on the handle as if she'd never seen anyone hold a suitcase before.

'Aren't you going to have a cup with me?' I asked. 'Or let me guess, you prefer tea that tastes like steeped lawn clippings?'

She laughed.

'I thought so.'

'Oh, hey, I almost forgot. There was a delivery on your porch.' She went over to the box on the floor next to the fridge and lifted it on to the kitchen table. My name was written in capitals on the top. The handwriting looked familiar, but I couldn't place it. I fetched the scissors from the knife block and sliced through the tape. Atop a mound of shredded paper was a card that read:

> *Dear Geri,*
> *We thought you might like a surprise goodie box of gourmet treats and some novels – latest releases from the bookshop so you don't have to worry about returning them or incurring a fine. Hope you get better soon.*

Love from all us at the library – Karen, Betty,
Hugh, Sam, Andrew and Julie.

Inside were deluxe after-dinner mints wrapped in blue foil, a gourmet biscuit tin, some specialty teas, blackberry preserve, a bottle of pink Prosecco and four books. It was one of those bottle-me moments I wished could last forever . . .

I became aware of Lottie speaking.

'Shall we take them out?'

I displayed the food items along the bench under the window and placed the novels in the middle of the table, bookending them between the salt and pepper shakers. We admired them for a minute before Lottie reached into her backpack for the library book she had selected for me. 'I'll try and come by tomorrow, if you like.'

'You don't have to.' I looked at Jack. *Things are on the up now, aren't they, Jackie-boy?*

'But I'd like to,' she said.

'In that case, that would be nice.'

PART THREE

700 The Arts, Recreation and
Outdoor Life

The Big, Endless World

In anticipation of Lottie's visit and in light of my new resolve, I decided to give myself a spring clean. Normally I have the healthy tanned colour of a Werther's Original toffee, but my skin now had the hue of Camembert rind – white with a grey tinge. My lips were a cracked salt lake and my hair a silver pot scourer. If Lottie was going through a blue period, I had been through a grey one.

I ran a bath, threw in some congealed clumps of old bath salts and, on my face, smeared the mask Crystal had given me before she went away, until I looked as if I'd fallen into a vat of Tippex. I soaked and scrubbed and hair-washed, then moisturised and deodorised. I put on a fresh blouse and dressed it up with black slacks and ballet flats passed on from Linda, who was no longer able to wear them due to heel spurs. I combed my hair, cleaned my teeth, sprayed on perfume, and found years-old foundation and rouge to revive my skin tone. Lastly, I got out the only two lipsticks I owned. I liked them both and couldn't decide on a favourite so swiped the 'Peachy Peach' across my top lip and the 'Coralicious' on the bottom. I stepped away from the vanity and took in the new me in the mirror. If I could say so myself, I lit up the room like the sun appearing from behind a storm cloud.

Except two things were missing.

And there they were, glued with sticky toothpaste residue to the bottom of the toothbrush holder. I ran them under the tap, dried them on a towel and slid them on to the fourth finger of my left hand. Holding them up to the wall light, they shone.

'That's better, isn't it, Jackie-boy? I don't want to let the side down.'

When Lottie knocked on the door at nine o'clock, I was on to my second Baileys and re-admiring Jack's cake in the pantry, doused yet again in brandy.

'Hey, you look lovely,' she said. Oscar romped around her ankles.

'Likewise,' I replied, noting the girl's floaty olive skirt, clean white T-shirt and her choice of lipstick, which matched the one on my top lip.

'I thought we could take Oscar for a walk, get some fresh air and tissues . . .'

'I went out earlier to get the newspaper from the doorstep,' I said proudly.

'That doesn't count. How about we get a coffee? Oscar could do with some café experience.'

'Me too,' I agreed. 'There are probably new coffee combinations I've never heard of.' I started giggling, then burped, and the unexpectedness of that made me giggle again.

'I'm glad to see you happier today, Mrs Verne. So, what do you think . . . ?'

I eyed the street. The sun was in full regalia, scorching my lawn and wilting the weeds. The sky was clear and bright and shiny like my rings. There were two dog walkers and a straggle of kids late for school. The big, endless world was alive and kicking and waiting for me to re-engage with it, just like Jack wanted. For what were the alternatives? Colouring in newspaper photos or alphabetising the spice rack?

'Okay,' I said and felt my heart do a crazy hip-hop move in my chest.

'Do you want to take the suitcase as well?' she asked, nodding to the case and my white knuckles on the handle.

'That would be nice.'

I looked beyond Lottie to the front gate, the footpath and the road leading to the shops, and realised how much would be required of me to get down the path and out the gate.

'Just a second. I'd better lock the back door,' I said, scuttling to the kitchen for another slug of Baileys. By the time I returned to Lottie, I was hiccupping.

'Are you all right?'

'Sure,' I said, raising my palms to the ceiling as if to say, can't you see my rouged cheeks and smart attire, my tamed hair and clean teeth, which were hopefully masking the effects of a rapid heart rate and tingles in my extremities.

'Have you been . . . ?'

Conveniently, Oscar cocked his leg on a veranda post. 'Oops, doggy needs a wee,' I said and made a note to hose down the post when we got back.

'Are you ready?'

I rolled back my shoulders, lifted my head to the sky and took my first steps away from the house. At the letterbox, I stopped and pretended to check the mail, wishing I'd decanted some Baileys into a water bottle for disguise.

'Okay?' Lottie asked. 'Look, you can virtually see the high street from here,' she said, pointing down the road. 'See the church spire, it's just there.'

I nodded but preferred to focus on Jack. I sensed he was trying to give me advice. Something along the lines of, 'Come on, Geri, you can do it, I know you can.'

'Perhaps you'd like to hold my hand?' I suggested. 'The pavement gets uneven up ahead and the roots of the trees are beginning to crack the concrete.'

With Lottie's hand in mine and Jack in the other, I felt much better. At as dignified a pace as Oscar could manage in his eager yet uncoordinated puppy state, we turned right at the front gate and slowly made our way down Richmond Road in the direction of the cafés. Jack followed closely at our heels, his wheels rattling on the pavement like a hospital trolley.

We had to make regular stops so Oscar could sniff and pee on random objects like cigarette butts and lamp posts. I appreciated the moments to pause as they helped acclimatise me to the world beyond my front gate. Life came at me from every direction. It was at once anxiety-inducing and tantalising. A falling leaf skated on to my head. I pulled it from my hair, held it in my hands, smelled its leafiness, then let it go. Piano music rose and fell on the breeze. A siren sounded in the far distance. A cat at number forty-one hissed. Sawdust clouds filled the air on the front lawn of number thirty-three from builders cutting wood. And still the warm sun stroked my skin, making me feel alive. *Hello, world, I'm here. I'm actually here.*

For the first few houses we didn't speak. It was as if Lottie knew I needed a moment to familiarise myself with the world beyond my front door. She also seemed focused on making sure she didn't let go of either my hand or the lead, at the end of which was her scatter-brained dog, who was becoming increasingly excited in direct response to the increase in sights, smells and sounds. At number twenty-three, Lottie started telling me about training Oscar to go upstairs.

'Guide dogs have to learn to wait at the bottom of the first step, but Oscar still hasn't got the hang of it,' she said.

Poor Oscar looked as if he never would. At number eleven, Lottie began talking about looking after guide dog puppies.

'It takes more than two years and thousands of dollars to raise, breed and train a guide dog,' she said as Oscar licked chewing gum stuck to the pavement. 'But they're not ready until they're fourteen months old, which is why volunteers are needed to look after them from when they're eight weeks. You have to have a fenced garden and commit to not being away from home for more than four hours at a time, which is fine for me because I work from home. Are you still okay?'

Although I was feeling hot and over-dressed and the effects of my morning tipple were wearing off, I felt elated to have reached the junction. *Nearly there, Jack!*

And bingo! In four hundred metres, I'd made it.

When we first moved to the area the high street had a coffee shop, a butcher, a newsagent, a post office and a couple of women's clothing shops. Now, there were two butchers, five coffee shops, eight clothing shops, a bookshop, a toy shop and an optometrist. Parking was at a premium and you only got two hours free instead of all day. At the first café on the strip, we took a table on the footpath and Lottie said she'd go and order.

'What would you like?' she asked, tying Oscar to the table leg.

'Coffee with a dash of milk, thank you,' I said. *You'll just have to share mine, Jackie-boy.*

'Anything to eat?'

I declined, but as soon as Lottie left, I had a change of heart given I'd only had liqueur for breakfast. I went to the entrance but couldn't bring myself to go inside. I stood in the doorway and eyed up the array of baked goods in glass stands on the counter.

'Yoo-hoo,' I called out, waving a hand to get Lottie's attention. Heads turned in my direction. 'Can I have a scone, too? Any flavour,' I added in case there were options.

Back at the table, I sat facing the footpath and smiled at everyone who passed. I was revelling in my achievement. *Hi, world, it's Geri, here.* I grinned. I was even warming to Oscar, despite him drooling over my shoes, and when Lottie returned, I couldn't help but give him a piece of scone.

'We're not supposed to feed the dogs at the table,' Lottie said.

'Pretend I'm his grandmother.'

She laughed.

'So, how are you doing since the fiancé incident?' I asked.

'So-so,' she said. 'My granddad had a great word he used when my grandmother died – "misslieness". It's an old Scottish word meaning the solitary feeling you get from missing someone or something you love. That's me.'

'It's a good word,' I said and subtly put a hand on Jack. 'I understand completely.'

'It must be really hard for you since you were married for so long.'

'It's not a countryside ramble,' I admitted. 'But I think grieving helps prevent the memories of my husband from fading.'

'I doubt they would, even when the grieving eases.'

'You know what it's like, you're supposed to try to get on without them, but love keeps getting in the way. Anyway, take solace in the notion that there are more Joshes out there and, if I may say so, more considerate ones.'

'I hope so. I'm thirty and single again. I'd like to think I'll meet someone who wants to share the rest of their life with me.'

'You will,' I said.

She nodded and looked at the hand I'd put on her shoulder. I stared at it, too, unaware of having put it there. 'Nice top,' I said. 'Good quality cotton.'

She smiled. 'Thanks, Mrs Verne.'

Then my name sounded loudly and clearly from a few metres down the street. Sue from number twenty-eight was waving and speed-walking towards us, her high-vis vest flapping in excitement. 'Geri, Geri! How wonderful to see you. And look, no sling, smart clothes, make-up . . .' Sue opened her mouth so wide in admiration that if I'd been quick enough, I could have thrown her a few crumbs of scone, too.

'I'm distributing Neighbourhood Watch leaflets advertising our inaugural workshop around the area,' she said, dumping a pile on the table. 'Everyone needs to be forewarned and forearmed where home security is concerned. Give them to friends, family, frenemies; anyone really! Now, tell me,' she said, leaning close, 'any word from Len? I haven't seen him around in a while and, well . . . he's such good company.'

'He's away,' I said.

'Ah.' Sue nodded.

'But, Sue,' I whispered, 'he has a girlfriend.'

'I heard, but who knows how long that will last. Holidays are notorious for break-ups. That's what happened to Kathleen and Paul. Do you remember? It was a disaster. Then they had to sit next to each other on the plane all the way home. In economy, too.'

'Oh,' I muttered.

'Well, anyway, let me know when Len's back. Do you think he secured his home properly? I hope he did.'

'I do, too, Sue.'

We watched Sue march towards the shops, the bag of pamphlets banging her hip, and once she'd faded into the crowd, I clinked my coffee cup against Lottie's. 'Here's to outings,' I said.

'Here's to outings,' Lottie laughed.

Paper Planes and Knitwear

When we got back to 51 Richmond Road, I stood on the veranda, looking out at the street, taking in how far I had ventured. I felt full to the brim with sunlight and a sense of accomplishment.

'You should have a seat out here,' Lottie suggested, bumping Jack up the steps.

'I did once.'

'Do you want me to get a kitchen chair for you?'

'Why not?' I said. 'How about two?'

When Lottie returned, she placed the chairs where the cane seater used to be. I wheeled Jack over to one, sat down and slid off my shoes. I patted the other seat for Lottie to join me.

Across the road, Ruby and Benny's mother was leaving the house. I waved and she waved back. 'That's . . .' I started but realised I didn't know the woman's name. How remiss of me, I thought, and made a note to ask Sue. She was bound to know. At the thought of Sue, I pulled out a leaflet from my handbag, opened it and folded it. I was feeling jaunty and carefree.

'What are you doing?' Lottie asked.

'It's the perfect day for it,' I said and made it into a paper aeroplane. Holding it like a dart, I threw it over the veranda railing. It quivered and fluttered to the ground. 'There's a trick, you know, to the folding and throwing. And that one had poor aerodynamics.'

I pulled out another and tried again. 'This could be a new way for Sue to deliver her brochures.'

'Oh, you're being naughty,' Lottie laughed.

I made a new plane and sent it up and over her head.

'Now you're just littering.'

'It doesn't count if it's in your own home. Here, why don't you make one?' I gave her a leaflet and started on another. I folded, threw, chuckled, folded and threw again. I hadn't felt this alive in a long time. A woman walking past startled as she saw one of my better examples from the corner of an eye. It was never going to reach her, so she needn't have worried.

'It's about Neighbourhood Watch,' I called out. 'Feel free to come in and pick it up. It contains important information on the initiative in our area.'

The woman hurried on, which was probably just as well as I wasn't sure I was ready for a complete stranger to fossick on my lawn for a folded bit of paper.

'The trick is to throw it gently rather than launch it at speed. There are other fancier designs, but I'd have to look them up. Six two nine point one Aviation includes paper aeroplanes, if I remember correctly.'

'This is hilarious,' she said, launching her plane.

I pulled out more leaflets and started on a new one.

'We can't use them all up.'

'I want to see if I can get one to the letterbox.'

Unfortunately, it didn't get anywhere near the letterbox but got taken by the wind and trapped in the crab apple tree. I looked at Lottie and we burst out laughing. She flung hers, too, but as laughing takes up more energy than you realise, her plane only flew ten centimetres at most before landing on Oscar's head, which made us laugh even more.

'Do you think we should stop?' I said.

143

'Probably,' she agreed.

'Why don't you take some so you can keep practising?' I suggested.

'Or I could distribute them around my apartment block?'

'Or you could do that.'

'Sue might prefer it.'

'She might,' I agreed.

'Well, thanks for the entertainment,' she said.

'Thank *you*,' I replied.

I watched her head towards her car with Oscar, picking up the paper-plane litter as she went.

'Don't worry about that,' I called out.

'All good, Mrs Verne.' She raised an arm and waved. I noted how the sunlight caught her silver hoop earrings and threw its shine back to me.

I waved, too, and didn't stop waving until her car had disappeared out of sight. You'd think I had regal pretensions the way I was carrying on.

For a minute or two – or maybe thirty, I wasn't sure – I stayed in the chair on the veranda. With my eyes closed and legs stretched out, I luxuriated in the world around me doing its thing and how it didn't bother me like it used to. The lawn mower next door, the fly on my arm, the crying baby in the pram. They were sounds and movements that came and went like the tide, lulling me into a snoozing state. Until Sue panted up the path and brought me back to life.

'Didn't I tell you how wonderful a seat would be here?' She was very loud.

I opened one eye at a time and realised I didn't get the urge to run inside and shut the door. I didn't even bother sitting up, but secretly praised Lottie's earlier foresight to clear the lawn of paper planes.

'I've just finished the leaflet drop and thought I'd pop by now that you're out and about. You see, I meant to say before how sorry I was about your fall and to apologise for barging in when it happened.'

'I did appreciate your concern, Sue, even if I didn't show it.'

'Oh, and I brought you this,' she said, handing me the package she'd been waving around as if having forgotten she was holding it.

I undid the wrapping and out popped a strawberry tea cosy – red with flecks of yellow and a green leafy top. 'Gosh, how . . . fruity,' I said. 'Thank you.'

'It's my latest creation. I'm doing a range of fruit and vegetable tea cosies to sell at the markets. They should do well, shouldn't they? People love a pop of colour in their kitchens.' I wasn't sure where Sue got her information from, but she seemed convinced. 'Anyway, time's marching on.'

'Actually, I had something to ask you, too,' I said. 'You know the house across the road – the one with the yellow door? Do you know the name of the lady who lives there?'

She glanced in the direction of Ruby and Benny's house then squeezed her eyes shut. 'Tamsin,' she answered. 'Works in marketing. A very good tennis player. My ex belonged to the same club.'

And then she was off, practically skipping down the steps and on to the street, the image of an eager and enthusiastic suburban crime-fighter.

Once Sue was out of sight, I picked up the cosy and put it on my head. It fitted surprisingly well and was less itchy than it appeared. I was impressed by its multi-functionality and decided to keep it on to tame my hair in the wind that had picked up. The absurdity of wearing it made me laugh and I wished I could remember how to take a selfie on my phone because I'd have sent it to Len if I could.

The next morning, I wanted to be sure that the previous day hadn't been an anomaly. I moved our morning cup of tea to the veranda. It was most pleasing to detect neither heart palpitations nor excessive sweating. I had picked up the newspaper and was reading any news item I thought Jack would be interested in when my phone honked. It was a text from Lottie.

> *Would you like to go on another outing? I was thinking the natural history museum on Sunday given you have a room full of butterflies.*

My husband and I used to go there all the time, I replied.

> *Is that a yes?*

> *I suppose it is.*

I slid the phone back in my pocket, contemplating what I had just agreed to. Two minutes later, it pinged again. It was Len.

> *Hey, Geri, we're on our way home. Back Thursday, so we'll come and see you.*

I held the phone to my chest and smiled.

But going on an outing with another person is quite different to doing it on your own. I knew that if I was going to start properly living again, I couldn't rely on other people to come with me. I decided to practise walking to the letterbox by myself. The distance was only about nine metres and I could go as slow as I liked. I could stop and sniff the weeds, wave at a neighbour, get a suntan.

I chose dusk to accomplish my mission, favouring diminishing light and fewer passers-by. I parked Jack at the top of the stairs so I didn't have to worry about getting him down the steps and took a moment to stretch my calves and roll my shoulders. The sky was an ink blot of apricots and blues, and the air scented with jasmine. I went down the top step, then the next. One step, two steps, three steps, four, until I was on the path. My heart rate was slightly elevated but manageable. I kept on walking, my focus only on the letterbox. When I got there, I rested my hand on its roof and paused to appreciate my achievement. Then, in case anyone was wondering what I was doing, checked the letterbox for mail, before turning and beginning the twenty-five-step return. In what felt like no time at all, I was back on the veranda with Jack in my hands. Easy!

That night I slept so well, you'd have thought I'd conquered the summit of the neighbouring hill, not a mere solo trip to the letterbox.

The following morning, still in my nightdress and dressing gown, I got the urge to sit in the car to familiarise myself with it again. Our car lived in the carport to the right of the house. It was a basic model, metallic-blue hatchback. It was an unfashionable colour at the time and is still unfashionable ten years on, but we tended to prioritise price and practicalities over aesthetics and extra features. I found my car keys, parked Jack on the porch and went to the carport. The grass was dewy from the night before and the air a little crisper than it had been.

The driver's door cracked open loudly. Keeping the door ajar, I got in, put the keys in the ignition without turning it on. I put the seat belt on, adjusted the rear-view mirror, and took hold of the steering wheel. When a small voice close to my head said, 'Hello, Mrs Verne,' my bottom levitated an inch off the seat, which would have been highly inadvisable had I been driving.

'Good god, children,' I swore, holding a hand to my heart.

Ruby and Benny stood by my door, school backpacks on their backs.

'What are you doing?' Ruby said.

'Driving,' I answered.

'But the door was open.'

'I was testing everything worked.'

'Mum says we have to walk to school,' Benny said.

'And Mum would be right. How are you two, anyway?'

'Good.'

'Still dog walking?'

Ruby shook her head.

'Bloody dogs,' Benny said, exaggerating an eye roll.

'Benny!' Ruby elbowed him. 'The dog wasn't easy,' she said by way of explanation.

'You should do another cake stall,' I suggested.

Ruby shrugged.

'I could give you some of my favourite recipes to try, if you like? Have you made a funfetti cake before?'

They shook their heads.

'It's filled with rainbow sprinkles and vanilla icing.'

'Yum!' Benny shouted.

'Okay, let's start with that one.'

'Thanks, Mrs Verne,' Ruby said.

'All right, then, off you go to school.'

I watched them scamper away, their backpacks bouncing and Benny whooping at the thought of being let loose with rainbow sprinkles. I jiggled the steering wheel, pressed the foot pedals and whacked the heel of my hand on the horn. It gave a single shriek, which stupidly made me jump and alerted the neighbourhood that Geraldine Verne was once again gearing up to step foot in the outside world.

The Letter

As promised, Len and Crystal visited after they got home on Thursday. It was a bright and sunny afternoon and for the second time that week, I wore my sunglasses. I felt like a movie star.

'Hey, hey, hey, Geri, we're back!' Len called as he came up the path and saw me on the veranda. 'Look at you out here all dressed up . . .' He made a wide arm gesture and grinned.

'Oh, stop it, Len.' I batted his words away, but I was tickled all colours of the rainbow.

'But, Geri, you're looking so well,' Crystal sighed.

'You are, too,' I said, even though I thought they'd got too much sun and their faces now resembled Jack's favourite burnished brown leather belt. 'I guess it was a good trip. I'd love to hear all about it, so long as you don't bore me with an Egyptian slide show.'

'Ha-ha, of course not. But tell us, what's been happening? I see the sling is off and dare I ask about the Meals on Wheels?' Len asked hesitantly.

'In the end it wasn't too bad. I even went for a dog walk with one of the volunteers on Tuesday.'

'Did you?' Len and Crystal exchanged a look. 'Well, that's excellent, Geri, really excellent.'

'She's asked me to go out with her again.'

'And?'

'I've said yes.'

Len gave me the sort of smile you'd give a child who's made you so proud you're rendered speechless.

'Anyway, you must stay. I've got a treacle tart ready and waiting.'

'I can get it,' Crystal said. 'You take that seat, Lenny, and I'll put the kettle on and get another chair while you two catch up.'

'Good idea, Cryssie.'

As soon as Crystal was out of earshot, Len, who'd suddenly taken on a twitchy demeanour, hurriedly sat down and moved closer to me. 'While we've got a minute to ourselves, Geri, I have to tell you something. I need your advice.'

I leant into him, too, wondering what he could possibly wish to tell me.

'So, this is the thing. I got a message via Facebook from a woman called Gail who says she's my daughter.'

'What?' My mouth dropped open in surprise. If my teeth hadn't been my own, they may well have fallen out. 'A daughter?'

'Uh-huh.' He nodded. 'You know, the daughter I don't have?' Len's tan bleached.

'I never thought I'd hear those words coming out of your mouth.'

'Me neither.'

'What are you going to do?'

'That's just it, I don't know.'

'What does Crystal think?'

'I haven't told her. I mean, she's closer in age to this Gail woman than she is to me, which makes it even more weird.' He ran a hand over his scalp, looked around to check we were still alone, then spoke again. 'I'll be quick. What she told me was this: she's fifty-one. Her mother had her when she was seventeen and she was raised by her grandparents. She only found out when she was eighteen that her sister was her mother and her mother was her grandmother. Her mum pretended she didn't know who her father was, and it wasn't until she died that she left Gail the name of her father. It was *my* name, Geri, *my* name. Are you following?'

'Gosh, Len,' was all I could muster. I can see how it would have been unnerving to come back from a holiday to that but, I have to say, I wouldn't have minded being in his position. Len already had three sons, whereas I was childless and not by choice. If I'd got a message like that, I'd be dancing and singing as if I'd been offered a role on Broadway.

'Did she say anything else?' I asked. 'Is there a way of working out if what she's saying is true or not?'

'She said her mother's name was Anne. But that's a common name and I went out with two Annes when I was younger. She also mentioned my brother's name, Leslie, as being another relative. But that could be the name of the sister I don't have. Nothing is conclusive.'

'There is one way. If you really want to know . . .'

He looked at me, aghast. 'I'm not doing that.' He shook his head vigorously and was now the colour of a mouldy peach. 'That's so invasive.'

'I thought all you had to do was swab the inside of your mouth?'

'Either way, I'm not ready for that.'

'You could delete the message and pretend you never got it.'

'What if she contacts again?'

'She might not.'

'What if it's true?'

'What if it's not?'

'Geri!'

'I'm offering possible alternatives, that's all. And I bet there's a tonne of Leonard Goodmans out there.'

'I suppose,' he said, although I suspected he had never entertained the idea of there being more Leonard Goodmans in the world.

'Anyway, she may have the wrong person.'

'Yeah,' he agreed. 'She may have the wrong person.'

'And she's probably sent the same message to others.'

Len nodded, pleased with these latest scenarios.

'Or, it could be wonderful news – an unexpected but happy surprise in your life,' I added. 'Right now, you're in shock, you've just come back from a holiday. I'd give it few days before doing anything.'

'Yeah.' He nodded, as if relieved to have someone else tell him what to do, and kept nodding as if a chink of neck vertebrae had come loose.

It was then that Crystal stepped on to the veranda with a tray of mugs and slices of tart.

'Thanks, Cryssie.' Len took the tray from her so she could go back for another chair. 'But do you think I should tell . . .' he whispered and flicked a head in Crystal's direction.

'I don't see why not. She'd like to be included, surely.'

'Yeah, okay.' He leant back in the chair and started recounting the history of a royal Egyptian tomb as if that's what we'd been talking about all along.

When Crystal returned, Len handed out the teas and the plates of tart, and said, 'Hey, we got you something, didn't we, Cryssie?'

Crystal reached into her bag and pulled out a box of Egyptian butter cookies stuffed with dates and a turquoise-blue china scarab beetle.

'Sorry they're not wrapped,' Len said.

'It's for good luck and symbolises the restoration of life,' Crystal explained, pointing to the beetle, which, if I'm honest, looked like the sort of thing I'd whack with rolled-up newspaper if I found it crawling around the kitchen. But I appreciated the sentiment and how auspiciously appropriate it was.

'Thank you,' I said. 'So, all in all the trip was a success?'

'Amazing, wasn't it, Len?'

'Oh, sure,' he agreed. 'We're already planning another. A cruise around Turkey and Greece.' His eyes lit up. 'I know, why don't you come with us?'

'Me?'

'I reckon you'd like it.'

I looked at Jack. Going on a cruise in another country would certainly be an adventure but was I ready for that? Len noticed me eyeing up the suitcase. I suspected he knew that Jack was the main cargo, but he had never pried. I sensed he wanted to talk about it now.

'You've still got this, then?' He pointed to the case.

'I do, Len.'

'You know, when you're ready, we can help you sort out Jack's stuff, can't we, Cryssie?' Len looked at his girlfriend, who, I suspected, despite having a sunshiny heart, had no desire to clear out the belongings of her boyfriend's dead friend. 'There's no hurry, of course,' he added.

'No,' I agreed.

'We're here to help!' Sometimes the boy scout in Len made surprisingly eager appearances.

'You've been nothing but helpful, Len. And on that point,' I said, glad to be able to change the subject, 'I don't want you wasting any more of your money on me than you already have. I doubt I qualify for Meals on Wheels anymore.'

'You're already in the system so I wouldn't worry about that. I'm happy to keep it going for a bit.'

'*I* should be paying for it, not you.' I felt bad leaching Len of potential holiday funds.

'Don't you want to keep seeing your dog-walking friend?'

'You mean I have to pay to get friends these days?' I smiled.

'You know what I mean,' he laughed. 'Anyway, I'd like you to come back to the club and challenge Crystal at bingo. She keeps winning the goddamn thing!'

The Museum

On Sunday morning, Jack and I waited for Lottie on my chair on the veranda. A gush of warm wind ruffled the frill on my cream shirt and tickled Jack behind the ear. The sun spun its shiny web around us, making the suitcase handle sparkle. Lottie was also in denim jeans, although hers were zippered and ripped, not elastic-waisted and hole-free.

'Ready?' she asked.

'Ready,' I said, pinging my waist band.

I appreciated her help getting Jack to the car without question-ing his presence and for the first time in three months, I became a passenger in someone else's car.

The museum was just as I remembered it, with the gargantuan skeleton of a sperm whale hanging in the foyer as it had done for more than a hundred years, its glossy marble staircase worn from thousands of footfalls, and the café that used to sell very good egg sandwiches with cress. As Lottie went to fetch a map and find out if there were any special exhibits on, I felt, for a moment, very small and insignificant – an average woman of average height dwarfed by a majestic whale in a monumental building with her husband in an urn in a suitcase. Until I remembered that I'd just travelled several kilometres into another suburb and that wasn't something to be sniffed at, as Jack would say.

However, my elation was short-lived, because when Lottie returned, she told me I had to check the case into the cloakroom.

'But it's only a silly old suitcase,' I said.

'I know. I'm sorry.'

'Let me talk to them.' Spurred on by a sense of accomplishment and a dollop of indignation, I went over to the ticket counter. 'Hello, there,' I began. 'I know rules are rules and all that, but I had an accident a few weeks ago and am still unsteady on my feet. I'm on a waitlist for a walker but my doctor said a small wheelie suitcase would be an excellent substitute. There's nothing in it for you to worry about and I'm sure you'll understand that an old woman's safety is of paramount importance.' I smiled and probably showed more gum than was desirable if I wanted to project the demeanour of a sweet-but-injured lady of senior years. Sue would have given me the thumbs up, but the cloakroom woman didn't. She may have returned the smile, yet her tobacco eyes were steely.

'I appreciate your concern, madam, but we don't allow bags of that size into the museum. There are lifts if you don't wish to use the stairs and plenty of seating. If you wheel it around here,' the woman continued, 'I'll give you a ticket so you can reclaim it at the end of your visit.'

I tightened my grip on the handle. I had not anticipated being separated from Jack, nor how the idea of handing him to a stranger would upset me.

Lottie, now next to me, put a hand on my arm. 'I know you don't want to,' she whispered, 'but they really won't let us in with it. It will be totally safe in there.'

What could I do? Have a tantrum and say I wanted to go home? A part of me felt like doing that, except a part of me also wanted to stick it out for myself and for Jack. To prove that I could, if not enjoy the museum experience for the both of us, at least do so without having a panic attack. *You'll still be with me in the building*, I told Jack. *That's something, isn't it?* I reluctantly let go of my husband.

Offering me the crook of an arm, Lottie said loudly, more for the woman's benefit than for mine, 'Here we go, Mrs Verne, you can hold on to me now. Shall we start with the birds and insects?'

'Thank you.'

Once in the bird and insect atrium, Lottie took me to the butterflies. 'Come on, this is what you'll love,' she said, pushing buttons to light up the cases. 'Hey, don't you have some of these?'

Beneath the main display cases were drawers and drawers of butterflies and moths, their dusty feathers spread wide, pinned and labelled.

'Check out the colours and patterns . . . What about the Himalayan one with its pretend eyes and spiky bottom wings?'

How many times had I looked in these drawers and studied the specimens? But always and only ever with Jack.

'And what about the markings on this one?'

I tried hard to concentrate on the insects and offer suitable responses to Lottie's comments but came over with the most peculiar sensation. It felt as if my husband – the real, live, living Jack – was standing next to me. As if I could reach out and take his hand, or at any minute he'd tap me on the shoulder. I moved away from the butterflies to the larger exhibits that lined the walls: the spiders; flies; beetles; sucking insects; wrens; water birds; hawks; and falcons, with their glassy eyes and talons, hairy legs and feathered wings in all their beautiful, frozen glory. And Jack was still with me. He even started talking: 'Look at those wings, Geri. The detail of every feather and hair. They are perfectly formed.'

I glanced around the room, wondering if anyone else had heard.

Thankfully, Lottie spoke and drowned him out. 'Hey,' she said, beckoning me over. 'This is what Darryl would look like if he was stripped bare.'

A large sulphur-crested cockatoo, all bones, no muscle or feathers, hovered mid-flight in one of the display cases, as if about to curl over tree-tops, slide in the slipstream of another's flight, teeter above water and swoop high into the sky. I looked but wasn't really looking. I tried focusing on the minutiae of bones and the bird's long wingspan, rather than thinking about Jack holed up in a dark, airless room and standing next to me at the same time.

'Did you know that a bird's breast muscle powers their wings?' Lottie pointed at one of the diagrams. 'I've often wondered what it would feel like to be a bird. A friend of mine did a skydive a couple of years ago and asked me to do it with her but Josh didn't think it was a good idea. You can die skydiving, you know.'

'You can die doing anything,' I said, which in hindsight was an unnecessarily grim comment, but I was feeling churlish without the case. 'I once read about a man who laughed so hard watching a TV show he went into cardiac arrest.'

Lottie pulled a face.

'I think that would be a good way to go. Happy till the very end,' I said.

'I'd rather not think about it, if you don't mind.'

I followed Lottie to the next section with the stuffed owls, parrots, common birds, sea birds, a bird's nest, an emu egg and a hummingbird egg, but couldn't summon any enthusiasm. Not only did I wish Jack could experience it with me, the exhibits reminded me of his predicament. Birds that had once been free were now frozen in time with nowhere to go. They were dead and trapped, just like my husband.

'I think I've had enough,' I blurted.

'But we haven't seen any of the other exhibits.'

I felt bad ruining the outing, but it occurred to me that it was one thing banishing your husband to the shed – which had been on my terms and on my property – but it was quite another navigating your way in the big wide world without him. What I'd not envisaged – or perhaps, hadn't wanted to – was a future where there was no urn and no suitcase. And that scared me more than the thought of laughing myself to death.

'Perhaps you'd like a break? A coffee and a sit down?' Lottie suggested. 'We could make paper planes with the serviettes?' She laughed.

Ordinarily, a coffee and a sit down would have helped, especially in the café where egg sandwiches may have been on offer. But this time I knew it wouldn't.

'Or we could go and look at the dinosaur exhibition, which is just across the way?' Lottie persisted. 'Do you know dinosaur means terrible lizard in Greek? Just a bit of useless information I picked up from when I illustrated a children's book on them.'

I shook my head.

'Come and sit down then.' She took my arm and led me to a seat.

'I'm sorry, Lottie, I don't want to.'

'Oh, okay.' Lottie looked put out. We stood halfway between the glass exhibits and the bench seat facing each other. I couldn't hold her gaze. 'Aren't you enjoying it?' she asked.

'It's hard to explain,' I muttered. 'I don't see why it matters to you, anyway.'

Lottie didn't answer but looked at her sneakers.

Feeling the need to make her feel better and put a positive slant on my decision, I added, 'Why don't you think of it as me giving you more time to do other things – things you actually *want* to do.'

'I want to do this.'

'But why?' Finally, I was given the chance to ask something I had been curious to know: why did she care to spend time with me?

Except Lottie was being as elusive as I was. She shoved her hands in her pockets. 'It's hard to explain.'

'We're even then.'

'I guess so.'

'So, can we go?'

Lottie nodded and headed for the exit.

Favourite Recipes

Back at the house, Jack in tow, I needed to do something to cheer myself up. I fished around the desk to find an unused notebook, took it to the kitchen, and went to find the recipe for the funfetti cake in one of my recipe books. I didn't want the children thinking I'd forgotten about them. On the first page, I wrote 'My Favourite Recipes' in large cursive font, extravagantly curling the 'y' and the second leg of the 'r'. On the second page, in my neatest, most legible writing, I wrote out the funfetti cake recipe, adding extra tips, such as the importance of getting the fridge ingredients to room temperature to ensure even baking and an extra smooth batter. Next, I had to decide which other recipes to include. I had a lot of favourites but would have to be considered in my choice. I wanted to avoid ones they may already know and those that would be too challenging or time-consuming. The chocolate fridge cake was a good one – it looked fancy like panforte but was easy and didn't require baking. Then there was the white chocolate banana blondie, which with the addition of fruit would please their mother, and finally, the pink jam slice with its traybake sponge and marbled icing. That would be enough to get the children started.

On Monday, Lottie arrived with veal schnitzel and salad. It was a little awkward seeing her again and to start with we pretended it wasn't.

'We're in Austria today,' she announced in the kitchen as if we were on a cruise and had arrived in a new port. 'Have you ever been?'

'No,' I answered.

She slid the meal on to a plate and into the microwave.

'Do you want to share it with me?' I meant it as a peace offering.

'We're not allowed to do that,' she said.

'No, of course.' I nodded. 'I'm sorry about yesterday.'

'Don't worry about it,' she said, taking the plate out of the microwave 'You haven't opened any of your gifts?' She pointed to my presents under the window.

'They're too good to open.'

'It's nice to have things to look forward to, isn't it?' She picked up the beetle. 'Another gift or a new purchase?'

'My friends who went away. They bought me that and Egyptian date biscuits.'

'Fancy.'

Lottie looked as if she was about to say something more but also as though she was about to go. I waited to see which it would be. It wasn't until we got to the front door that she spoke. 'Look, I know the museum trip didn't go so well but would you like to try again? I'm going to the zoo on the weekend as I've been commissioned to illustrate elephants for a children's storybook. I want to get some inspiration and photograph the animals. You could come too.' She shrugged as if she didn't mind whether I did or not.

I weighed up the pros and cons. I knew I had to get out and about again and there was no question that a zoo visit appealed, yet I was still spooked by our trip to the museum. I looked to my husband for an answer, but I'd left him in the kitchen.

'Have a think about it,' Lottie said.

'Yes, okay, I'll think about it.'

Later Len phoned as I was snacking on frozen peas on the veranda. I was trying to catch them in my mouth and also hoped to spot Ruby and Benny to give them my recipes. I put him on speaker phone so I could continue throwing.

'I thought you'd like an update on Gail,' Len said.

'Oh yes? Have you made a decision?'

'I phoned her. I pretended I was someone else and made out like I'd got the wrong number. I wanted to hear her voice.'

'Was it a good voice?'

'It was a bit husky – a smoker's perhaps – but I found out that she's a teacher.'

'An honourable profession,' I said and threw another pea. I missed again.

'I know. That sealed the deal. I called her back and told her who I was. She laughed about my ruse, which was a good thing, too. She sounded really pleased to hear from me. Like *really* pleased. I've decided I want to meet her.'

During our unsuccessful baby-trying years, when Jack was becoming disgruntled by our lack of progress, I tried a few times to tell him the secret I'd been keeping. Yet each time, I failed. I felt ashamed and didn't want him to think badly of me. What's more, when it happened, I had promised not to talk about it with anyone ever again. No one must know, my mother told me. No one must know, my father said. No one must know, Harry had insisted. So I told no one. I metaphorically hid the experience in a compartment in my head never to be opened again. Not only did I wish to forget about it, I wanted to pretend it hadn't happened at all. Yet now with Jack gone, all I felt was more shame and a cupboard-full of guilt, and I hadn't forgotten about it at all. But what if things had turned out differently? What if I had taken a different course by having the baby and putting it up for adoption and I was now sitting in Len's chair? I may not have known whether the pregnancy could have lasted full term, but what if it had?

After hanging up from Len, I was about to go inside when I saw Ruby and Benny's mother walk past. I called out to her and waved. She turned and came in the gate.

'It's Tamsin, isn't it?' I said. 'I've got something for the children. Do you mind waiting a minute while I get it?'

I scuttled to the kitchen to fetch the notebook. Realising I hadn't put my name on it, I quickly added 'by Mrs Verne' on the first page and returned to the porch.

'I hope you don't mind but I've written a few recipes the children might like to try.'

'How lovely,' she said, taking the book.

'I don't mean to presume that you don't have cake recipes or can't bake, of course.'

She laughed. 'Based on your Louise cakes, I have a feeling you're far better than me. I'll be sure to give this to them when they get home.'

After twenty-four hours, I decided I'd thought enough. I accepted Lottie's invitation to accompany her to the zoo.

612.6 Pregnancy and Childbirth

Halfway through 1975 I lost my fourth pregnancy. I had just come home from work, pleased to have helped thirty-seven people find the books they were searching for on topics as wide-ranging as 133.8 Psychic phenomena, 343 Military law and 485 Classical Greek grammar, and returned 102 books to their proper homes on the shelves. I had discounted my stomach cramps as having over-extended myself during the course of a busy day. It wasn't until I got home that I realised they meant so much more. I refused to believe it. But the more I tried to pretend it wasn't happening, the more I thought I'd lose my mind. Not misplace it temporarily or forget where I'd put it or leave it outside in the rain, but actually lose it. I went to the bedroom, slid off my shoes and lay on the bed. I decided to stay there, keeping as still as possible in the desperate hope that the pregnancy and my mind could somehow be restored to their rightful places so that when Jack came home from work, it would be as if nothing untoward had ever happened.

It was not to be.

My fourth pregnancy escaped the nest before it could even fly.

When Jack came home and saw me there, he let his shoes join mine and held me tight. After a few moments, he spoke quietly, gently, as if loud noise would make things worse.

'I don't think we should do this anymore, Geri-pie,' he whispered.

'Don't say that,' I said.

'I can't bear to see you in so much pain.'

'It will be worth it.'

'But what if it doesn't happen? Never happens? Isn't part of our fate?'

'I don't want to give up.'

'But Geri . . .'

'Please.'

The ceiling light swayed ever so slightly from the breeze that had slipped in through the window and made me shiver. Jack squeezed my hand. 'I don't like seeing you like this,' he said.

I thought about telling him then, but it didn't seem the time – much like how the other times hadn't seemed right either. Instead, I said, 'Just once more, Jackie-boy. Please.'

'Well, all right, Geri-pie. But only if you're up to it.'

After that, I sought solace and advice in the library, reading up about conception in section 612.6 Pregnancy and childbirth. Legs in the air post act. Brazil nuts for Jack. Bananas for me. It made us giggle, but we did it all. I heard about scientists in London experimenting with in vitro fertilisation and dreamed a dream beyond our reach.

When I became pregnant for the fifth time, I wanted to lie on the bed for nine months without moving, which was not far from what my doctor suggested. He told me not to get stressed or over-exert myself, and that I should only continue working provided I wasn't on my feet for more than an hour at a time. I obeyed the rules as if they had been written up and published in 321.9 Authoritarian systems. I felt vindicated by my determination and due diligence, until at ten weeks my fifth pregnancy ended. I wondered if Jack was right. Maybe sometimes, enough is enough.

The Zoo

Saturday morning began layered with haze, the air thick with heat and the sun trying to break free. I gave Jack a few twirls before getting out of bed. I was excited about another trip and felt like dancing with him at any opportunity. I dressed in my most comfortable shoes, a favourite but faded summer dress and floppy fabric hat, then I generously sprayed myself with perfume, put on sunscreen and combed my hair that didn't wish to be tamed. It occurred to me that if I dyed it red I could lose myself in the orangutan enclosure.

'The orangutans, Jackie-boy!' I laughed, abandoning the comb and using my hands.

Jack didn't respond. Neither did my hair. Perhaps my next outdoor achievement could be a trip to the hairdresser?

I watched for Lottie's arrival from the window seat in the bedroom and as soon as I saw her car, took Jack and went outside. Although I hadn't been timing myself, I believe I achieved a personal best walking to the letterbox, my reduced anxiety and heightened level of anticipation more than compensating for the aerodynamic drag of my dress and hat. It was a good start to the morning. It was even better when Lottie hoisted the suitcase into the car without a second's hesitation. I sensed a change in the air, like when winter turns to spring. I savoured the tang of transformation and wondered where it might lead.

When we arrived, I thought it best to make Jack appear as inconspicuous as possible – as much as I could given the suitcase's colour and size. I tucked him behind me when we went up to the ticket counter and spun him in front of me as we left. Although on reflection, a late-age woman in a dated dress and over-sized hat looking like she was planning on spending the night at the zoo was probably the least inconspicuous I could have been. Nevertheless, no one questioned me or my dress sense.

'So,' Lottie said, studying the map, unaware of my concerns, 'the elephants are on the far right-hand side of the park. Let's make our way there, stopping at whatever other animals we want to see.'

The haze had lifted to reveal a cloudless sky and with it a sun that enhanced the sweet smell of animal manure scenting the air. We paused at the Komodo dragon enclosure with its lone large lizard whose loose, leathery skin was disconcertingly like the skin on my elbows, before moving on to the lemurs, meerkats and gorillas. We overtook a man with two squealing toddlers and a crying baby who, if you asked me, could have benefitted from quiet time in the sloth enclosure. Lottie asked several times if I was all right, which was understandable given my behaviour on the last excursion. And I did feel all right. Despite being further afield than the coffee shop and out in the open with strangers, I felt protected from the outside world, as if its vast expanse allowed for both a sense of freedom and a feeling of security. It was the perfect mix of just a little but not too much. I decided to practise making small talk and ask Lottie about her latest project.

'It's for an educational book on elephants for children,' she explained. 'The publisher wants realistic drawings with a sense of fun, which is code for "not boring". I have to include pictures of a baby elephant, elephants eating, a family of elephants, that sort of thing. I've brought a sketch pad and camera with me so I can record what I see today. I hope you don't mind waiting while I do it. Or you can go and look at some of the other animals, if you like.'

'I don't mind at all. I'm planning on eating ice cream and hot chips and savouring them for as long as I can.'

Lottie laughed.

'I'm not joking.'

'Well, okay,' Lottie said, looking at the map again. 'Perfect. There's a food market opposite the elephants.'

In the rainforest aviary where the sky was lush with tree canopies and bird sounds, I thought to ask about Darryl.

'To be honest, he's like an annoying friend,' Lottie said, hoisting the backpack higher up her shoulder. 'Which probably sounds weird.'

'It does when you know he's a bird.'

Lottie laughed again. 'It's the fact he talks to you, albeit in repetitive phrases that don't make sense when strung together. When I come home, he greets me with a "Hi, Lots" just like Josh used to – the same pitch and intonation, except squawky. It was off-putting at first but now I don't mind. Oscar doesn't talk to me like that.'

'Oscar's a dog.'

'Yeah, and not that bright. I don't think he'll reach guide dog status.'

I didn't like to say I'd spotted the puppy's mental deficiencies on the first day I met him.

'You should consider getting a pet, especially now that . . .' Lottie started. I knew what she was going to say, but what she didn't realise was that I already had a pet of sorts. Jack needed exercising, feeding, talking to . . . even patting.

Then we were at the giraffes. Lottie wanted a photo with one in the background. She did it so fast, holding her phone up, pulling me closer, saying 'cheese', that I didn't have a chance to prepare myself. I attempted a smile but feared it was too late. Finally, we got to the Asian elephants. While Lottie found a seat close to the enclosure, Jack and I went to buy ice cream. The pungent smells of hay and dung threatened to overpower our chocolate-covered vanilla ice cream cones, but it didn't matter. Jack and I were on an outing – at the zoo, no less – and we hadn't been separated and that's what mattered the most. We sat quietly watching Lottie sketch. She worked swiftly with her pencil, first drawing a mother elephant eating from a grass piñata, then sketching her baby. She was so focused I dared not speak, until I got the urge for a cold drink and knew just the thing. I stood up and wondered if I could get to the shops and back on my own.

'I fancy some Fanta,' I said. 'Do you want some?'

'Sure. You can leave the case here, if you like?'

I looked at Jack. *You'll be all right for a few minutes, won't you, Jackie-boy?*

I moved him closer to Lottie, gave him a pat and went to the food market to buy two cans of Fanta. It was a relief to be out of the sun and after purchasing the drinks, I sat for a few minutes under cover outside the zoo shop, watching tourists buying fluffy crocodiles and penguin pens. When I returned, Lottie and Jack were gone. I wasn't worried. I figured Lottie must have wanted to capture a different view of the elephants. I looked around for a lanky girl in a purple cap with a backpack and red suitcase. Deciding it was better to wait for them in one spot rather than go searching, I parked myself at the end of the bench we'd sat on earlier, next to a middle-aged couple indistinguishable from each other in matching tracksuits. After ten minutes, I had to tell myself not to worry. Jack was safe with Lottie.

After fifteen minutes, I did a circuit of the elephant enclosure. For once, I was thankful the suitcase was red. I walked with purpose, weaving between a crowd that had formed around a keeper giving a talk, all the while searching, looking, scanning.

Come on, Lottie. Come on, Jack. You can come out now, I said in my head. *I'm not keen on playing hide-and-seek and I've got Fanta, Jackie-boy.*

I still couldn't see them. Don't panic, Geri, unless you're a two-year-old you can't get lost in a zoo. Can you?

Then, I heard my name.

There it was again. A bouncing backpack and a waving arm, not coming from the elephants but from the Rainforest Trail. Lottie was running towards me. She looked like a giraffe on the move but with a shorter neck and distress dripping down her face. What was she doing down by the giant tortoises? And where was Jack?

'It's the suitcase,' Lottie panted. 'It's gone.'

The colourful lanterns overhead swayed in the breeze like Christmas tree baubles, blurred and went black. I came to with my head on Lottie's knees, my hat on the ground a metre away, and a pool of Fanta next to my arm. A zoo first aid official was taking my pulse. For a few seconds it was pleasant gazing at the sky, listening to the bamboo creak, enjoying a horizontal moment on bitumen, at one with nature and the world, until I remembered why I was there. I thought I might faint again. Where the hell was my husband?

'I don't know what happened,' Lottie babbled. 'I wanted to take some photos over on the other side, so I packed up my stuff and wheeled the case with me. As I was leaving the elephant barn, here at the junction of the Rainforest Trail, a kid ran past, fell over, burst into tears. She'd lost her mother. I picked her up even though she didn't want me to. She was wriggling and crying, and her knee was bleeding so I ran to try and find her mother. I'm so sorry but I left the case where it was; it was only for a few minutes, I swear. But when I came back it was gone. It was here. Right here.'

My heart leapt out of my throat and tumbled down the hill towards the pigmy hippo enclosure. I watched it disappear and wondered if I'd ever see it or my husband again. The zoo official with a badge-name of Al told us that it would be all right, they would find it, but I had to try to calm down because my heartbeat was going through the roof even though we were under no roof and my heart had rolled away.

'We have to look for it,' I said, getting up.

'Careful, Mrs . . .' Al said.

'Verne,' Lottie replied.

'You might have another turn.'

'I need to find the case. It's important.' Running was too glorified a word for what I was doing; it was a floundering fast-walk, limbs and mind in disarray, as if I was trying to demonstrate butterfly stroke on land. The zoo staffer called out for me to stop. I ignored him. Lottie caught me up at the sun bear enclosure, where a solitary bear was rubbing his back on a tree trunk.

'Mrs Verne, please stop. It could be anywhere. We can't search the zoo on our own.'

'How else are we going to find it?'

'The first-aid guy says there are lost property drop-off points. Someone may have left it at one of those.'

'But it's been stolen. Why would they do that?'

'Because they might decide they don't want it?' Lottie said meekly.

'Why would someone *not* want it?' I cried, which in retrospect was an absurd comment as the only person who wanted it was me. The thought of a stranger discarding Jack made me sob noisily, breathlessly, as if my body couldn't keep up with the force of my emotion, making the people around us stare.

'It's okay,' Lottie said, putting her arms around me. 'It will turn up.'

But I didn't think Lottie believed it would. The suitcase was gone and there was no way we were ever going to see it again.

663.6 Soft Drinks

When Jack died, I had been at the hospital vending machine getting two cans of Fanta – which perhaps sounds foolish and frivolous, but it was only because the day before we had been reminiscing about the first time we tried Orangina during a trip to the Poitou-Charentes region in the south-west of France in pursuit of butterflies.

'That must have been thirty years ago, Jack,' I said, pulling the chair close so I could pat his arm. An eyelid may have flickered, I couldn't be sure. I kept talking.

'I think you told me at the time that Poitou-Charentes is home to nearly half of the two hundred and forty-seven species of butterfly found in France. Isn't that right?' I didn't wait for an answer. 'You see, I do remember. I also remember how we decided to go punting down the Poitevin Marsh – the "Green Venice". It was so romantic, wasn't it? Until you spotted a butterfly on the back of a swan and fell into the bog, scaring a bunch of beige cows and scattering the swans. You helped dredge the marsh of sludge that day, didn't you, Jackie-boy?' I chuckled. Jack wanted to chuckle, too, I knew he did even though he was in a coma.

The next day, when I was by his side again, the memory of Orangina was still on my lips and I got the urge to find some. How wonderful it would be to pretend we were back in France, enjoying

Orangina with a picnic lunch, I thought. Although I didn't want to leave him, I wasn't planning on being long.

'I'm just going to nip out, Jack,' I said, getting up.

It wasn't until I got to the soft drink vending machine at the far end of the corridor in the palliative care ward that I realised the absurdity of my search. Of course there was no Orangina in the hospital. But there was Fanta. Oh yes, I thought, if we closed our eyes and used our imagination, we could recreate the memory. It wouldn't matter if Jack couldn't sip, let alone suck through a straw. I could put droplets on his lips at the very least. I slid enough money for two Fantas into the coin slot and watched the cans slide out, roll down and land with a tinny thud.

If my first mistake had been to leave Jack's side, my second had been buying two cans instead of one. As I walked happily back to his room with the drinks, my shoes echoing in the corridor, a nurse came out to meet me. I didn't like the look of the downward turn of her lips and the angled frown of her eyebrows.

'I'm so sorry, Mrs Verne,' she said.

It was all she needed to say.

The cans left my hands and just missed my feet as I rushed to Jack's side.

'I got Fanta, Jack,' I said as I held his hand and watched his inert pale body pool and blur in my eyes. 'One for you and one for me. To remind you of France. To remind you of us.'

Basket Case

I sobbed on Lottie's shoulder, wishing for the second time in my life that I hadn't left Jack to buy Fanta. I only lifted my head because Al the zoo attendant came to ask us if we'd like to lodge a lost property claim.

'You have to do it at the main office,' he explained. 'I can take you there.'

'Thanks,' Lottie said. Then to me, 'Come on, let's do that.'

I wiped my eyes, took her hand and, together, we followed Al. At the office, I filled out the required form and asked the woman behind the counter if we could wait on the seat outside.

'You might be waiting a while,' she said. 'It's not until the end of the day that the lost property is collected from all the drop-off points and brought here. Sometimes, it doesn't happen until the next day. If you leave us your number, we'll give you a call if it turns up.'

I ignored her and went to sit in the shade.

'Are you sure you want to wait?' Lottie said. 'I don't mind taking you home and coming back as soon as we get news.'

'I'd rather stay. But I understand if you want to leave. You have other commitments.'

'Don't be ridiculous, I'm not leaving you. Anyway, how will you get home?'

I shrugged.

'Oh, Mrs Verne, please . . .'

'Please what?'

'Please, be sensible.'

'Sensible?' I felt my composure cracking but couldn't seem to do anything to stop it. 'How sensible was it to leave my suitcase unattended?' I snapped. My face reddened.

'I know and I'm sorry.'

'Sorry isn't good enough. The case has been stolen and who knows what's going to happen to it.' A young couple with a baby turned in our direction but I didn't care how loud or screechy I sounded. We were at the zoo, after all.

All possible scenarios played out in my mind. If someone had taken the case, they wouldn't return it to lost property; they'd run off with it and throw it in their car to open somewhere far away from the location of the theft. Even if thieves were disappointed with its contents, it was doubtful they'd be Good Samaritans and return it to the place they had found it. No, they would dump it somewhere for another person to take – perhaps someone who fancied using the suitcase for their own travel purposes, who would leave the contents on the roadside for another to paw over.

'We have to stay positive,' Lottie said. 'We don't know that it's been stolen.'

'It's not wheeling itself around the zoo on its own, is it?'

'No, I guess not.'

'I'm telling you it's not. All you had to do was stay with the case.'

Lottie looked about to cry but wiped a hand across her eyes and retaliated with, 'Well, who takes a suitcase everywhere with them, anyway?'

'I do.'

'Why?'

'It's none of your business.'

'It is now.'

'Yes, unfortunately that seems to be the case,' I said, immediately regretting the pun I hadn't intended to make.

'What's in it that's so important?'

'It's private.' I looked away.

'If it's that important and private, why take it out of the house in the first place?'

'You wouldn't understand.'

'Try me.'

As if I was going to rip open my soul like it was an eagerly awaited present. Lottie scuffed her feet on the path. I gritted my teeth and looked to the sky that was so beautiful and sunshiny it was now nauseating. How could it look so cheery after what had just happened?

'Listen,' Lottie said eventually, 'however angry you are with me I'm not leaving you here on your own.'

'Do you think I'm completely incapable of doing anything?'

'No, it's just . . .' But Lottie didn't finish and I had no interest in furthering the conversation. I crossed my legs, crossed my arms and crossed my heart. Wafts of lunchtime condiments – vinegar and tomato sauce, fried oil and meat pies – came in waves; monkey cries and bird calls sounded in the distance; people meandered by oblivious to me and my distress. I felt exhausted and hot. As the world turned, it felt as if mine had stopped and all that I was and all I would ever be was a seventy-two-year-old woman fixed to a guano-gilded seat in a zoo mourning, once again, the loss of her husband.

Eventually, Lottie spoke again. 'I took some more photos. Do you want to see?'

I nodded, even though I wasn't fussed. But it was good to have her by my side, I realised.

After another half an hour, a zoo official approached.

'Are you the people who lost a suitcase?' asked badge-name Steve. His bald head and khaki-coloured uniform gave him the look of an olive-and-cheese party skewer. I used to like them.

'Have you found it?' I asked, my heart rattling as if it was the last biscuit in the tin. I clasped my hands together and prayed for the discovery of my husband.

Steve shook his head, sloth-like. 'Sorry.'

'It's red,' I said, in case he had been mistaken. 'Well, not as red as it was when we first bought it. It's a bit tired now and one of the wheels is chipped.'

'Nah, sorry.'

I emitted a sound like a violin whining. If I heard the word 'sorry' again, I thought, I might slap the speaker with my floppy hat. Lottie took my hand.

'Yeah, look,' Steve continued, 'I was coming over to tell you there's no point in hanging around. We may not know anything for up to forty-eight hours. You're better off making the most of your zoo visit then going home. We'll let you know if anything turns up.'

'But I don't want to go home,' I said.

'It's okay, Mrs Verne,' Lottie said. Then to Steve, 'You *will* promise to call if a red suitcase is found?'

'Yes, of course. It'll be safe here for a day or two if you can't get back straight away.'

'We *would* come back straight away, don't you worry about that,' I said. 'And it has to be kept safe. *Very* safe. You see, it's not just any old suitcase. It holds very important cargo. *Very* important.' I jabbed the air with a finger.

'I know . . . well, I don't know but I apologise again for what has happened and we'll do everything we can to find it.' I sensed he was regurgitating a stock-standard response from a stock-standard customer service booklet. 'Why don't you come with me and I'll get you some complimentary tickets for next time?'

'I don't think there'll be a next time,' I muttered.

'That's very kind of you,' Lottie said.

'I really don't want to leave, Lottie,' I whispered, sensing I was gripping her hand too tightly.

'I know you don't but waiting here isn't going to make any difference. They've promised to call as soon as there's news and I'm happy to bring you back when there is. They'll kick you out at closing time anyway.'

I knew Lottie had a point, but still, I couldn't bear the thought of going home without Jack. Yet, if I was being honest, I also didn't fancy sitting on a bench in the zoo by myself with strangers walking by, staring at me as if I was an animal exhibit. Reluctantly, I got up and we headed after Steve.

In the car, I tried not to think about my husband. Yet how could I *not* think about him? I did nothing but wonder where he was and who he was with when he should have been lying in the back seat of Lottie's car, applauding the wonderful day we'd just had. I stared blankly and silently out the window, my desire for making small talk having vanished with Jack.

Arriving back at the house, Lottie tried giving me the complimentary zoo tickets again.

'They're meant for you,' she said.

'Keep them for future research.'

'But if you change your mind . . .'

'I doubt I will.'

'I'm really sorry, again, Mrs Verne. We just have to be patient. The case will turn up, I'm sure.'

I nodded and smiled but wasn't convinced. As I walked up the front path on my own, my thoughts were consumed by the terrible prospect of never seeing my husband ever again.

Losing Heart

The click of the front door shutting echoed loudly before the house fell quiet – the loud kind of quiet that was disturbingly deafening. I felt hollow, like the scooped-out shell of an avocado. I couldn't bring myself to look at the photos of Jack on the hall table and was too scared to move without the clack of Jack's wheels on the floorboards to accompany me.

Eventually, I went to the kitchen. The quiet followed me there. I made tea but barely sipped it. I gained no solace from admiring my gifts, had no desire to turn on the radio or watch television. I had no appetite for the cannelloni earmarked for Saturday's meal and couldn't even be bothered to throw it out. Worse, seeing the baking I had made and having no husband to share it with only highlighted the dreadful state we were both in.

There was nothing for it but to go to bed.

I slid under the covers feeling as dispirited as a non-alcoholic beverage. I kept the phone on the bedside table just in case. But the only telephonic activity was a text from Lottie, checking up on me. Come morning, I was spent and despairing, made worse because I wished more than ever that he was with me to twirl around and cheer me up, to read the newspaper to and have a giggle with. It was as if Jack had never existed at all.

I called Len instead and asked if he had time to drop by. 'I still have treacle tart that needs eating,' I said.

When he arrived, he could tell I wasn't myself before I'd said anything, let alone invited him in.

'What's happened?' he asked, looking smart in a linen shirt, chinos and dark sunglasses, holding two takeaway coffees.

'The suitcase has been stolen,' I said.

'Stolen? From the house?'

'No. I was at the zoo.'

'The zoo?'

'Look, come in. I'd rather not tell the whole neighbourhood.'

'Here, caffeine to perk you up,' he said, stepping inside and handing me a coffee.

We went into the living room, where I'd set up the tart on the coffee table. 'And another thing, Len, I think it might be good idea to cancel the Meals on Wheels now. Help yourself,' I added, pushing the tart towards him.

'Hang on, can we backtrack? What were you doing at the zoo and what happened to the case?'

I slumped into an armchair, took a sip of coffee and recounted the events of the previous day as succinctly and calmly as possible. Len said nothing until I'd finished.

'Right, so let me get this straight,' he said, 'it's only been twenty-four hours since the case went missing?'

I nodded.

'There's hope is what I'm saying. Always look for the hope.'

'I know . . .' I blew my nose into a floral paper serviette.

'It's hard, Geri, I get it. What I don't get is what this has to do with Meals on Wheels?'

'Because if the suitcase isn't found, then how can I keep seeing Lottie? I know she didn't mean for something to happen to it, but

I don't think I'll be able to forgive her if it is gone. And anyway, I don't need it anymore.'

'But what if Lottie wants to keep seeing you?' Len said.

'Why would she want to do that?'

'Well, why has she been taking you out? It's not part of the service.'

'I don't know. She's a nice person. Anyway, at the zoo she was doing research for her book.'

'But she didn't have to invite you.'

I reached over to slice some tart since Len hadn't moved. 'Come on, you know you want some,' I said, pushing it towards him.

He poked at the tart with a fork before saying, 'I know you might not want me to ask this, but it needs to be said: what were you doing taking the case to the zoo in the first place?'

I looked away.

'I think we need to talk about the suitcase, Geri. It's been the elephant in the room for . . .'

'Don't talk about elephants!' I blurted, which was, on reflection, an unnecessary outburst, probably made worse by me raising my hand to Len like a stop sign.

He startled, then said my name softly with feeling. 'Geri, I haven't pushed you to talk about the suitcase before. I haven't pushed you to talk about anything, really, since Jack passed. I've let you get on with things your way and hoped you knew I was around to help or be an ear whenever you wanted, just like you were with me. But you've got attached to that case in a way that's not, well, you know . . .' He paused and took a bite of tart. 'You see,' he said gently, 'I've recently heard about a condition called CGD, Complicated Grief Disorder. Withdrawal from social interactions, refusal to leave home, strong attachment to mementos of the deceased . . .'

'I'd rather call it Compulsive Groundhog Day, if you don't mind. Anyway, there's nothing wrong with staying home if you don't feel like going out, is there?' I said indignantly. 'But you're changing the subject. It doesn't alter the fact that the suitcase is gone.'

'No, I know, and I'm really pleased you've been getting out and about. Does the case contain anything valuable? I mean, other than . . . you know. Should the police be involved if you think it's been stolen?'

It hadn't even occurred to me that the police might need to be alerted. Could this criminal act be classified as a kidnapping? I blew into the serviette again.

'Geri, it's causing you so much angst. Isn't it enough that you've lost Jack?'

I gasped. That was it! I hadn't just lost my husband once; I'd lost him twice.

'Twice!' I exclaimed.

'What?' Len frowned.

Thankfully, I didn't have to explain as my phone pinged. Could it be? I hoped, fumbling in my dressing gown pocket.

'Who is it?' Len asked eagerly.

'Only Lottie,' I sighed, ignoring the text. A plane thundered overhead, sounding low and large. If it fell from the sky right then, I wouldn't have minded. At that moment, I'd have taken death by dislodged aeroplane toilet seat over my current circumstance. 'So, do you think you can cancel Meals on Wheels for me?'

'Yes, okay,' Len said. 'Do you want me to also call the zoo?'

I shook my head. 'I don't think it will make any difference. In this instance, no news is bad news.'

'Please don't lose heart. Try to stay positive.' He put a hand on my knee.

'I feel like I've already lost my heart, Len. Nothing positive about that.'

I looked out the window into the street. A light rain shower was sprinkling tears over the lawn. We sat quietly like the last two people at the cinema waiting for the movie credits to roll. Until Len looked at his watch.

'Sorry to take up your morning,' I said. I may not have shown it enough, but I really did appreciate what he did for me.

'It's fine, Geri; I don't mind at all. But I'm afraid I have to go. You'll never guess who I'm meeting . . .' He paused then grinned. 'Gail.'

'Are you? Finally, someone has good news to share.'

'Yeah, I'm nervous but excited.'

'It'll be fine.' I patted his hand still on my knee.

'Will you be okay on your own?'

I nodded, even though I wasn't sure I would be. This was going to be the biggest test of my aloneness. For I was now more alone than I had ever been before.

'Call me when you hear something. Promise?'

As soon as Len left, I went back to bed and stayed there for the next twenty-four hours.

All Present and Accounted For

At first, I thought a goose was honking in my ear. I rolled over to make it go away but then it was in my other ear. Not only was it *not* a goose, it was a car horn coming from my phone. I reached under the pillow, pulled it out and answered. It was a short call – barely even a two-way conversation – but I had to replay it in my head a few times before the woman's words properly computed. One eye opened. Two eyes opened. My heart opened to welcome in the world. I sat up and punched the air. You'd think I was at a sports game and my team had won. I sat up and called Len. I hadn't even finished speaking when he said, 'I'm coming over.'

Never had I got ready so fast. Face washed, teeth cleaned, hair combed and perfume sprayed in a matter of minutes. I used lots of perfume, too. I didn't want Jack to think I hadn't made an effort. I waited for Len on the porch and as soon as he drove up, I went down the path speedier than I ever had before.

'Gosh, I haven't seen you move so fast since winning the meat tray in the pub raffle that time,' Len joked through the open passenger window.

'This isn't comparable to winning a meat tray, Lenny,' I said, getting into his car.

But just as Len was about to drive off, Eve and Doug from Meals on Wheels pulled into the parking space in front of his car. Not only were they early but I was surprised they'd turned up at all having asked Len to cancel them.

'What are they doing here?' I said.

'I'm sorry I haven't called them yet. They were closed over the weekend.'

Eve and Doug were now out of their car and had their heads in the boot.

'You'd better let them know you're going out,' Len said.

I sighed and wound down the window. 'I'm over here,' I called out.

'Oh, hello, Mrs Verne,' Doug said, coming over to us. The slowness of his walk rankled. I wanted to get going.

'You'll have to skip me today,' I said. 'I've got an important matter to attend to and it can't wait.'

'We could come back in a couple of hours, at the end of our round?' Doug suggested.

'Don't bother. Give someone else a double helping or have it for lunch yourself,' I said. 'Think of it as my donation to the cause.'

'Um . . .' Doug looked at Eve.

'We're not allowed to do that,' Eve said.

'I won't tell anyone. And where's Lottie?'

'She called in sick.'

Perhaps she hadn't wanted to see me either. 'I'm sorry but I've got to go!' I closed the window and shot an arm out in front of me. 'To the zoo, Lenny, my friend!'

The second worst thing to having lost the suitcase was watching strangers go through it. My excitement at being reunited with Jack was thwacked abruptly on the head when we entered the lost property room. For there, on a table, was the red suitcase lying flat and open, its contents laid bare for all to see as if it were an anaesthetised body cut open for surgery. My stomach did a triple somersault in the tuck position. A zoo staffer, badge-name Justin, stood behind the table and smiled as if I should be overjoyed to see a stranger rifling through my belongings.

'Hi there,' he said. 'Is this your case?'

'What are you doing?' I asked. 'Why have you opened it?' I stood tall and put a hand on my hip.

'We need to check for hazardous materials and to verify it belongs to you,' Justin said. 'Standard procedure, I'm afraid.'

'Hazardous materials?' I gasped.

'A bomb, gun . . . that sort of thing.'

'Are you kidding?'

'I'm sorry, it's a security measure. If you don't mind, can we confirm that the contents are yours?'

I gripped Len's hand, probably too hard, as he made an un-Len-like grimace.

'It's okay, Geri, they're just doing their job,' he said. I suppose he was trying to reassure me, but I don't think anything would have. Jack and I were being denuded in public and it wasn't pleasant. 'Where did you find it?' Len asked Justin as I seemed unable to fill any conversational gap.

'It had been abandoned in bushes. Probably by teenage boys pulling a prank. We had a busload of school kids at the zoo on Saturday. It's the sort of stupid thing they might do. Funnily enough, it wasn't far from where it had been left but was hidden by foliage, camouflaged by the bushes' red flowers.'

Unbelievable. Not only had I gone through unnecessary angst when the case had not been kidnapped but discarded close to where we'd been, but the irony of Jack's luggage colour choice had proven to be completely ineffectual just when we'd needed it to stand out the most.

'Mrs Verne?'

'Pardon?'

'Can we verify the contents?'

'What if something's been stolen?' I asked. Just because it hadn't been nicked by professional criminals didn't mean something untoward hadn't happened, did it?

'Then you need to say so.'

I took a step forward. Part of me was nervous to look inside in case things were missing, while another part of me wanted to quickly zip it up before any more of this investigative nonsense could continue. Len gave my hand a squeeze as I tentatively made my inventory. And there it all was. An envelope of photos, letters Jack had written to me over the years, the letter I once wrote him, his wallet, a tin of baked beans and Jack himself in the pewter urn. *All present and accounted for, Jackie-boy.* There was no doubt that anyone who opened the case hoping for more – a wad of money or a laptop, perhaps – would have been most disappointed.

'It's all there and it's all mine. You can close it up now,' I said firmly.

But Justin left it open. Worse, he picked up the wallet, the one I gave Jack for Christmas seven years ago. It was caramel coloured and now crinkled and worn like my knees. He looked inside.

'Was there much money in here?'

'What? No. I don't know. I can't remember,' I said, getting flustered. 'Do you mind?'

He ignored me and pulled out Jack's driving licence. 'Who's this?' he asked.

'My husband,' I answered, reaching for it. 'This is a breach of privacy, you know.'

'His name?'

'Jack Verne, for goodness' sake.'

'Is this really necessary?' Len asked.

'And . . . this?' Justin asked, holding up the urn.

'That,' I said, as dignified as I could, 'is also my husband.'

Justin's mouth formed the perfect opening for a balled-up sock as he realised what I meant. He carefully placed Jack back inside the case, returned the licence to the wallet and put the wallet next to my husband. 'I'm very sorry, Mrs Verne, that's all we needed to do,' he said, zipping up the case. 'We didn't mean to cause you any distress.'

I couldn't leave the zoo quick enough.

'Come on, Len, let's get out of here,' I said, tugging on his shirt and yanking Jack.

'Yes, okay,' he said. 'But I think you should slow down. We don't want another accident.'

I wasn't slowing down for anyone. I kept going, my head lowered as if battling an oncoming wind. I felt violated and embarrassed at having the suitcase contents exposed as they had been. It had never seemed wrong or shameful to wheel Jack and his belongings around in a case either in my house or out in public. On the contrary, it had felt perfectly and utterly right. As right as it did to wear two different lipsticks at the same time or your friend's knitted tea cosy on your head. But now that all had been revealed in so public a manner, I saw it for what it was: sad and pathetic. I wanted to go home and zip myself into the other red suitcase and never come out.

When we got to the car, Len hoisted Jack into the back seat and I slid in next to my husband. I wished I was even closer to him – glued to him like one of his wheels.

'All right?' Len asked.

'All right, Len,' I said. 'You don't mind acting like a taxi driver for the ride home, do you?'

'Not at all, Geri,' he replied, shutting my door and getting into the car.

I leant an arm on Jack and felt an overwhelming sense of protectiveness. It was a possessiveness fuelled by love so strong I wondered how on earth I could have ever banished him a few weeks back. Len put the radio on and found a channel playing easy listening music. I welcomed his attempt to create a soothing ambience for the drive and for not bombarding me with questions or chatter. I needed a moment with my beloved, unstolen husband and to appreciate having him in my arms once again. When we returned to Richmond Road, Len helped me get Jack to the house. Exhausted from emotion, I flopped into one of the chairs and pulled the case close.

'Why don't you stay, Len? We could have some warm Prosecco and after-dinner mints to celebrate? They're on the bench under the kitchen window.'

'The Prosecco might be nicer cold,' he said.

'Probably.' I nodded.

'Then save it. I can get something else. What would you like?'

'Actually, I don't need anything.' I put a hand on Jack; I had everything I needed now. 'Why don't you sit down? You haven't told me how it went with Gail.'

His face burst into joy. 'Oh, Geri, it was brilliant,' he said, pulling up a chair. 'She was . . . what's the word? Effervescent. Yes, that's the one.'

'I'm so pleased.' I patted his knee.

'Yeah, she was friendly and chatty, and wanted to know about me and my life. She said she has Italian genes, too, and has done an ancestry DNA test.'

'Do you think she *could* be your daughter?'

'I reckon there's a good chance. I mean, she even looked like the Anne I once dated, a younger version with long, straight, black hair, high cheekbones and short stature. The facts add up, too. I found a photo of Anne – did I tell you? – with a group of us at the beach. I showed Gail and she recognised her mother immediately.'

'That's lovely, Len.'

'And you'll be pleased to know I've also told Crystal, who got quite excited. Here's me worrying about telling her.'

'What about your boys?'

'I'll tell them in due course. I want to know for sure before I do. I reckon they'll like her, though.'

'Does that mean you're going to do the parentage test?' I asked.

He nodded. 'I think we should. I'd rather know the truth now. Gail thinks we should meet up a few more times before we do it, though. But next time, I'm going to bring Crystal.'

'I'm so happy for you, Len.'

'Yeah, happy days.'

'You could say that again.' I smiled and subtly stroked Jack.

'Speaking of honesty,' he said. 'Have you told Lottie the case has been found?'

'Not yet.'

'She'll be worrying.'

'I know.' I nodded.

'So, do you still want me to cancel the Meals on Wheels?'

The Unzipping

For the next twenty-four hours, I did not let Jack out of my sight. Whether I went to get a glass of water or go to the bathroom, he came too. I even decided to have him sitting on the sofa next to me rather than on the floor at my feet. I practised raising him off the ground to test my previously injured wrist and then, when that seemed doable – despite the dead weight – I heaved him up, bending both knees and grunting for an extra power boost. The sofa cushion sank beneath the load, but I liked that we could be the same height as one another. *Equals again, Jackie-boy.* I decided to do that with him in a chair on the veranda, too, to ensure he had the same view I did. And that's where Lottie found us, with our heads resting against the chair backs, wallowing in the gloriousness of reunion. I must have been half asleep as I heard neither the gate opening nor footsteps coming up the path. She seemed to appear out of nowhere on the top step.

'Hi, Mrs Verne,' she said, holding two swan plant milkweeds. 'Sorry to scare you.'

I sat up. 'Oh, hello.'

'I wanted to apologise for what happened and I bought you these. They're to attract Monarch butterflies.' She put the pots at my feet.

'*Ascelepias fruticosa,*' I said.

'Yeah, them.' She nodded.

'You didn't need to bring me a present.'

'I thought it might be nice to have real butterflies in your garden alongside the preserved ones in your house.'

I felt one of the leaves. A dribble of milky sap oozed from a tear in the branch on to my fingers. 'They're actually weeds, in case you didn't know, and not particularly attractive ones, don't you think?'

'Yes, I suppose they are,' she agreed. 'I mean, if you don't want them . . .'

'On the contrary, I'm touched.'

'I've been feeling so bad about what happened. I know the suitcase means something to you, even though I don't know what, and was worried sick it wouldn't be found.'

'Thankfully, it was, so you don't need to worry about it anymore.'

'I just . . . well, I don't want to fall out with you. I don't want you to think badly of me.'

'I don't think badly of you and I don't like falling outs either,' I acknowledged.

'So there was nothing stolen from the case?'

'No. Teenage boys apparently.'

'Bloody boys,' Lottie joked.

'Yes. Bloody boys.'

She smiled. 'I'll see you later then,' she said and looked about to go.

'Ah, Lottie?' I added. 'You should probably know that I've cancelled Meals on Wheels.'

'Oh, I see. I suppose you don't need it anymore.'

'That's right. I've got two working arms, two working legs and my desire to leave the house is increasing exponentially.'

'That's great, isn't it?'

'It is.'

There was a moment's silence as if neither of us knew what to say.

'Well, if you'd like help planting the milkweeds . . . ?' she began.

'I've got two arms now, remember?' I smiled, waving my hands as if I might break out into a vaudeville act.

'I mean, just because you're not keeping up Meals on Wheels doesn't mean we can't see each other, does it?'

'Technically, no,' I said. I was hesitant to give away too much as I wanted to know Lottie's feelings on the matter. Why *did* she want to see me?

'Technically?' She looked both hurt and flummoxed. 'Don't you want to see me again? You don't like my company?'

'No, that's not it.'

'Then . . . ?'

How could I tell her that I feared getting attached to her and then somehow losing her, too?

'What do you want with an old woman like me?'

'I've never had someone like you in my life. And, by the way, you're not that old.'

'I could be your mother or even your grandmother.'

'Exactly.' She nodded.

'Is that why you're volunteering for Meals on Wheels? To find a surrogate elderly relative?'

'No!' She shook her head. 'No, not all. I can't believe you'd say that. It's been an unintentional and enjoyable by-product. Some of the other clients we deliver to are . . . well . . . greige would be the best way to describe them. You're not like that. You've listened to my boyfriend woes, given advice . . .'

'Advice?'

'Yes, like your shoe analogy. About how being in a relationship is akin to being a pair of shoes, where each half brings out the best in each another.'

'Did I say that?' I tried to remember. 'That sounds quite good.'

'It is.' Lottie nodded. 'I thought the suitcase incident would make you reject me and it would feel like I was being rejected by my mother and Josh all over again. I know I've got Dad, but I've never wanted to burden him with stuff. He's had a hard time as it is with Mum leaving him to raise me and my sister on his own. I don't want him worrying about me. I haven't even told him that Josh and I have broken up. I just can't bear to.'

'But what about friends?' I asked.

'Yeah, I've got friends. This is different. You're funny. You've been married for fifty years. That's inspirational! My parents were only married for ten. I love the love you have for your husband, even though he's not here anymore.' Lottie paused, as if taking in for a moment the amount of love Jack and I shared. 'I'm only telling you this so that you understand. I'm not asking you to adopt me or anything weird like that.'

I closed my mouth that had, at some point during her speech, dropped open. All this time Lottie had been admiring *me*?

'Sorry, I've probably said too much,' Lottie added, looking embarrassed. 'I'm not trying to barge into your life. Enjoy the plants,' she said and turned to go.

'Wait a minute,' I called out.

She paused on the steps.

'If you describe some of your other clients as greige, what colour do you think I am?' I asked.

Lottie's mouth turned up at the sides like the gentle curve of a banana. She thought for a minute. 'Probably puce,' she said. 'Like sometimes you're brown and other times purpley-red.'

She said it so seriously that I burst out laughing. It wasn't just the ridiculousness of being attributed to a colour; it was from joy. Lottie looked at me as if relieved I seemed more crazy than dismissive and started giggling with me. We became a pair of laughing kookaburras disrupting the peace. When I could laugh no more and my cheeks had returned to their relaxed, jowly state, I said, 'If you want to stay, you'll have to bring out another chair from the kitchen.'

'Thanks, Mrs Verne. I would but I'm on a deadline with the elephant book.'

'Ah, yes, the elephants,' I said. 'I feel more amenable to talking about them now. Perhaps you could show me your drawings sometime?'

'Sure.' She nodded.

'And thank you for the swan plants. They'll be a lovely addition to the garden.'

I smiled and she smiled, and our teeth bounced joyously around the veranda as if they were marbles.

I sighed and patted my husband. Maybe it was because a zoo official had opened the case and reminded me of its contents, but I felt a sudden and overwhelming urge to reminisce. I took Jack off the chair and wheeled him into the living room. I laid the case on the floor, sat in the armchair and unzipped it. The lid flopped open to once again reveal its contents. There was a rip in the black lining and a musty, airless smell. A week after Jack died, I had been so distraught and so full of – what was the word Lottie had used? . . . misslieness – that I'd collected some of Jack's things I hadn't wanted to throw away. It was as much a symbolic act as it was practical, one that made me feel as if Jack hadn't completely gone. I thought that if I gathered together important pieces of him, I could try and make him whole again. That if I put them in a suitcase, he got legs, became transportable. I was pleased with myself when it was done.

Grief? Pah! I told myself. I had found a way to cope and everything was going to be all right.

Slowly and carefully, I took out each item, starting with Jack's passport, now expired, its pages stamped randomly with all the places he had been. I ran a finger over his photo and gently pressed my lips to his. Next, some of the letters he had written to me and the notes he often left lying around the house in his scratchy, left-leaning handwriting. Silly ones, like *Have gone to the shops to get milk. I miss you already* or *I've gone out for a beer with Len – wish it was with you.* The sentimental old fool. I put the letters on the coffee table to read properly later. Then, a tin of baked beans whose innocence disguised so much. It would have been a simple, honest meal that summed Jack up if you had to reduce him to a dish: easy-going, unpretentious but full of goodness. I hugged the tin to my chest and squeezed away tears. *I shall put them next to my gifts on the kitchen bench, Jackie-boy. That way, we can savour the thought of eating them together.*

There was Jack's wallet, which I'd not bothered going through at the time because he never carried much cash on him. When the zoo man asked if there was money in it, I hadn't been able to think straight. Who knew, maybe Jack had left a decent amount and I never realised. I looked through it now, and found a twenty-dollar note, some coins, Jack's driving licence, credit card, healthcare card, a receipt and an old lottery ticket in the zip pocket. Thankfully, nothing to have worried too much about apart from the credit card, which I took out to destroy later. There was an envelope of photos – a motley bunch of pictures I'd had in my bedside-table drawer which included one of Christmas dinner a year ago, a photo of Jack and his sister two years before she died, one of Jack giving a speech at a friend's seventieth birthday party, and one of him standing next to his framed butterflies. All photos that had yet to be put in an album or ones that had once been framed and replaced with something else. I fanned them out on the carpet and wondered if I had any spare frames to put them in, or whether I would have to buy some more.

Then the urn, the most important item of all. I rubbed the pewter with the bottom of my sleeve. It didn't polish up like silver but had the sheen of grandeur and two bands etched around the top as if representing the two of us. I placed it in the middle of the coffee table.

'Maybe I was wrong to wheel you around in a case, Jackie-boy. Instead of kerbside scroungers taking you to use as a vase, perhaps I should have you on display. And if I go out, I can pop you in a shopping bag. That way, you'll still be with me and you won't get lost again.'

I nodded to myself, pleased with the decision.

And finally, underneath them all, in a crinkled yellowed envelope a letter I had written years ago. It wasn't strictly Jack's, but it should have been. And that's what made my lips quiver and face collapse as if that was what I was scrunching in my hand and not the envelope. I had written it with the intention of giving it to him after our fourth miscarriage. Why hadn't I? Because sometimes the truth is more painful than keeping a secret. Because of the guilt I felt at having already kept it quiet. Because I had tried, as everyone had advised, to forget about it. Because I felt ashamed – ashamed that it may have been the reason we couldn't have children, ashamed that I had been with a man like Harry who didn't deserve to have children, ashamed that I had acquiesced to others' demands when, deep down, it wasn't what I had wanted.

'I should have given it to you, Jack,' I admitted out loud. 'I kept a secret from you and that was wrong. You had a right to be told and I never gave that to you.'

I unscrunched the envelope and flattened it out. But I didn't think I could bring myself to read it. What would be the point? It would change nothing and only serve to reignite all those feelings that were already beginning to bubble to the surface.

I was nineteen when I met Harry, a crystal-eyed boy whose breezy nature and pluckiness captured my heart and hung it high on the flagpole of love. He wasn't the first boy I had dated, but he was my first proper boyfriend, the one I had thought might be 'the one'. I had just turned twenty when I told him I was pregnant. The romantic part of me dreamed of his embrace, a spontaneous offer of marriage and desire to raise the child with me. But the look he gave me after I told him immediately squashed the romance. His face drained of colour; he looked like he was about to be sick. 'For the record,' he said, 'if you want to keep it, go ahead, but I want nothing to do with it. If you get rid of it, I don't want to talk about it again.' I opened my mouth to speak but no words came out. His lack of compassion was shocking. Where had the blitheness gone? Where was the Harry I had thought would support me in a time of need? I went to my mother, but she had the same idea. 'You can't keep it, Geraldine. Much better to be rid and get on with your life.'

And so I secretly and traumatically terminated the pregnancy. It wasn't the same between me and Harry after that. The 'what if' loitered between us and I sensed his feelings towards me had changed. In hindsight, I realised I resented what I had been made to do. I never stopped wondering: what if I had kept the baby? What if I'd been able to have more children? So many what ifs littered my mind. I let the envelope drop in my lap and asked myself if there was any point in continuing to wonder. I couldn't change the past; I could only look to the future. Wouldn't it be a little brighter with someone like Lottie in it as well?

The next day, I put the empty red suitcase on top of the wardrobe next to its sibling. It was time to acknowledge that its travelling days were over. I stood Jack's wallet and passport in the centre of the kitchen table, put the letters and notes he had penned me with his most recent letter on top of the books by my bed, and the tin of baked beans took pride of place on the kitchen windowsill next to the Egyptian scarab beetle. The urn accompanied me wherever I went, but the letter I had written all those years ago got torn into bite-sized pieces and sprinkled into the paper recycling bin.

Back in the kitchen, I cut two slices of treacle tart for me and Jack to boost our drained blood sugar levels.

Gardening

The next day I found myself rifling through Jack's *National Geographics* in the butterfly room where I knew I would also find some old women's magazines. I had been unable to stop thinking about the extraordinary notion of gaining a pseudo-daughter/granddaughter in one's seventies. What did it mean? How were you supposed to act? What did it look like when nappies and school runs had never been involved? Would the library section 649 Parenting have any relevant books? I wondered if I could model myself on a women's magazine agony aunt. Was it such a silly thought? But after finding the magazines and reading some of the letters in the agony aunt column, whose queries ranged from what to do about lopsided breasts to how to kiss a man in a canoe, I questioned whether I was cut out for the job. Instead, I decided to kick-start our new relationship by accepting Lottie's offer to help plant the swan plants.

I had not returned to the shed since rescuing Jack from banishment. The only signs of my stopover were used nuggets of nose-blown toilet paper. I picked them up, stuffed them in my pocket and went in search of soil and gardening tools. Behind the golf clubs was a bag of near-empty potting mix and next to that, a trowel, spade and gardening gloves. I gathered them up and placed them near the spinach that had gone to seed and a dead tomato plant in the plot along the left-hand side of the garden.

'What do you think about this spot for the milkweeds?' I asked Jack, whom I'd placed on the outdoor table under the kitchen window. 'It gets a fifty–fifty mix of sun and shade. The old plants will come out easily since they've given up on life, and Lottie will be able to help dig the holes.'

'Talking to yourself again?'

I jumped and dropped my sun hat.

'Sorry. You weren't answering the front door, so I thought I'd see if you were out here,' Lottie said, appearing from the path down the side of the house.

Regretting bringing Jack outside, I went over to him as nonchalantly as possible and flung my hat over him. He looked surprisingly good as a hat stand.

'What's your plan?' she asked.

'The first thing you should know about swan plants is that they like being in a wild garden with unkempt soil. You will notice' – I gestured – 'the suitability of my back garden. The only thing distinguishing the lawn from the flower bed is the stone garden border. Those withered stalks with dead leaves are rose trees in disguise and around them is a hideous border, usually called an herbaceous border when plants are thriving. And, you will note, there is a proliferation of weeds flourishing so well they're more attractive than the plants.'

Lottie chuckled.

I surprised myself by enjoying the role of teacher. I wouldn't want to offend Lottie by comparing her to a child, but it wasn't totally dissimilar to toddler story time at the library.

'As you've probably gathered,' I went on, 'this is more a lesson in how *not* to garden. Neglect and starvation are words plants don't like. I was suggesting to myself when you arrived that we put the swan plants here along the fence line. But first, we need to get rid of the tomato plant that no longer produces tomatoes and the spinach that looks as if, in a reversal of the story, it has eaten Popeye. Would you like to dig around the roots and I'll pull?'

Thankfully, Lottie didn't risk dislocating a shoulder as the plants flopped out with ease. I threw them on to the path.

'Although this goes against usual gardening practice,' I said, 'I think we'll leave the smaller weeds, because from a distance and if you squint, they give the appearance of a country garden. Wild in the romantic sense rather than the feral. I'll deal with them later.' I picked up the trowel and made rough holes for where I thought the milkweeds should sit, allowing some space between them for their roots to spread. 'Perhaps you could dig two decent holes, here and here,' I suggested.

Lottie nodded and started digging. When the holes were ready, I sprinkled the last of the potting mix into each and together we moved the swan plants from their pots into the holes.

'They're hardy plants. You don't have to be too fussy. Shove them in, cover them with soil and give them some water.'

'Is that it?' Lottie asked.

'That's it. Gardening one-oh-one.'

'Now what happens?'

'We wait.'

'When do you think the butterflies will come?'

'Hopefully, it won't take long. All you need is a pregnant female to lay some eggs.'

'Then?'

'It takes about a month for the whole metamorphosis: three to five days for the egg; nine to fourteen for the caterpillar; and eight to fifteen for the chrysalis. I'll keep you posted, don't worry.'

'Thanks. I'd like that.'

'Now, for the final act, we must have a cup of tea and admire our handiwork. Perhaps you could put the tools back in the shed – anywhere will do – and I'll put the kettle on.'

I went inside to make the tea and, in the jubilant mood I was in, decided to dust off my expensive china teapot and use Sue's knitted strawberry tea cosy.

'In keeping with the gardening theme, I thought I'd christen a recent gift,' I announced on my return, carrying it all out on a tray.

'That's cute,' Lottie said, touching the leafy tea cosy top.

'It was made by my friend you met at the café.'

'It's kind of funny.'

'I'm not sure if it's real kitsch or ironic kitsch. It's hard to tell with Sue. She's making a range to sell at the markets.' I spun the teapot several times one way, and a couple of times the other, and realised I missed spinning Jack, for the urn was disappointingly untwirlable.

'My sister loves that kind of thing. Does she knit other fruit?'

'She mentioned vegetables.'

Lottie looked as if she was contemplating the ideal vegetable for a knitted tea cosy or if, indeed, one existed.

'I can find out what other varieties she does, if you like? Milk? Sugar?' I asked.

'Milk, thanks.'

I poured the tea and wondered if it was the right time to formally acknowledge our newfound friendship. 'I was thinking about what you told me the other day,' I said. 'You see, I have never entertained filling a hole as if I was Polyfilla but I'm up for the challenge. Take this as an official acceptance of the role.'

'What do you mean?' Lottie frowned.

'As a pseudo-mother figure.'

'Oh, I see.' She smiled. 'Look, I probably overstepped the mark saying what I did but I've been so emotional with everything that's been going on.'

'Actually, I appreciated your honesty. Are you still having problems with . . . what's his name?'

'Josh.' She nodded. 'It's more problems without him.'

'You're still wearing the ring,' I noted.

She held out her hand and admired the ring's sparkle.

'It's very pretty. I can't bring myself to take it off.'

I thought about the letter I had recently torn into tiny pieces. 'Sometimes letting go takes a symbolic act,' I said.

'Is this another bit of advice?'

'I've got all sorts of advice if you really want it. Like where to store excess newspapers, the benefits of turning underwear inside out so you can wear them twice, how to keep yourself company, how to pretend you have company when you've had enough of your own . . .'

Lottie laughed.

'I could go on. How to freeze cheese, how to save money, how to bake . . .'

'I wouldn't mind learning how to do the last one.'

'There, you see, I knew we'd find something you'd want my help with.'

'Honestly, Mrs Verne, I don't want you to feel you have to play a role. It's enough that you've forgiven me.'

'On the contrary, I was touched and, please,' I said, leaning closer, 'call me Geri. All my friends do.'

'Okay.' She smiled.

We watched a ladybird land on my hat and I desperately hoped Lottie wouldn't ask what sat beneath it, but thankfully she was preoccupied with twiddling her ring. The ladybird raised its wings once, twice, then, *pop*, it was gone.

'You know what you said about letting go?' Lottie said. 'What did you mean?'

'Toothbrush holder,' I replied.

'What?'

'Put the ring in your toothbrush holder. That way it's out of sight and gets cleaned at the same time.'

'Now you're being silly.'

'It's true. I've done it.'

'But you're wearing your rings.'

'It wasn't a lasting thing.'

'When did you do that?'

'A month or so ago. I was in a mood with my husband.'

'Now you're not in a mood with him?'

'Correct.' I leant forward again. 'I'll let you in on a secret,' I whispered. 'Before you found me in the shed, I had been trying not to love him as much anymore.' I flicked my eyes to Jack. I had never discussed my love for him with anyone else – the times when love diminished and those when it expanded like dough rising. It felt strange but also strangely right.

'And how did that work out?'

'I couldn't do it.'

Lottie nodded and thought for a minute. 'Isn't that what grief is, a form of love?'

I shrugged. I hadn't thought of it like that before.

'But why be angry with him when he couldn't help what happened?'

'It's complicated. I was trying to move on.'

'So we're the same, then, you and me?' she said. 'We're both trying to let go.'

I looked into my teacup and took a large gulp of tea without acknowledging what she'd said. Until I was deafened by a squeal. Lottie had my sun hat and was thrashing it around. 'Get off, get off!' she cried.

'What is it?'

'A wasp!'

'You'll make it angry whacking it like that.'

'I don't care.' She thwacked the air a few more times, until I told her the wasp had gone. 'Thank goodness,' she said, fanning her face. 'That's better. Thanks for the hat.' She was about to place it over Jack again when she paused, studied the urn and looked at me questioningly. 'Is that what I think it is?'

'It depends on what you're thinking it is,' I said casually, hoping she'd think it was a coffee thermos left out from the day before or a Middle Eastern souvenir from my Egypt-visiting friends.

'Your husband?' she asked and, without looking aghast, added, 'He's probably getting hot out here. Shall we take him inside?'

796.6 Cycling Sports

Six weeks before Jack's death, when I'd been in the back garden pruning the roses that were already showing signs of neglect, he showed me a bike hire website on his laptop to which I'd said, 'Is that what I think it is?'

It's one of those teasing phrases where the recipient has to decide whether to take it positively or negatively. Jack did the former. He grinned, waggled his eyebrows and gave me a thumbs up.

'I'm feeling good at the moment and we haven't done something like this in such a long time,' he said. 'And when will I ride a bike again?'

I wished he hadn't said that because we both knew he never would. Yet all I could say, leaning over his shoulder as my eyes smarted, was, 'You might be feeling good now but what about when you get on a bike?'

'In that case, let's do it now!' he exclaimed.

'What?'

'It doesn't have to be a full day. You can hire by the hour and it's near the city park. What's stopping us?'

He had a point. It was a Saturday morning after all, and I knew Jack had only small windows of energy throughout the day, which were usually in the mornings.

'Okay. I suppose I'd better go and put some Lycra on,' I joked.

'Me too,' Jack laughed.

It was a decision I not only never regretted but wished Jack had suggested weeks ago so we could have done it again. For one hour we wobbled and giggled and pretended we had baskets on the front filled with French baguettes and rounds of cheese and were riding the streets of Paris. For one hour and for the rest of that day, our worries left us. For one hour, I felt as carefree as a five-year-old on a bouncy castle and afterwards, suddenly ravenous. We had lunch at the park café with a glass of wine and dessert. It would turn out to be Jack's last restaurant meal: prawn linguine and poached pears with ice cream.

Craft for a Cause

In the kitchen, I tucked the urn at the back of the bench next to the microwave, as out of sight as possible. I didn't wish to have him on display like he was an exotic gift or a focal point for conversation. Although Lottie didn't mention Jack again, I couldn't stop thinking about him. I may have renounced the suitcase, but I was still clinging on to the urn. By transporting it everywhere like it was a security blanket, was I in danger of jeopardising my friendships as well as my future? How close I'd been to cutting ties with Lottie after the distressing incident at the zoo. Had I done so, I would have never known how she felt about me, and our friendship would never have progressed. Even Len was beginning to lose patience with me and 'the elephant in the room' as he called it (*sorry, Jack*). And look how happy Len was with Crystal. He had managed to bring someone new into his life without dismissing what he'd had with Pam. I may not have wanted to find romance again, but did I want my life to be constrained by an urn full of ashes?

Then there was Jack's final request. We'd been married for fifty years and I could name his favourite toothpaste, butterfly and song but had been unable and unwilling to choose the best way to send him off. What kind of a wife doesn't honour her husband's last wish? There were so many lasts Jack had had to make during his final weeks and days but this one relied on me and I hadn't done it. The reality was, Jack was still in my care, just as Lottie's ring was still in her care, and maybe, just maybe, it was time to let go.

It was difficult to concentrate on anything else after that. Even when Lottie showed me her elephant sketches, my husband was still on my mind. Even when Ruby and Benny spotted me on the veranda waving goodbye to Lottie, Jack lingered like the smell of a ripe Brie long after it's been put in the fridge. He had given me his blessing to look forward to the future. But what exactly did my future hold?

I would have gone inside had the kids not called out to me.

'Mrs Verne, Mrs Verne,' they said, crossing the road with a large Tupperware container.

'Hello, children.'

'We made your cake.' Ruby grinned so wide her mouth looked about to split in two.

'Did you?' I smiled. 'Well, come up here and let's have a look.'

They bounded up the steps and handed me the container. They hadn't made just one cake, they'd made two and layered them with the same vanilla buttercream that iced the top, and a flurry of rain-bow sprinkles to make it pop with colour.

'We did it all by ourselves,' Benny said.

'Kind of,' Ruby said. 'Mum was around.'

'But I was in charge of the mixer,' Benny added proudly. 'No one else was allowed to turn it off or on.'

'I'm impressed. It looks perfect. Shall we do a taste test or are you saving it for something?'

'Taste test, taste test!' Benny jiggled and jived.

'It's for you, Mrs Verne,' Ruby said.

'I can't have it all; you must share it with friends. But I am keen to try it.'

'We did what you said and whipped the butter and sugar together first for four minutes and used the long, skinny sprinkles so the colours didn't bleed.'

'Good work.'

I went inside to fetch a knife, plates and forks. When I returned, the cake was on a chair and the children were sitting on the steps playing paper, scissors, rock. I cut three slices and handed them around. They made room for me on the top step and I sat in the middle like a chunk of dry old cheese between two fresh slices of bread. If I could have pressed pause right then, I would have. I'd have stayed there for the rest of the day with those two, eating a cake they'd made for me from one of my recipes.

'Do you like it, do you like?' Benny turned to me, his eyes sparkling. His face was so close I could count his freckles.

'I do like it, Benny. You should be pleased with yourselves. Now, I think you should go home and share it around.'

'Thanks for the recipes, Mrs Verne,' Ruby said.

'There's plenty more if you want them.'

The children's surprise gift reminded me to call Sue about her tea cosies. I dialled her number.

'I'm interested in your cosies, Sue,' I said. 'What vegetable varieties are you knitting and are they organic?'

I had to hold the phone away from my ear while she laughed.

'That's good, Geri; I like that. I've got pumpkin, swede, aubergine and tomato – technically a fruit, I know. Plus, I'm doing cupcakes. Pale pink and lemon. I've also decided to sell them at the next Neighbourhood Watch meeting to raise money for our committee kitty to pay for things like stationery, stickers, signs, etcetera. If that's successful, I'll do more for a community safety project I have in mind. I'd like to transform the small area next to

Dave Whistle's house into a pocket park. Do you know Dave? His dog looks like it ran into a door.'

'It sounds like a lot of knitting. Watch out for occupational overuse syndrome,' I said, surprising myself by proffering Sue a health and safety message.

'Indeed, Geri. I'm also thinking of knitting cosies for my front window featuring the letters of Neighbourhood Watch. I've done the maths. If I put two or three letters on each cosy that's eight or nine cosies in total. Perfectly doable, and I'm getting quicker. Now I can knit, talk and watch television at the same time!' Sue's pride streamed down the phone line. 'I've also set up a Facebook group. You should join.'

'Mmm,' I said non-committally.

'The thing is, Geri, it's not all about burglaries. There are plenty of things we can talk about at our get-togethers: winter fire safety, using environmental design to prevent crime, internet scams, especially relationship ones. You might like to come to that one, if you want to get back on the dating scene.'

I laughed half-heartedly.

'I'm not joking,' she said. 'Anyway, drop by any time. I've got plenty of each variety. And Geri . . . ?'

'Yes, Sue?'

'I was thinking of asking you a favour since you're feeling better and all that . . .'

'Yes?'

'Would you consider doing some baking for the Neighbourhood Watch meets?'

After hanging up, I texted Lottie about Sue's tea cosies.

They sound awful, I wrote, *but if you want a giggle over a cup of tea . . .*

I think they're fun, Lottie replied. *My sister has a purple kitchen that she insists is called aubergine. Her birthday's coming up, so perhaps I should get her an aubergine tea cosy.*

Also, I added, *would you like to do some baking with me? I could teach you how to make vanilla cupcakes?*

She replied in the affirmative and Lottie's second life-skills lesson was set for Friday.

641.59 Cooking Characteristic of Specific Geographic Environments, Ethnic Cooking

My first date with Jack, back in 1966, was at Giuseppe's, a small Italian restaurant two suburbs away. I could remember exactly what we ate. As Jack was a regular, he suggested I order their signature dish: the spaghetti carbonara.

He told me, like a true man of the world, 'You can tell the quality of the restaurant by their carbonara.'

At the time, I could only speak with pasta-making authority on macaroni cheese, so took his word for it.

'I'm going to have the special of the day, veal scaloppini,' Jack said. 'I've never had it before, have you?'

'I haven't. I can't even spell scallop— what?'

'Here, use the menu,' Jack said. 'You'll be able to spell it forwards and backwards then,' he laughed.

It was a night of cream sauces and conversation. Once we were officially dating, I suggested we go back to properly savour the dish.

'Do you think Giuseppe might tell me how he makes it?' I asked Jack. 'Then I could cook it whenever we feel like it.'

Giuseppe obliged. I listened carefully and took notes on a paper napkin. But no matter how many times I tried, my spaghetti carbonara was never as good. I often wondered if there was a secret ingredient Giuseppe had omitted from his list, or whether it was simply confirmation that baking was my forte.

Mamma Mia

Having become reacquainted with sitting on the veranda, I was now enjoying being in the back garden, which, in retrospect, would have been a better place to begin my acclimatisation into the world beyond my front gate. There, no one could see me and I couldn't see them – unless I stood on a stepladder and peered over the fence into the neighbours' property. Come Monday, late afternoon, Len and Crystal found me out the back checking the swan plants.

Len appeared at the back door with a cooler bag of beer. Crystal, a few paces behind him, looked like a pot of pink blusher and smelled like a department store floor of cosmetics. I realised I must have forgotten to lock the front door, which was another thing I was getting lax about. Yet it didn't faze me. It was pleasant to have friends drop by unannounced.

'Hey, Geri? What are you doing out here?' Len asked.

'Checking for caterpillars,' I said, pointing to the swan plants.

'Oh, right, have they always been there? Are those the ones Jack planted?'

'No, they were a gift from Lottie.'

'She really is a nice person, isn't she? Does she know you've ended Meals on Wheels?'

'Yes.' I nodded. 'I told you I didn't want to be buying friends, didn't I?'

Len smiled. 'Any action on the plants?' He flicked his head in their direction.

'Not yet.'

'You'll have to tell us when there is, won't you?' Crystal said.

A bunch of crickets started up as dusk began sucking away the day. I pulled my cardigan around me. 'Shall we go inside?'

'Sorry to drop by unannounced but Len's got some good news, too,' Crystal explained as we went to the kitchen.

'Hang on, Cryssie, let's crack open a beer first,' Len laughed. 'Do you want one, Geri?'

'Sure.' Fetching a bottle opener, I also pulled out a tea towel. After pretending to use it to wipe down the bench, I threw it over Jack, who was sitting next to the bottle of Prosecco at the far end, and joined Len and Crystal at the kitchen table. 'So, tell me your news.'

'It's two bits of news, as it happens,' Len said. 'One, I got my ancestry DNA results back and I can confirm that I am Italian. *Mamma mia!*' He exaggerated an Italian accent.

'That would explain the prolific hand gesticulations then,' I laughed, raising my beer bottle to his.

'Very funny. It's only fifteen per cent, mind you, but hey, I reckon it gives me licence to eat all the pasta I want.' Crystal chuckled. Len continued. 'It would have been better if they could have pinpointed the exact area in Italy I'm from, but the testing isn't quite there yet. Still, I'm tossing up whether I'd prefer to be Roman or Milanese . . . Anyway, you know what it means, don't you? A trip to Italy. I'm hoping that because the DNA results are linked to the ancestry website, I might get some family matches and we could tour Italy meeting the rellies!'

'Sounds wonderful,' I said.

'I told you Gail has Italian ancestry, too, didn't I?'

'You did.' I nodded.

'So that's the other news. We've met Gail twice now and have booked to do the parentage test on Friday. They like you to do it at the same time and it's only a week's wait for the results.'

'Gosh, Len, no mucking around.'

'But she's so nice. I can't believe it. We hit it off immediately.'

'She's very warm and kind,' Crystal added.

'She's had a really hard time of things, though,' Len said. 'She grew up with her grandparents and there was little money to go around. Then, after thinking she'd fallen on her feet with her husband, he left her a few months ago *and* she found out she's got an autoimmune disorder. What was it again?' He turned to Crystal.

'Graves' disease. It affects the thyroid.' She pointed to the side of her neck where the thyroid wasn't located.

'You see, she's been accumulating medical bills like you've no idea and being a primary school teacher, she doesn't have a high salary.'

'Poor thing,' I agreed.

Len nodded and took a swig of beer. 'I said I'd give her some money to tide her over.'

'Really?' It was hard to disguise my shock. 'That's very generous of you when you don't even know if she's your daughter.'

'I have a hunch she is. Anyway, I think it's the right thing to do. Crystal agrees, don't you, Cryssie?'

'Oh yes,' she said. 'If you met her, Geri, you'd want to help too. Her story is so sad.'

'It'll only be a few hundred dollars. I'm not going to hand over my life savings.'

'I guess,' I said, although I wasn't convinced it was something he should be rushing into.

'Another beer?' Len asked, handing around more bottles. 'Look, do you want to see?' he said, pulling out some paper from the side pocket of the cooler bag. 'My DNA results.'

I tried to appear interested, but the percentage breakdown of someone's genetic heritage is really only of interest to its owner.

'Hey.' Len suddenly looked around the kitchen. 'I've just realised – no suitcase?'

'It's in a safe place.'

'Is it, now? You're not going to lose it again?'

I shook my head.

'We're still happy to help you sort out Jack's stuff, aren't we, Cryssie?' He patted her knee under the table.

'Thanks. I might take you up on it some time.'

'Well, I'd say that's another piece of good news. Let's toast to a trifecta!'

I clinked my bottle against theirs. Yet, while it didn't seem as daunting a notion as it once had, I knew there was something else I had to do before I could begin sorting through Jack's belongings.

Vanilla Cupcakes

I spotted the first Monarch butterfly five days after the swan plants had been planted. I was eating strawberries at the small outdoor table in the back garden. The butterfly fluttered on to the back of the chair opposite mine. I froze, a strawberry halfway to my mouth. *Don't move, Jack, don't make a sound.* Slowly and gracefully, it opened and closed its wings, showing off its stained-glass-window markings. There were no black spots on its hind wings, which meant it was a female. Had she just mated or was she in search of a mate? I got up to try and lead her to the swan plants but, *flit*, she darted off.

Hang on, Jack, there she is. She was higher now, her white spots flickering like lights, heading towards the plants. I shoved the strawberry in my mouth and followed her. Overhead, a dark cloud was spreading like mercury, elbowing out the last vestiges of blue sky. A drop of rain plopped on to my shoulder. The butterfly flew erratically higher and higher until she was impossible to follow. I went to the swan plants and inspected the leaves for eggs. Nothing. Not yet. I hurried inside, gathering Jack and the strawberries as rain fell like strings of fish roe around me, excited a butterfly had finally found us.

That afternoon, once the rain had stopped and the scent of pollen hung in the air, I decided to venture out for the first time on my own to buy ingredients for Lottie's visit. I put Jack in a sturdy, reusable shopping bag with a small thermos of tea so we could make a proper outing of it. My idea was to have a pit stop in the park on the way to the shops to enjoy a moment with my husband somewhere other than inside the house. It was an idea I very soon regretted. After finding a park bench, I was so preoccupied taking in the view and hoping no one would invade our personal space by sitting next to us that instead of pulling out the thermos, I grabbed the urn and started unscrewing the lid. To think, I could have drunk my husband! My heart went into overdrive and in no time was speeding down a racetrack. It took several minutes before I could even think about opening the thermos. Except by then, the moment I was hoping to have with Jack was lost. I left the park and hurried to the shops and home again so I could put my husband somewhere safe, all the while unable to dismiss the incident as a blip in my day.

By Thursday morning, there were several clusters of eggs like white sprinkles on the underside of the swan plant leaves. I was excited to tell Lottie.

On Friday, in anticipation of her visit, I set up the kitchen for our cooking class, with the non-perishable ingredients and utensils laid out on the table and my favourite cupcake recipe on the book stand. I left the front door open so she could come straight in without having to knock.

'So, I've brought an apron,' she said, pulling one from her bag. 'Josh gave it to me. He thought it might inspire me in the kitchen, but I think he only bought it for himself.'

Featuring the curvy headless body of a woman in a red bikini, I could see how it might have appealed to her ex-fiancé. Lottie looked neither impressed nor like she wanted to put it on.

'Why don't I wear it?' I suggested. 'I've not worn a bikini since the eighties.'

'Okay,' she laughed.

'You can wear one of my mine,' I said, pulling out options from my apron drawer. 'The choices are: a festive Christmas tree, a fifties-inspired frilly floral number, or one that says "Stand back, I'm about to cook".'

'The latter. That's me!'

We swapped aprons, put them on, had a giggle at how ridiculous I looked and got started. I let Lottie do it all but gave instructions and advice along the way, as I did with the children, passing on important tips that recipes don't normally tell you. Once the cakes were in the oven, I put on the kettle and handed Lottie the wooden spoon.

'You have several years of spoon-licking to catch up on,' I told her. She laughed and took the spoon from me. That's when I noticed. 'Do I see that something's missing?'

She smiled and waggled her ringless left hand. 'I won't lie; it was really hard. Not to get it off but to keep it off. It was two nights ago when I was watching *The Bachelor*. Don't ask; I know I shouldn't love that show but I do. I realised I was wearing a ring that foretold a future that now no longer existed. I took it off and kept it off for the rest of the night. But when I woke up the following day, it felt weird, so I put it back on. Then I tried again and, because I was really busy with work, was able to forget about it for a bit. It helped that I had only put it in the jewellery bowl on my bedside table, mind you. It wasn't like I'd thrown it out or anything. It was in a logical place ready for me to wear again if I wanted. But in my rush at the end of the day, I raced out the door to meet Dad for dinner and forgot I wasn't wearing it. Of course, he noticed. I considered saying it was getting fixed or something, but I've never been good at lying.' Lottie paused for a moment to gather her thoughts and lick the spoon.

I passed her the spatula. 'Here, I think you need to lick this too.'

'I was so scared to look at Dad's face after I told him but, dear Dad, he took my hand and squeezed. That was it. That was all I needed. When he dropped me home, we opened the whisky you gave me.' She gave the spoon one last lick and put it in the bowl in the sink.

'You've done a very brave thing,' I said.

'I don't know if it's brave.'

'Courageous, then.'

'Still, the thought of starting over . . .' Lottie sighed and consoled herself with the batter-smeared spatula.

I reached for three mugs and dropped a tea bag in each. 'Maybe you should do something to mark the occasion.'

'What do mean?'

'Something out of your comfort zone. Something you wouldn't have done if you were still with Josh.'

Lottie frowned. 'Like what?'

'You mentioned skydiving that day at the museum. Something like that.'

'Oh, I don't know if I want to do that anymore.' Lottie shook her head. 'It was my friend who had been encouraging me.'

'Something will come to you.'

'Have *you* done something to mark an occasion?'

I thought of Jack's fruit cake and an occasion I hadn't yet marked, which had been coming to mind more and more frequently now that Jack was out of the suitcase.

'I can't think of anything,' I muttered and returned to the tea making.

As I was doing so, Lottie noticed the photos on the fridge. 'Is this your husband?'

I nodded. 'See the one on the right? That was when Jack got the butterflies framed. He was so proud that day.'

'The butterflies in the room off the hall?'

'The Butterfly Room,' I said. My chest swelled with pride. I hadn't referred to the room in that way – spoken aloud and in capitals – for such a long time that I wanted to do it again. '*Our* Butterfly Room,' I added. I took the teas to the table, holding two in one hand and one in the other.

Lottie put the spatula in the sink and joined me at the table. 'Do you realise you've made three teas?'

The comment made me jerk. The tea sloshed and splattered over Jack's passport and wallet still standing in the centre of the table. I wiped them with my apron. 'It's thirsty work, baking,' I said.

'Were you planning a trip?' she asked. 'Don't do what I once did and turn up at the airport with an expired passport.'

'They're Jack's,' I said.

'Suddenly Jack is everywhere,' she laughed. 'Have you been doing a clear-out?'

'Sort of.'

'After Granddad died, Dad found a hundred dollars in a pair of trousers he was going to throw out, so it's a good idea to check everything. All pockets. All drawers. I wanted to go through Josh's wallet when I found out he was cheating on me but couldn't bring myself. I didn't want to see a receipt for a dinner for two to which I hadn't been invited.'

'Probably sensible. No need to torture yourself,' I said. 'My husband's wallet isn't particularly interesting. There's a receipt for

226

dry cleaning, a measly amount of money and a lottery ticket – an obsession of his that proved time and again to be entirely pointless.'

'Have you checked it?'

'No, it's old.' I drank tea from both mugs to keep up my façade of thirstiness.

'I think you can still claim, even months later,' Lottie said.

'Jack never won more than a few dollars. It became a standing joke.'

'Still, I think you should check it.'

'I don't approve of the things.'

'It could be a last hurrah for your husband.'

It was the words 'last hurrah' that did it. The farewell, the parting song, the epilogue yet to be made, sung and written. My eyes pricked. I looked away.

'Sorry,' she said, touching my hand. 'Here's me worried about taking off a stupid ring when you've had to let your beloved husband go. It must have been so hard.'

I tried sipping some tea but it's not easy drinking when you also want to cry. I squeezed my eyes shut and tried not to think about my husband. But it was as impossible as it was not to cry. For thinking of Jack didn't only bring about sadness or longing or feelings of love, it also brought on guilt. I'd thought I'd avoided honouring Jack's last wish because I'd wanted to get it right. But now, I realised, it was also because I hadn't wanted to let him go. Because if I let him go, what would be left? The half that was me. One left shoe without its partner.

'Geri?' Lottie said softly. 'Do you want to talk?'

I shrugged, even though I wanted to talk much more than I ever had before. 'Sometimes I worry that if I stop grieving my memories of Jack will fade,' I whispered.

'Memories only fade if you want them to and I can't imagine you'll ever let that happen. Look at all the photos you have around you.'

She was right of course, but still . . .

'You know, when Mum left Dad, he reckoned he went through a form of grieving. He said it was like losing a part of yourself, while at the same time trying to regain it.'

'Yes, I suppose that's it,' I agreed. 'For the past five months, I feel like I've been walking with a limp, literally and figuratively. I want to bring him back so badly it hurts. That's why I like to . . . you know . . . keep him close.' I glanced at the urn in its safe spot by the microwave. 'It didn't make sense to scatter his ashes, let alone do so how he wanted. You see, I made a promise to my husband and I haven't honoured it.'

'Go on.'

I looked at all the Jacks stuck to my fridge. 'Well, just before he died, he asked me to take him – his ashes – somewhere exotic. Except I never knew – and never found out – what he meant. I discarded the notion as impossible, too hard. I decided the only way I could keep on living was to hold on to him. But not only have I risked losing him in undesirable ways, he's become a safety hazard. At the zoo, he could have been stolen, then discarded and sent to landfill. And the other day . . . I nearly drank him.'

'What?'

'I know. Can you believe it?'

She looked at me with her big brown eyes, then burst out laughing. 'I'm sorry,' she said. But I was already laughing with her. We laughed for a solid minute – it may have been longer – and I wondered if Lottie had undisclosed therapeutic superpowers she was unaware of.

When we got our breaths back, Lottie insisted we do some brainstorming. She rattled off potential ash-scattering opportunities as if she was in a quick-fire round on a quiz show.

'What about at his favourite holiday spot or over the sea with flower petals?' she suggested.

'Jack didn't really have a favourite holiday spot. He liked trying new places and was prone to seasickness,' I said.

'How about putting them in an hourglass? That's what my aunt did with my uncle so she could use him as an egg timer.'

'An egg timer?' I pulled a face.

'Just an idea.' She shrugged. 'Or, an obvious one, which I'm sure you've thought of, is sprinkling him in the garden.'

'It's just not very exotic, is it?'

'You could take him overseas.'

'Where?'

'Anywhere.'

'I've thought about that, but the cons outweigh the pros: the cost of the flight, the need to travel out of the country, having to comply with local ash-scattering regulations . . . I'm sorry to sound so negative. You can see how it's become a dilemma.'

'You know, when Dad owned the pet shop,' Lottie said, 'he often had people asking him what to do with their pets when they died. One family got a concrete statue done of their cat where the ashes were mixed into the mould, and another made a soft toy version of their dog that was literally stuffed with its ashes.'

I tried to picture Jack as a stuffed toy but couldn't do it.

'What if you split him into quarters and pick four of the best ideas? A quarter could be scattered over a park, a quarter over some plants and so on.'

'I don't think so.' I couldn't split Jack up as if he was the winnings of a horse race that needed divvying between a syndicate: a leg going to the park down the road, his head over the swan plants.

'If I think of any other ideas . . .'

Lottie was trying hard, but I was beginning to wonder if Jack's last request was another of his conundrums he'd bequeathed me to mull over long after he was gone. Then Lottie snapped her fingers.

'I know! What about a helium balloon so he could float away on his own adventure?'

I thought about the Christmas tree in the living room, of the many times I had decorated it with balloons for, not just his birthday, but our wedding anniversaries and Christmas. I thought about the concept of Jack flying away, going in a plane to a foreign, maybe even an exotic, place, like a butterfly taking a ride on a bird or a dolphin hitching a lift on the back of a whale. Jack loved flying because usually it meant some sort of novel experience awaited. But flying didn't have to mean in a plane, did it? It could also mean a balloon. And who knew where a balloon might take him. He could go on multiple adventures on the one trip and I wouldn't have to leave the country. Lottie's eyes had lit up like a string of Christmas tree lights in delight at the idea. I wondered if she had hit on the solution.

Until a smell distracted me. I sniffed. Singed sugar scented the air. 'The cupcakes!' I rushed to the oven. The tops of the cakes were bubbled black like volcanic rock. 'Last tip for the day,' I told Lottie, 'set a timer so you don't burn your baking. I was going to show you how to ice them, too.'

'Never mind,' she said.

Pop! The cupcake came out like a golf ball. 'This is probably the worst baking I have ever done.' *Pop*, another came out, still steaming like barely cooled lava.

'They're pretty bad,' Lottie agreed.

'Let's get them out before they set in the pan and are stuck forever.' I gave Lottie a knife and we chipped away until all twelve came unstuck – a batch of inedible cupcakes delectable to no one.

'I won't tell you off for throwing them in the rubbish,' Lottie laughed.

'Good, because that's where they're going.'

After Lottie left, I lingered on the porch a little longer. I felt lighter, clearer, calmer. The sky seemed brighter and the air sweeter. Back inside, I turned on the radio and swayed with Jack to the music. It was a shame it was an ad for underarm deodorant, but it was a catchy jingle and we could jiggle to it without having to worry about fancy footwork. When the news came on, I was reminded that it was the day of Len's DNA paternity test. Leaving Jack on the bench, I went to find my phone.

When Len answered, his greeting was lacklustre and un-Len-like. 'So . . . ?' I asked tentatively. 'How did it go?'

'It didn't,' he mumbled.

'Oh, Len, you sound like someone whose white suit got shrunk at the dry-cleaners.'

'I was all geared up for it, that's all.'

'What happened?'

'Gail cancelled at the last minute. Something came up at school. She said she'd rebook for next week.'

'Oh, that's okay, isn't it? For a minute I thought she'd reneged on the whole thing. It just means another wait.'

'Yeah,' he sighed.

'Chin up, Len, it'll happen.'

'I get impatient, Geri. I know I can take a while to make up my mind on something but when I do, I just want to get on with it.'

I was tempted to open up to Len, too, and tell him my plans for Jack which I thought might help cheer him up. But I wanted to have it all arranged, so I could send Len a proper invitation. Instead, I told him, 'I would offer a bunch of clichés to make you feel better, but they'll only make you annoyed. Trust me, I know.'

'Thanks, Geri. I suppose I have plenty to do in the meantime,' he said, sounding perkier. 'More genealogy research, for starters, and tomorrow it's the semi-finals of the golf competition. I was even thinking of signing up for Italian cooking classes. Crystal and I have always wanted to learn how to make pasta. Anyway, what about you, Geri? What's been happening?'

'Oh, not much,' I said and left it that.

PART FOUR

The High Street

Come Monday, the air seemed sweeter still. And it wasn't solely from the lingering scent of scorched cupcakes in my kitchen. No longer did I feel like an older woman with no direction except the circumference of her property. For the first time in months, I felt I had a purpose. I had a proper reason to leave the house: tasks to do which could not be achieved over the internet. Going to the high street to look for helium balloons may sound like an odd way to begin reclaiming your life, but you've got to start somewhere.

In order to regain my life, it was time to do what Jack had wanted all along: to think of myself and work out how I was going to live without him. Not how was I going to preoccupy myself for the next hour or the next week, but how I would fill the rest of my days. Instead of slowly dying inside, I had to find my new place in the world and properly live again. Already I had Lottie to gift motherly instruction, Ruby and Benny to help with their baking and Sue to support with her Neighbourhood Watch initiative. I could also do a full garden makeover – starting with the planting of my namesake rose – and help the neighbours revive Jack's nature strips. I could join the garden club for inspiration and restart my old book club. There might even be a place for me at the library again. I'd have fitted in anywhere – section 305.26 Elderly persons or even

398.245 Unicorns. That would be fun. Just to be back there, to be helping out, to feel like I was a whole person once more.

I slung Jack over my shoulder in a shopping bag – this time without the tea thermos – and headed to the party shop on the high street. Inside, it was like being slapped in the face with a disco ball. Rather than trawling the shelves, I went straight to the sales assistant behind the counter, whose smile was like one of their foil party banners.

'I'm looking for helium balloons,' I explained. 'Large. Possibly red. Possibly heart-shaped.'

'We have heart-shaped red ones or clear balloons that you could put red heart confetti into,' she told me. 'With our custom helium range, you can fill them with almost anything like feathers or even smaller balloons.'

'I was hoping to include a surprise,' I said, realising what it might sound like if I explained exactly what I wanted to do with my husband.

'Sure, but we'll have to check it can be done. We take orders in advance but pickup is as close as possible to when you want it because the balloons only stay inflated for up to sixteen hours.'

'And the cost?'

'It depends on the balloon size and all the extras. The biggest clear balloon is ninety centimetres and starts at fifty dollars. It's more if you want to put something inside, extra for the helium, a decorated ribbon and a weight.'

'Fifty dollars for one balloon?' I gulped, before reminding myself that I shouldn't skimp on Jack's final send-off. Even so, it was an outrageous price. 'In any case, I won't need tassels and definitely no weights.'

'You'll need something to keep it down otherwise it will float off and you'll never see it again,' the girl laughed.

I smiled. Little did she know.

I left with their business card and a packet of mini red balloons, which I thought would look lovely on the tree at home.

Afterwards, I headed to the newsagents to get some wrapping paper for the present I was giving Lottie, and some extra to have on hand for times of unexpected gift-wrapping. I picked out three rolls of white paper with gold dots and headed to the counter.

That's when I heard someone ask for twenty dollars' worth of scratch lottery tickets and realised I'd left Jack's wallet at home. I'd intended to do the right thing by checking his ticket before throwing it out. I cursed my forgetfulness and was about to exit when I had a change of mind. I could do it later.

Yet . . .

No, I'll wait. I've more pressing things to do.

But . . .

Something niggled. It was like Jack was tapping my shoulder, twisting my arm from the afterlife. I dropped the wrapping paper in the chocolate display and left the shop. Better to know for sure that I could bin the ticket guilt-free. Or perhaps Jack merely wanted me to have another go at making a solo round-trip to the high street.

Forty minutes later I was back at the newsagents and started all over again. I picked up my wrapping paper and joined the queue. A woman ahead of me was dithering over the selection of novelty letter-shaped keyrings on display. I wanted to tell her to hurry up, some of us have things to accomplish. Maybe the Geri of two months ago would have blurted that out but the new one managed to keep her emotions contained.

Finally, it was my turn. 'Can you check this?' I asked the sales assistant, whose stringy ponytail made me think of a pull-chain on an old toilet.

As he slid the ticket into the machine, I picked up one of the novelty keyrings shaped as the letter A and tried to work out the attraction. But all they seemed notable for was their use of plastic.

'Lady,' said the assistant, tapping the counter. 'Hey, lady.'

'All done?' I asked, replacing the keyring and reaching for the ticket.

'You're a winner!'

I rolled my eyes. 'It's not the first of April, you know,' I said.

'No, honestly, you are!' he said loudly, even though I was only a metre away.

I wanted to tell him to quieten down, he was making a fool of himself. 'Well, how many keyrings will it buy? Five? Ten?' I asked, humouring him.

'More keyrings than we stock.'

'I'm being serious. How many? A ballpark will do.'

'I dunno, hundreds?'

This man was so good at pranking, I was beginning to believe him.

'Look, lady, you've won nine thousand dollars! Hey, everyone, this lady's a winner!' he announced, pointing at my head.

He had successfully attracted the attention of every customer. A chorus of clapping exploded around me. 'I think you should check it again,' I said. 'Jack's never won that amount before.'

'The machine doesn't lie.'

'Please do it again.'

'I think he's made a mistake,' I said to the clapping customers.

'All right, everyone,' the assistant announced to the group that had formed around me, 'at the customer's request, I'm checking it again.' You'd think *he* had won the way he was carrying on.

There was a palpable intake of breath.

'And . . .' The man, who seemed to have pretensions of being a game show host, drum-rolled his fingers on the bench. 'You are indeed the winner of nine thousand dollars!' Another cheer erupted.

My jaw went slack and out slid the words, 'I was going to burn the ticket . . .' Because that was the first thought that went through my head.

'Whatever you do, don't do that!' he said. 'She was going to burn the ticket, everybody,' he told the crowd. Then, to me, 'That's not a good idea, let me tell you. Here's what you *do* do. Take a copy of it for yourself, fill out this claim form and send it off with the original ticket. And very soon, you will have nine thousand smackeroos in your bank account. Hey, do you want that wrapping paper as well?'

I looked at the rolls of paper I'd put on the bench but couldn't immediately remember what I wanted them for. 'I think I'll leave it,' I said, pushing them away.

'You could afford to buy all our wrapping paper now,' he laughed. 'Anyway, if I were you, I wouldn't be wasting my winnings on stationery. I'd go out and get a spoiler for my car. Here, don't forget the ticket and don't lose it either.'

I nodded and floated out of the shop. I slid the ticket and claim form into the zip pocket of my handbag, and turned to head home, almost forgetting that I was meant to be stopping by Sue's.

795 Gambling (Recreation)

When Jack bought his first lottery ticket, he said he was going to buy me earrings to match my engagement ring and, for himself, a set of quality binoculars. It was towards the end of 1969, the year man first set foot on the moon. The year The Beatles performed their last public performance on the roof of Apple Records. The year Graham Greene published *Travels With My Aunt*. We were engaged and Jack had been given a pay rise. To celebrate he went out and bought a lottery ticket. He didn't win a cent. But it didn't stop him buying another one a couple of months later.

'This time, if I win big,' he said, 'I'll get us a car.'

I rolled my eyes.

'Darling, you won't be eye-rolling when this beauty cashes in,' he said. 'You'll be rolling with me down the road in the latest Fiat 124.'

That didn't happen either. He didn't even win the cost of a bus ride to sit in the driver's seat of the latest Fiat 124 in a showroom. For a few seconds, disappointment flashed across his eyes. It didn't last long, which pleased me as I didn't fancy feeling sorry for him over what I considered a pointless, money-wasting exercise. Yet something else happened to my husband that day. He got hooked on the wishing, the ticket-buying, the anticipating. A few weeks later, he bought another ticket, rubbed his hands together, made another wish, and kissed the ticket before slipping it into his wallet. He won five dollars, which was enough to make him continue. I quickly realised my eye-rolling was doing little to curb his addiction. For it didn't take long for his wishes to grow more extravagant and the purchasing more regular, until it settled into a modest weekly ritual which gave him such a thrill it seemed unfair to deny him.

Knit One, Purl Won

'Geri, so lovely to see you.' Sue's face lit up when she opened the door, which warmed my insides.

Until I came over all light-headed and weak-kneed and had to steady myself on the side of the house.

'Geri, are you all right?' She took hold of my arm.

'Just feeling a little faint, Sue,' I said. 'I might need to sit down.'

'Of course. Come inside and I'll get you a glass of water. Have you been overdoing it? It's so hot today.'

I was about to tell her how I'd just won at the lottery but knew she wouldn't approve of such public announcements, having once warned me how friends can take advantage of friends as much as strangers can. I also knew that divulging the win would require an explanation of so many things. Like why I hadn't bothered to check the ticket before now; why Jack's wallet had been hidden away; how much I had won; and what I was going to spend the money on. Sue would ask questions I didn't have answers for or didn't want to disclose. I said nothing and let her take me to a chair in her front room. I rested my head between my knees as Sue went to get some water. When she returned, the sensation had passed.

I noticed then that she'd had a makeover. 'A new do?' I asked of her hair that was now cut into a bob, its colour no longer two-toned but a more flattering, if still obviously dyed, single shade of brown. Her clothes, too, were less over-sized and more figure-hugging.

'Yes, do you like it?' she said, doing a twirl. 'I could give you the name of my hairdresser, if you like? The thing is, Geri, I've met a man.' She winked.

I didn't reciprocate the wink but offered an enthusiastic response of, 'Oooh', thinking how pleased Len would be.

'Do you remember . . . ?' she started. 'Oh, you probably don't, but when you had the accident a policeman – Rog – accompanied me to your house. He waited for me in his car, thinking I'd need someone to talk to after the stress of it all. We ended up going for a drink and I saw him a few more times when I went to the local police station to discuss the Neighbourhood Watch. Then he asked me out. I hadn't realised he'd been thinking of me in that way, nor I him, to be honest. But I can't believe I've found someone who is as passionate about home security as I am.'

I would have laughed had I not known she was being serious. Still, I was pleased for her and told her so.

'And how about you, Geri?'

'I'm well, thanks,' I said, until the surprise of the win hit me again. 'Actually, I'm better than that. I suppose you could say that sometimes life throws up unexpected surprises which makes one very happy indeed.'

'Doesn't it just? Do I detect the need for a haircut?' She said it with so much subtext, I had to set her straight.

'I don't have a new man in my life, nor am I on the lookout for one, if that's what you mean.'

'But why not? You'd be surprised at how invigorating it is. You know, Rog has a friend – an old colleague, now a widower – who's offered to give a talk on credit card fraud. I could introduce the two of you.'

'I'm only in the market for tea cosies, thanks, Sue.'

'Think about it and let me know.' She winked again and I wondered whether, in fact, she had developed a twitch. 'So tell me, which cosies did you want again?'

'An aubergine and a cupcake, preferably yellow.'

Under the window of her front room was a large plastic container with an arsenal of fruit, vegetable and cupcake tea cosies. She rifled through and pulled out a dark-purple woolly aubergine with a bright-green leaf and a pale-lemon cupcake with cream icing and tufts of coloured sprinkles.

'Check you're happy with them. Remember they all have slight variations because they're hand-made.'

'How much are they?'

'As you qualify for the friends and family discount . . .' She started doing the maths in her head.

'No, no, I'll pay full price,' I said, feeling the effects of win-induced generosity. 'I'd like to support your cause.'

Sue put a hand to her chest. 'Thanks, Geri.'

'In fact,' I added, 'I was thinking about your request the other day and I'd love to do some baking for Neighbourhood Watch.'

'That would be wonderful.'

'Perhaps a giant lemon cake, as a reminder to people to avoid being lemons with their security,' I laughed.

'Oh, Geri, yes!' she said with more enthusiasm than I was expecting.

'I was joking, Sue.'

'But why not? Crime prevention doesn't have to be boring.'

'Perhaps cupcakes would be more practical, then you wouldn't need to use a knife, given you're all about safety,' I suggested, thinking Lottie and I could revisit the baking lesson and make several batches, this time unburnt and iced.

'Good idea. Community safety should be our number one priority and you never know what types may come to the

Neighbourhood Watch meetings. Maybe the cupcakes could be lemon-flavoured instead?'

Back home, I took Jack out of the bag and placed him on the kitchen table. I rubbed his curves with my sleeve and then fished out the lottery ticket and claim form. The morning's events felt unreal.

'Nine thousand dollars, Jack,' I said softly at first, then hooted it to the ceiling. 'Nine thousand dollars!'

I stared at the ticket and saw rows of dollar signs instead of numbers. I flapped it in front of him so he could see, too. 'It's a winner, Jackie-boy, a winner! Can you believe it?'

I wanted him to swing me in his arms and kiss me in excitement. Although woozy no longer, I felt queasy with disbelief and joy and I had an overwhelming urge to tell someone. The obvious person was Lottie, for she was the only one who knew of the ticket.

As soon as she answered, I skipped over any greeting. 'It's a winner,' I said. 'A winner.'

'What?' she asked.

'The lottery ticket. I took it to the newsagents like you said.'

'And you've won?'

'Nine thousand dollars.'

'Wow. Just wow.' She beamed happiness down the phone line.

'If you hadn't told me to check it, I would have burnt it and added it to the ashes.'

'And now you can.'

'Yes, I suppose I can,' I said, realising I'd given no thought as to what came next. But then, 'Actually, no, I can't. I need to send in the original with the claim form.'

'Make a copy and you can burn that.'

245

'Oh yes, the man at the newsagents said I should make a copy. I could have done it while I was there, couldn't I? Goodness, I can't seem to think straight.'

'Have a cup of tea. Isn't that what you like to do to make yourself feel better?'

That was what I liked to do but I felt too stunned to do anything. I nodded, lost in thought.

'Geri? Are you there?' Lottie asked.

'Uh huh.'

'Have you decided what you'll do with the winnings?'

'No idea.'

'You'll have to treat yourself to something.'

'I could splash out and get two helium balloons instead of one?'

'Surely you can do better than that.'

'To be honest, I don't know. I'm still in shock.'

'You don't have to rush it.'

'No, I don't,' I agreed. 'And another thing, I told Sue I'd do some baking for her Neighbourhood Watch meeting. Would you like to have another go at the cupcakes?'

'I'd love to, but I won't be free until the weekend.'

'That's all right. The meeting is on Monday, so how about Sunday? Come for lunch.'

I skipped to the living room – actually skipped like I'd knocked sixty years off my life – taking with me the claim form, my husband and the pack of red balloons. With the television on in the background, I blew up all twenty balloons, even though eight was more than enough with which to decorate my table-top tinsel tree. I threw two up into the air and watched them float down like big red love hearts. One landed next to the library books Lottie had given me that were now overdue. I was reminded of my next task: to visit the library and pay the fine. I would also have to go to the post office to send off the claim form and buy supplies for two batches of cupcakes: lemons, yellow food colouring, extra muffin pans and paper baking cups.

Unfortunately, the post-win delirium didn't last and soon I began to feel like a balloon deflating. It felt wrong for me to be happy when the one with whom I most wanted to celebrate was no longer around. When Jack had his first lottery win, I surprised myself by how excited I got. Gaining five dollars didn't warrant the zeal I exhibited – dancing Jack around the kitchen and whooping as if I was at a football game. My reaction was not so much because he'd won something but because I knew how much he wanted to win. And now that he had, I felt sad he wasn't around to enjoy it. I lay on the sofa, rested my head on its arm and had a moment of silence in homage to his absence.

After a few minutes, I flicked a couple of balloons loitering by the sofa into the air. They bounced up and fluttered down around the urn. I thought about Jack's instructions to me in his letter: *Promise me you won't stop living. Life is to be treasured and I want you to treasure yours. Live life now for the both of us.* So I decided to be joyful all over again.

The Library

I arrived at the library an hour after opening, having already been to the kitchen shop, the grocer's and the post office. Karen was easy to spot at the front desk. Her hair, once brunette, was now neon pink and her loud voice made heads turn.

'Geri, you're back!' She jiggled in delight.

'Well,' I said, trying to downplay things, 'I don't think I ever really left. Think of it as a temporary hiatus. You're looking well.'

'Do you like the hair?' She preened proudly.

'You remind me of a Post-it note,' I said, hopefully not unkindly. 'Don't tell me you've met a new man, too?'

'Goodness, no,' she laughed. 'I'm still with Dave. It was book week last week and I dressed up as Thelma the Unicorn for the kids. I kept the hair for fun. Shame you couldn't have been here. Maybe next time?'

'Yes,' I said, thinking how that could be something else to include on my 'how to keep on living' list. I put the two books I was returning on to the counter and whispered, 'Sorry, they're a bit overdue.'

Karen opened the back cover of the top one, checked the date, then glanced around and whispered, 'Don't worry about it.'

'Thanks, Karen,' I said, giving her a low-down thumbs up. 'Actually, what I'd really like to do is make a donation. I know funds can be tight and you can never buy enough books, can you?'

'Aw, Geri.'

'I've come into some money, you see,' I added, thinking it didn't matter if Karen knew; I could trust her.

'That's so kind. As you know, we won't say no! You'll have to fill out a donation form. We've got one somewhere . . . Are you going to hang around? Get some books out?'

'I think I will,' I said. 'I also need to use the photocopier.'

I left my shopping bags with Karen but kept Jack over my shoulder. I was only going to make two copies of the lottery ticket but in the end made four: one to keep in case the original got lost, one to frame, one to burn and mix with Jack's ashes, and one for just in case. Then I headed to where I really wanted to be, deep in the heart of all the books, to wander the rows, savour the sounds of whispering voices amongst the quiet and bask in the beauty of people reading. I breathed in and inhaled one of the best smells in the world: the aroma of thousands of books. *Where shall we start, Jackie-boy? Section 410 Linguistics, 560 Fossils and prehistoric life or 130 Parapsychology and occultism? Or shall we just begin at the beginning, 000 Computer science?*

I walked slowly, running my fingers along the plastic-covered spines, remembering what it was like to trawl the aisles, returning books and reordering those out of numerical sync, being the custodian of knowledge past, present and future. It was as if I'd never left. Then I was in 100 Philosophy and 300 Social sciences. I smiled and nodded at anyone I passed and occasionally pulled out a book, so I didn't appear suspicious, mad, lost, or all three. When I got to 641.40 Cooking, I paused to browse the books on baking. I pulled one out that caught my eye called *Icings on the Cakes* and took it to an armchair. For a good ten minutes, I became engrossed in fondant flowers before remembering where I was. I got up, tucked the book into the bag next to Jack and headed to the sports section, thinking I could find a golfing book for Len. He might like a few last-minute tips for his tournament. Without knowing a thing about golf or what books Len had already read on the topic, I chose one titled *A Hole in One: Swing it Like it Matters.*

I also spotted a selection of titles in 797.56 on skydiving: *Dive Right In; To Jump or Not to Jump; Skydiving for Beginners;* and *Spread Your Wings: Fly Like a Bird.* Hadn't Lottie once said she wanted to fly like a bird? I pulled out the last two and looked through them. Maybe I could borrow a book for her as well. It might inspire her to do something crazy and propel her out of her comfort zone. I added the books to my bag and headed back to the main counter.

'You've got a mixed bag here,' Karen exclaimed.

'I'm lending some to friends,' I said.

'That's nice. Will we see you again sometime soon?'

'I think you will now that I'm able to get out and out about.'

'Super,' she said. 'And here's a donation form. You can drop it back when you're next in.'

With four books, six lemons, three new muffin pans, two packets of baking cups, a couple of magazines, a bottle of yellow food colouring, plus Jack, I realised walking home was going to be tricky. For the first time in months, I hailed a taxi and didn't care about the cost or about being in a car with someone I didn't know.

I arrived home to find a container of baking on my doorstep with a note.

> *Dear Mrs Verne,*
> *Here is a pink jam slice we made for you. This time,*
> *we want you to have it all. We hope it's as good as*
> *you make it.*
> *Love Ruby and Benny*

The following day, I called Len to see how he was, and to tell him about my two solo outings and the golf book I thought could help him with his game. He didn't answer. He didn't call back or send a text either, which was unlike Len, but then he did have a maybe-daughter to keep him busy.

It was Thursday when he finally replied.

It's Gail, he texted. *She's gone AWOL.*

Sitting Duck

After receiving Len's text, I dropped the magazine I'd been reading, grabbed the urn and the children's pink jam slice and went to the car. We bunny-hopped out of the carport to see him. It was daunting being back behind the wheel again but also wonderfully empowering.

I hadn't been to his apartment for months, but it hadn't changed. He and Pam had down-sized not long before she died. They went from a two-storey, five-bedroom, rambling brick house to a more modest and modern three-bedroom apartment with a large outdoor deck and view. While I'd always been envious of how well Pam kept house, it wasn't until she died that I realised it was Len's doing as much as Pam's. For Len lived immaculately – it wasn't just the white suit he could effortlessly keep clean.

Crystal greeted me at the door. She smiled but it wasn't a usual Crystal smile.

'What's happened?' I asked.

'I'd better let him tell you,' she said. 'He's outside.'

I followed her through to the living room and on to the balcony where a view of undulating red rooftops and powerlines like tightropes underlined the sky. Len was on a cane chair, wearing sunglasses and a forlorn face. He raised a hand in greeting. I sat down and followed his gaze. A small cloud appeared and dispersed. It seemed disrespectful to speak before he did.

'You know,' he said quietly, 'it's not really about the money. It's the feeling of being duped. Being totally and utterly conned. I'm a fool, Geri. A complete fool.'

'Perhaps you could fill in the gaps in the story for me? I'm a little in the dark, Len,' I said.

He sighed. 'I told you Gail was going to rebook the parentage test, didn't I?'

I nodded.

'She made it for Tuesday at four o'clock, and so Crystal and I turn up at the lab ten minutes early 'cause we don't like being late. We wait for Gail and wait some more. But she doesn't appear. At four twenty, I text her. She doesn't reply. At four thirty, I call her. Still no reply. The lab assistant asks if I want to do the test and says Gail can do hers at another time to save me a third visit. I say no because at this point, I'm feeling a little uneasy. I tell myself I'm being silly and Crystal tells me I'm being silly, too, and that there will be a logical explanation. That evening, we go to the movies because Crystal can't stand me pacing the house. Still no word from Gail. When Wednesday comes, I notice that the second lot of money I transferred to her cleared the day before.'

'The what . . . ?' I interrupted but Len put up a hand to stop me saying any more.

'Please. Let me keep going,' he said. 'I call her again. Still nothing. I try to think of the name of the school she said she worked at so I could call her there. I couldn't remember it, so asked Crystal, but she doesn't think Gail ever told us. I look up her Facebook page only to remember that it's private. Even so, I send her a message via Facebook because that's how she got in touch with me in the first place. No response. Then today, I call her again and get a message saying the number no longer exists. Her number no longer exists!'

he repeated slowly. 'It's like *she* doesn't exist anymore, Geri. But my money did and now that's gone, too.'

'Hell, Len.' I suddenly felt nauseous as if it was my maybe-daughter who had made off with my money.

'Hell, indeed.'

'But perhaps there's a perfectly acceptable reason. Like she's run out of money and her power's been cut off,' I said, remembering my stack of unpaid bills.

'I thought of that and I'd like to think it's true. But she could have got in touch, explained why she didn't come to the lab. She could have used a friend's phone or a laptop. She could have turned up on my doorstep. That's another thing, she knows my address. I don't know hers. She knows a lot about me and I know nothing about her, not really. And now I'm beginning to think what I do know is a pack of lies.'

'What does Crystal say?'

'You know Cryssie, she can't bear to think the worst of people, but even she's beginning to doubt Gail's intentions.'

'We should tell Sue,' I said.

'Oh god, I'm not getting her involved.'

'No, Len, it's okay. She's got a boyfriend now. That policeman who turned up when I had the fall.'

'Really?'

I nodded. 'Maybe he could investigate.'

Len gazed at the dispersing cloud. 'What's the point?'

'To stop her doing the same to others,' I said. 'To see if you can get your money back.'

'I doubt that will happen.'

'It's worth a try.'

We watched another cloud move across the sky. One minute it was a face, the next a dragon. 'So . . .' I said tentatively, curious as to exactly how much money Len had given the woman. 'How much?'

'A thousand dollars,' he muttered. 'I know I was probably premature offering her money, but she promised to pay me back. I felt sorry for her, you know. I thought I was doing a good deed, helping tide her over while she was going through a rough patch and, to be honest, I was convinced she was my daughter. *Convinced.*'

'I'm sorry, Len.'

'I never thought something like this would happen to me.'

'You got caught up in the moment.'

'I got conned, Geri; that's all there is to it.'

'She must have charmed the hair off your chest. I mean, I got excited for you, too – although I would have been more cautious about giving her money. But that's because I don't have it to throw around . . .' I said, temporarily forgetting I was now nine thousand dollars up.

'I wasn't throwing it around!' Len exclaimed.

'No, I know, sorry. I didn't mean it like that,' I said hurriedly.

I didn't know what else to say but to offer more sympathy. A humid breeze wrapped itself around us and brushed the leaves of the clematis climbing the walls at either end of the deck. I lifted my head to capture the last of the summer sun, before reaching for the tin containing the pink jam slice.

'Here, this might cheer you up. The children across the road made it from one of my recipes. I think they've done a pretty good job.'

'Thanks, Geri.'

He took a slice but left it resting on his knee as if unable to muster any enthusiasm for eating.

'And speaking of money . . .' I said, producing my wallet and pulling out a copy of the lottery ticket.

He took off his sunglasses and peered at the ticket. 'Another of his gambling purchases?'

'I found it in his wallet.'

'You've only just found it?'

'I've only just checked it. That's a copy.'

He looked at me questioningly.

'I've won nine thousand dollars,' I said casually as if I was used to winning large amounts of money.

'Christ, Geri. Nine thousand?'

'I know.'

'Nine thousand?' he said again. Then, 'Poor Jack. That's mean, isn't it? Why does life have to be so mean sometimes?'

'I don't know, Len. Sometimes life is the darkest blue and other times, a cheery yellow. That's how Lottie looks at things, which I think is quite useful. If you imagine events in your life as a series of oil paints, all you need is some turps to wipe away the colours you don't like anymore. That way you can move on from the nasty times.'

'Oil paints?' Len rubbed his eyes as if my metaphor baffled him.

'Never mind,' I said. 'Have some cake, that'll do the trick.'

'Hey, this is pretty good.'

'It is, isn't it? I give it an eight out of ten.'

'Seems fair.' He nodded and finished the slice. 'So how come Jack had an unclaimed ticket in his wallet?'

'I think it was the one I bought him on our last walk together. When he told me he felt like a bar of chocolate. I'd completely forgotten about it.'

'You know, he used to say to me sometimes: "Lenny, I'm going to need a lottery ticket." He'd say it in those words. I'm going to *need* like it was some sort of medication or pain relief and if he didn't get it soon, he was going to go downhill pretty quickly.'

I laughed.

'I know you didn't approve of his weekly habit, but it could have been a lot worse.'

'I know.'

'Has he really won nine thousand dollars?' Len's face split into a grin.

I nodded.

'And he's not here to celebrate . . .' His smile dropped.

We had a moment's silence, wishing Jack could have been around to enjoy his win. I wiped away a tear and then another, and another. Len looked like his eyes were forming puddles, too. He came over to me and was about to give me a hug when he stubbed his toe on my bag on the ground.

'Christ, what was that?' he said, holding his foot.

'Jack,' I said.

'What?'

'Jack,' I repeated. There was no point lying about it anymore when I was about to invite him to the send-off.

'I thought now that you'd gotten rid of the suitcase, you weren't doing that anymore.'

'Same doing, different mode of transport,' I said. 'Anyway, that brings me to the other thing I wanted to tell you. I'm having a Jack-sending-off celebration and you and Crystal are invited.'

'Are you now?' I think he wanted to say so much more, but in the end he didn't. Instead, he said, 'Of course we'd love to be there, Geri.'

Then, carefully avoiding my husband in the bag, he sat down next to me and gave me a hug.

'At least you won't have to worry about stubbing your toe on him ever again,' I said.

That only made him hug me harder. I didn't mind because I'd read that hugs release feel-good chemicals into the brain and right then Len needed as many of those as he could get.

Ticket Number: 15091971

Jack had not been long in the palliative care ward when he asked me to go for a walk with him. He was barely mobile, but with a walking stick and my arm to lean on, he could just about do it.

'I fancy some chocolate, Geri-pie. What do you think?'

'Never say no,' I replied.

'I was thinking of a proper walk, though. Get out of this place if we can. There's a newsagent not far down the road.'

'Oh, Jack . . .' I started.

'I'll be fine. We can take it slowly. Stop and smell the roses and all that.'

I had to agree that leaving the hospital with its cloying smells of antiseptic and unfinished food trays was an enticing idea. I told one of the nurses of our plan and Jack said he'd bring them all back some chocolate, the charmer that he was. We walked through the hospital garden and on to a path that eventually took us to the main road. The newsagent was a block away, further than I thought, but Jack was determined. Whenever he said, 'It's time to smell the roses,' we stopped, took a moment and started up again. It would have been nice had roses been in season, but still, there was the pleasant scent of morning rain in the air and the sugary waft of doughnuts from a nearby bakery.

By the time we got to the shop, Jack needed to sit down. We stopped at the bus stop seat opposite and I told him to stay there while I went to get the chocolate.

'What would you like?' I asked.

'I reckon a decent slab of dark chocolate and something for the nurses.'

I nodded.

'Oh, and Geri? You wouldn't mind getting a lottery ticket, too, would you?'

'So that's what this was all about?' I rolled my eyes.

'It was a nice walk, though, wasn't it?' He smiled.

'You're cheeky, you know that? Well, go on, then, what numbers do you want me to get?'

'One five oh nine one nine seven one.'

'You said that quickly.'

'They're my numbers. I never get anything else.'

'Can you say them again? I've forgotten them already.'

'Fifteenth of the ninth, nineteen seventy-one.'

Even though he said it slowly and repeated it for good measure, it took me a few seconds to twig.

'That was our wedding day,' I said.

He grinned like a fairground clown. Then, 'Well, are you going to go in or not?'

I came back with two large blocks of chocolate, the latest *National Geographic* magazine I knew he'd enjoy and a lottery ticket. I sat down next to him, told him to put the ticket somewhere safe and broke off some squares of chocolate. 'Energy for the walk home,' I said.

As two buses came and went without us, we held hands and ate our chocolate, feeling like a newly married couple all over again.

The Last Supper

It was Sunday. I rose early to get ready for Lottie's visit, the lunch and her second baking lesson. Having neglected to buy the wrapping paper, I fetched a bundle of newspapers from the laundry basket and took them to the kitchen table. Lottie's present needed wrapping but I didn't want to encase it in bad news. I looked through the travel sections, hoping to find something more uplifting. It was on the cover of the weekend edition from a month ago that I found the perfect parcel centrepiece – an aerial view of tandem hang-gliders flying over islands in Hawaii. While Lottie hadn't talked about going hang-gliding, she had mentioned skydiving and I thought it might be an appropriate nod to help her move on without Josh. I wrapped the tea cosies, gulped down some toast and changed into my navy-and-white polka-dot dress. I always feel smart in that dress. It was one Jack complimented me on whenever I wore it. I ran a comb through my hair and put on my two lipsticks.

Next, I set up the outdoor table with the blue-and-yellow tablecloth we bought several years ago in France, paper serviettes left over from Jack's birthday four years ago and a small vase of flowers picked surreptitiously from the front garden of number forty-two. I buffed Jack with a polishing cloth and placed him in the centre. I took out plates, glasses and cutlery, and the artisanal bread and organic eggs I had bought the day before. I tidied the kitchen, making sure the dirty dishes were in the dishwasher and the labels of my gifts lined up under the window were facing out. Finally, I waited for Lottie on the veranda, the enticing smell of fried bacon from someone else's kitchen making me wonder whether I should have bought bacon as well.

Oscar dragged Lottie up the front path as if genuinely pleased to see me. I'd told Lottie she could bring him, thinking he could run around the back garden as much as he liked because any damage he did would go largely unnoticed. He licked my shins and bounced up as if he wanted to lick my face too. Silly dog.

'Down, Oscar,' Lottie shouted. 'Sorry, Geri, he's getting so boisterous.' She yanked him away with the lead and I suggested we head out the back before he found a particularly alluring scent on some furniture and cocked his leg on it. Straining on the lead, Oscar slobbered down the hall, while Lottie ordered him to heel in vain. At the back door, she let him off the lead and he bounded into the garden and started digging.

'Ugh, that dog; I'm so sorry,' Lottie said.

'Don't worry. He can get to work pulling out weeds and tilling the soil.'

'I can tie him up, but he'll crash soon and want to sleep.'

'I don't mind. He's happy.'

'How are the swan plants doing?' she asked, pointing to them.

'Have a look, if you like, while I get lunch started. The leaves are nearly decimated and the caterpillars are getting fatter.'

I watched her from the kitchen window. I was delaying the food prep, I knew, but I needed a moment to prepare myself. My hands began shaking as I removed the loaf of bread from its paper bag. I sliced it as best I could and put it in the toaster without

261

turning it on. I poured two glasses of orange juice and put them on Jack's tray with the cutlery, Lottie's gift and the two library books on skydiving. I took out a small frying pan, a pot and a can opener.

Finally, the tin of baked beans.

I pressed it to my chest and closed my eyes. 'Here it is, Jackie-boy.'

I breathed in and out, slowly, deeply, then opened my eyes and began. In went the beans, on went the toaster, and into the pan two eggs were cracked. Heating, toasting, frying, buttering, serving, then licking the wooden spoon of baked bean sauce. When it was ready, I carried the plates outside and returned for the tray.

'This may not be your usual kind of lunch,' I told Lottie. 'But let me explain . . .'

Thankfully, Lottie seemed unperturbed by the serving of baked beans or that it was the last meal Jack never got to enjoy. What's more, she thoughtfully raised her glass. The orange juice shimmered in the sun.

'To Jack,' she said.

'To Jack,' I said.

And then we ate.

Although I could hear my husband querying the fried egg sitting on top of what he would have called 'the perfect dish that needed no accompaniment', the egg was my choice. As we were a matching pair again, I wanted his final hoorah to be similarly symbolic. The beans were tangy as they should be and the runny yolk a tasty addition. The bread was grainy and thick and, pleasingly, didn't get soggy like the cheaper, white bread variety I usually bought. I ate slowly, thoughtfully, in reverence to my husband. Lottie ate slowly and thoughtfully, too, perhaps in reverence to me. The sky stretched out its blue wings, drying itself in the sun, the air spiced with baked beans, eggs and joy. For a few minutes we didn't speak for there was really no need to. Until Oscar bounded over to us and started sniffing Lottie's gift on the tray at my feet.

'Oh, yes, I've got you something,' I said, patting Oscar on the head and picking it up.

'What's this for?'

Taking the parcel, I was pleased Lottie remarked immediately on the photo featured on the front of the wrapping. 'Great picture,' she said.

'I'm glad you noticed. It's meant to be symbolic.'

'It is?'

'Yes, a symbol of letting go, of going outside your comfort zone. Plus, I've got so many newspapers, I thought I should start recycling them. If you'd like some out-of-date reading . . .' I laughed.

'Actually, I could use some newspaper for the bottom of Darryl's cage.'

'You can open it, you know,' I said.

Lottie ripped open the paper. 'You bought them,' she exclaimed.

'One for your sister and one for you. You said you liked cupcakes.'

'I do!' Lottie smiled. 'Please tell me how much they are.'

'Usually when someone gives you something wrapped, even if it is in repurposed newspaper, it means no payment is required. I don't know if you have a teapot or not, but even if you don't, you could wear it as a hat. I've worn mine and it's not as scratchy as you might think. Or you could use it to cover up a hideous figurine you've been given by a well-meaning relative that can be whipped off for display purposes whenever they visit.'

'Thanks, Geri,' she laughed.

We returned to the meal. I didn't want it to end; I wanted to savour every bite, even the sauce dribbles and crumbs on the plate. I estimated I had five mouthfuls to go but if I kept them small, I could make them last longer. Lottie was eating quicker than me and, naturally, didn't appear to be thinking too much about morsel size or the number of chews. I thought it best to give her the library books, so she had something else to focus on while I concentrated on my final mouthfuls.

'I borrowed these from the library for you, too,' I said, pointing to the books on the tray. 'I thought they might be inspirational. And you'll be pleased to know that skydiving – especially doing it tandem – is safer than you think. It's safer than your morning commute.' I was now on my fourth-to-last bite.

'Except I don't have a morning commute, remember? Are you trying to persuade me to do it?' She smiled.

'I just don't think you should let whatever Josh told you get in the way of doing something you might actually want to do. And somehow, I get the feeling you'd like to do it.' I pronged my third-to-last mouthful.

Lottie turned the books over and skim-read the blurbs. 'Take the plunge and get over your fears,' she read. 'It will be the ride of your life that you'll never forget or regret. Freefall for sixty seconds then parachute like a bird cruising languidly on a slipstream . . . Who wrote this?' she groaned.

'Didn't you say you wanted to fly like a bird?' I asked. 'The other day on the television, David Attenborough said gannets can dive-bomb into the ocean at speeds of more than eighty kilometres an hour. Just imagine . . . well, you wouldn't have to if you sky-dived. It's like the human version, isn't it?'

'I guess so.' She nodded.

I was on to my penultimate mouthful. I took my time, making it last as long as I could, until there was only one more to go. I closed my eyes and chewed very, very slowly. I pictured Jack sitting opposite me, relishing every bite. I imagined talking about butter-flies and plants and where our next trip might be. Until Jack's last meal was simply a tickle on the tastebuds.

Lottie gifted me a few seconds of silence in memory of my husband before resuming conversation.

'So, enough about *me* letting go, what about *you*? Are you still going to send off Jack in a helium balloon?'

'Oh, yes,' I said. 'I've decided to do it on the fifteenth of next month. We got married on a fifteenth, you see. I'd love it if you could be there and I'm going to invite Len and Crystal, too. I want to make a party of it and have cake and sausage rolls. Jack liked sausage rolls. The only thing is, I haven't told the party people I'm going to put him inside the balloon. I'm hoping they won't mind. Do you think they'll mind? They did say they can put all sorts of things inside balloons and I've got a kitchen funnel that should do the trick.'

'I'm sure it can be done,' Lottie said.

'I hope so. In any case, there's one other thing I wanted to do before we started baking. Do you mind helping?'

'Of course not,' Lottie said.

'It's the lottery ticket. I want to burn it.'

I doubted burning a photocopy of the ticket would bestow much ash; it was the point of it which mattered. Much like the pairing symbolism of baked beans and eggs, I had decided the burning could be divided into two parts: one for me and one for Jack. For me, it was a symbolic burning of something I disapproved of and for Jack, it was so he could be sent off with his last and, as it turned out, most profitable lottery ticket ever. It would be a win–win for both of us.

'Do you think we should do it inside?' Lottie suggested. 'Ash might blow everywhere otherwise.'

We moved to the kitchen and I set up what we needed on the bench: the ticket, a bowl, a lighter, the urn and a funnel. I put the ticket in the bowl and set it alight. It took easily, rapidly. We watched the orange flame devour the paper until all that was left was a grey powder.

'So what now?' Lottie asked.

'I was going to put it with Jack.'

'Oh.' She didn't look enamoured about the idea. 'How do we do that?'

'Kitchen funnel,' I replied, holding it up.

'Okay. How do you open the urn?'

'It's a screw top.'

We stared at the urn. Perhaps we were both thinking the same thing: what would my husband look like? Millions of burnt lottery tickets or the bottom of a fireplace? Would he be light and fine or heavy and coarse? Even I was beginning to get cold feet.

'If we do it together, we can make it quick,' I said.

Lottie nodded but her face had gone the colour of the pumice I use to rid my feet of dead skin. Perhaps I had overstepped the mark by including her in this part of my ceremonial plans. Yet we were here now; it seemed too late to stop.

'How about this,' I said. 'If you unscrew the lid, I'll put the funnel in and then the ash. We don't have to see a thing.'

'Perhaps you should transfer the ash to a jug?' Lottie suggested. 'It would be easier to pour.'

'Good idea.' Finding a jug, I slid the funnel on top and tipped in the lottery ash. We stared at the jug. We stared at the funnel. I feared if I didn't do it then, it would never happen. 'Are you ready?'

Lottie nodded but looked nervous.

'Why don't you hold the urn and unscrew the lid, and I'll pour?' I said. 'We'll do it on the count of three . . .'

She was still nodding.

'Okay?'

'Okay.'

'All right . . .' I drew in a deep breath and began, 'One, two, three.'

My heart dashed out of the starting blocks like it hadn't galloped in a while and clamped in my throat. When we were done, I hurriedly screwed the lid back on and we high-fived each other over the top of Jack, buried beneath his winning ticket.

That night I slept the sleep of five hundred satiated Meals on Wheels recipients as thirty-six unburnt lemon cupcakes with pale-yellow icing rested in containers in my pantry.

Neighbourhood Watch

The local church hall where Sue was hosting the Neighbourhood Watch workshop was on the corner of Derby and Miller Streets – only a twenty-minute walk from my house. Despite having two Tupperware containers plus Jack, I decided to go by foot, having realised that my recent outdoor activities – primarily, walking to the shops – had been invigorating. My intention had been to drop the cupcakes at Sue's earlier in the day but when I called to see when she'd be in, she was in such a flap with last-minute arrangements that she was unable to give me a coherent answer. She suggested leaving them on the doorstep, which only highlighted her agitated state because she'd neither considered the public visibility of her doorstep for opportunistic cupcake stealing nor its lack of shade. It seemed easier to drop them off on the night. I arrived at the hall at ten minutes past seven, twenty minutes before the workshop was due to start. Sue was still in a fluster. She was firing off orders to three helpers as if in a verbal darts-throwing competition.

'Right, what's that table doing there? We need it here. Can someone move it? Yes, that's it, much better. Now can we fan the biscuits on the plate? They're more appealing like that. Same with the tea cosies. Fan. Don't pile. Okay, so, where's the Blu-Tack? Anybody? Anybody? Oh, it's okay, don't panic. I've got it!'

Not wishing to disturb Sue in the throes of organisational mayhem, I headed to the small kitchen out the back. One of the other women had found respite there, too, and was having a drink by the water cooler.

'I'm just dropping these off,' I told her.

'Cute,' she said. 'There are paper plates on the table for food. Sue had safety concerns about using china. I'm Salma, by the way.' She put out a hand for me to shake.

'Geraldine,' I replied and was about to take her hand when Sue walked in.

'Heavens, Geri, you're cutting it fine, aren't you?' Sue said. 'Anyway, it doesn't matter. Let's get them on the table.' She took a container off me. 'Don't they look adorable? Have you seen them, Salma? Geri is an excellent baker. Now, there are paper plates somewhere . . .'

'It's okay, Sue, I can do it,' I said, putting a hand on her arm, for she looked about to explode. 'I think you need a breather.'

'No time for breathers, Geri! People will be here any minute.'

'Can I help with anything?'

'That's very kind, Geri. I think we're under control but perhaps you could arrange the cupcakes for me? Your baking is now the icing on the cake.' She threw her head back and laughed. She was borderline hysterical.

'I hope we've made enough,' I said. 'By the number of chairs set up, it looks as if you're expecting half the neighbourhood.'

'Wouldn't that be wonderful.' She put a hand to her chest and looked skyward. 'Now, don't be offended, but I didn't want to be caught short, so I bought a few packets of biscuits as well.'

'Don't worry, it will be fine.'

'I do hope so, Geri, I really do.'

Finally, Sue left me alone to set up the cupcakes. For a bit of fun, I decided to arrange them into letters and spell out the beginnings of Neighbourhood Watch. Unfortunately, I only had enough cupcakes to create the first syllable which made it look as if I was cracking a horse joke. As I was working out if I could change it to 'lemon', Sue approached with her arm around a policeman.

'Geri, I'd like you to meet Rog.'

Rog smiled through a beard. His gentle demeanour and calming presence were a welcome antidote to Sue's jitters.

'Rog is going to inform us of the latest crime statistics and field any concerns or issues people may have, aren't you, Rog?'

He nodded.

'Geri lost her husband, Rog; it was very sad.'

'I'm sorry to hear that,' he said.

I shrugged and realised I felt less upset about Sue's public description of me to someone I didn't know than I once would have been.

'I was going to tell you, Geri, that I'm planning a workshop on loneliness and vulnerability. Because if you're lonely and lack social contact, you're more vulnerable to criminal activity. Isn't that right, Rog?'

'Not if you don't pick up the phone or answer the door.' I said it light-heartedly even though I was deadly serious. It had worked for me so it could work for others.

'It's not always that simple.'

'I've found acting invisible an excellent roadblock to interacting with strangers.'

'The thing is, Geri, more and more older people are living on their own, alone, these days. I mean, look at you . . .'

'I may be on my own, but I haven't *been* alone.' I felt the need to defend myself against Sue's insinuations.

'I know!' Sue's eyes lit up, exposing the electric blue eyeliner she'd taken a fancy to wearing. 'You could be a guest speaker. Couldn't she, Rog? You could talk from experience, give advice.'

'Like how to keep your husband in a suitcase?'

But Sue was so preoccupied with writing her idea on the back of her hand that she didn't catch my comment. 'Pardon?' she asked, looking up.

'I said like how to rearrange your bookcase. I've found that to be a great activity to ease the pain of loneliness.'

'I think you're missing the point, but that's okay. We can have a debrief beforehand. Ooh, look, we've got arrivals. Why don't you grab a seat?' And Sue was off, greeting people at the door as Rog slipped away in the opposite direction, finding a quiet spot behind the tea cosy table.

Returning to the cupcakes, I picked up ones at random and moved them around, so the letters morphed into an arrangement that was more modern art than alphabetical. Hoisting the bag with Jack further up my shoulder, I made my way to the back of the room. I was about to take a seat at the end of a row when I spotted Lottie walk in with another woman. She saw me, waved and weaved her way through the chairs towards me.

'I didn't think you'd be here,' she said.

'Neither did I.'

'This is my neighbour, Jenny. She saw me mail-dropping Sue's leaflets in our apartment block and thought I was one of the organisers. I had to tell her my only contribution was the cupcakes and even that's tenuous. Geraldine is teaching me how to bake, Jenny.'

'Food always tastes better when it's free, doesn't it?' I said, noting how I was getting better at small talk with people I didn't know. 'I wasn't planning on staying for the whole thing, to be honest, but now that you're here . . .'

Even though I had secretly suspected an evening of bingo would have been more fun, to Sue's credit, it was an informative hour and her pre-meeting nerves belied her public speaking ability. Rog managed to make a joke while delivering crime statistics, which wasn't an easy thing to do to a crowd who took the health and safety of its community very seriously.

When the talks were over, the room was abuzz with chatter and Jenny said she was keen to try one of our cupcakes.

'I've got some news you might be interested in,' Lottie said as we ambled towards the snack tables. 'You see, I've been reading those skydiving books, and you were right; they are inspiring. They even make it sound fun rather than scary.'

'Does this mean . . . ?' I raised my eyebrows.

'Yeah.' She nodded. 'I'm thinking of doing it after all. I guess, more than anything else, I want to feel alive again. I realise now that Josh had been stifling that. I've also decided to move out of the flat, sell the ring and buy something with the money I wouldn't normally buy myself. And I'll definitely adopt Oscar if he doesn't pass the test.'

'That's wonderful, Lottie.'

'Then I had another thought. Why don't I skydive on the same day that you send Jack off? It could be two "letting go"s at the same time.' She grinned, clearly thrilled with the notion.

I had to admit I liked the sound of the idea. It gave me a warm glow to think I had helped her and now she was helping me.

'We could take photos of each other to mark the occasion,' she added as if to convince me further.

'Do you mean I'll need to schedule a hair appointment sooner rather than later?' I laughed.

She laughed too, and instead of thinking of an excuse to leave, I decided to stay for a cup of tea. Although I didn't fancy being badgered again by Sue to be the subject matter of another meeting, I felt an unexpected burst of rejuvenation, like a dehydrated plant that had just been watered. What's more, I was proud of myself for mingling with people I didn't know. I patted Jack, snuggled at my waist, knowing he wouldn't say no to refreshments either.

It was at the hot water dispenser that I met Len and Crystal, who had only minutes ago walked in.

'Oh, hello, you two. It's just finished,' I said.

'I know.' Len nodded. 'We've come to talk to Sue. I've been thinking about what you said the other day. That maybe you're right, others need to know there are people like Gail out in the community.'

'You still haven't heard from her?'

He shook his head.

Crystal patted his arm. 'It's terrible, Geri, really terrible.'

'You must talk to Rog, Sue's policeman,' I said. 'He seems a very nice man and will take your story seriously. I'll introduce you to my friend Lottie, too. She was with me a minute ago . . .' I looked around for her and realised she had found Jenny, who was holding two cupcakes and talking to Rog. 'Come on, they're over there.'

Eating Tea Cosies

Back home, I couldn't get Lottie's idea out of my head. It became a niggle that wouldn't budge. Like trying to remember the name of the woman who won Best Supporting Actress for *Murder on the Orient Express* at the Oscars in 1975 in the weekend's newspaper quiz (it was Ingrid Bergman). I went to bed with it rolling around my subconscious, then woke with it still on my mind the next day, and the next. It wasn't merely that Lottie wanted to go skydiving or that she had suggested she do it on the day of Jack's balloon send-off, it was her desire to feel alive again. For I had been feeling more alive myself, even though it seemed ridiculous to think that turning up to a Monday night Neighbourhood Watch meeting could induce a sense of vitality. I had been experiencing similar vigour walking to the high street, chatting to the postman and waving to the Kaneshes from across the fence. It made me wonder what else I could do to feel more alive. How I could properly embrace Jack's desire for me to live life for the both of us.

Then I had an idea – an idea so absurd, it made me laugh. An idea so out of this world that it could be deemed exotic. A notion which a year ago would have been unthinkable but now seemed simply out-of-the-ordinary. It would be an adventure for both of us, like nothing we had ever done before. I had two weeks to make the plan, which was more than enough time, providing I didn't also have a change of heart. First, I did some background research – forewarned is forearmed, as Sue would say. Second, I went to the doctor. Third, I told Lottie. Fourth, I invited Len and Crystal, telling them only the time and date. Fifth, I made daily checks on the swan plants while waiting for the big day to come around.

One week after the Neighbourhood Watch meeting and five days before Jack's send-off, chrysalises had formed, dangling like lime dew drops piped with gold. The air was now a little cooler, the seasons on the turn. Overhead the sun, somewhere behind the clouds, lit up the corrugated iron sky as if trying to push away the rain. I walked around the garden, pulling up large weeds, sweeping away the soil Oscar had flung on to the path and imagined what it would look like completely cleared – a clean slate with which to begin again. The idea excited me more than it ever had. I could start with that, then move into the house, I thought. I'd do a clear-out and a proper spring clean – even get the sofa recovered. Fifty-one Richmond Road could come alive again, too, just like I was.

Soon enough, it was the fifteenth of the month.

I woke so early it was still dark. My stomach twisted itself into a French knot. I felt like I'd eaten one of Sue's tea cosies. I put on my dressing gown and danced with Jack down the hallway so I could make his final jig last as long as possible. I made us two cups of tea and went to sit in the back garden. Everything was serene and still, the only sounds two distant birds rubbing their eyes and stretching their wings. We sipped our teas as an orange sun slowly swallowed whole the remains of the night. It felt like the dawn of a new era, which sounds dramatic yet seemed apt. The me of yesterday was different to what the me of tonight would be, as the me of three months ago was different to the me today. It made me wonder what the me in a month's time would be like or the me in a year. So many possibilities, so many different mes. When we'd finished our tea, we returned to the kitchen. I had one more task to complete before the day could properly begin. It was something I never thought I would ever do. Decant my husband.

'Come on, Jackie-boy, it's time to dust you off and get you ready for your final adventure.'

I took the funnel, two zip-lock bags and a large bowl to the table where the urn was waiting.

'This is it, Jack,' I said, the enormity of the task threatening to overwhelm me. It made the lottery ticket ash dispensing seem like a cinch. Yet, even though I had Lottie to help me then, this time I wanted to do it alone. I wanted Jack all to myself. It would be the last time, after all. The last time he was physically present. The last time I would make two teas for one person. The last time I would cling to him and he to me. I had found peace. I was ready.

But only if I imagined him as a bottle of red wine – a Cabernet Sauvignon or Shiraz that needed degassing and aerating before it could be drunk. And so that's what I did. I imagined my husband as a bottle of wine. Tears pooled in both eyes as Jack spilled into the two bags like sugar into a bowl. I placed them into a small toiletry bag and that into a larger bag along with leather gloves and Jack's cable knit sweater. Once dressed in my elastic-waisted pants and a long-sleeved cotton top, I waited on the porch for my friends.

Len came up the path carrying a bottle of sparkling wine, blowing a party horn.

'Hey, Geri, we're ready to party!' He had a revived perma-tan, wore a short-sleeved, pale-blue shirt and looked cheerier than he had in weeks. Crystal followed in a figure-hugging dress, also blowing a party horn, each blow making her wobble on her kitten heels.

'Ooh, Geri, I feel a bit overdressed,' she said, giving me a hug.

'Never base the dress code on what Geri's wearing,' Len laughed, whistling the party horn again.

'If we based it on yours, Len, we'd look like we were going to a seventies Miami fancy dress party,' I joked. 'Anyway, there's no dress code for today. Whatever you feel comfortable in.'

'I don't see why you can't tell us where we're going or what we're doing. Giving Jack a send-off could mean anything.'

'It's a surprise,' I told him. 'You'll find out soon enough.'

'How are you feeling, Geri?' Crystal asked. 'Are you all right?'

'I'm great, Crystal, thanks.'

'Are you sure? You'll tell us, won't you, if it gets too much? And you can tell Len to tone it down, too. He's all hyped up like a kid on candy.'

'Hey, I'm in a good mood, Cryssie,' Len said. 'I want this to be a happy day. It should be a happy day, shouldn't it, Geri? Jack would want that.'

'That's right, Len. No sadness. Just joy.'

'So can you tell us where we're going?' He winked.

'Len!' Crystal elbowed him.

'All right, all right,' he muttered.

'Lottie will be here soon. She's going to drive us,' I said.

'Oh, yeah, Lottie. Nice girl.' Len nodded.

To stop Len pestering about our destination, I changed the subject and asked if he'd heard anything from Rog about Gail.

'Well, yes, but I was going to tell you after because today is about you, not me, isn't it?'

'Have they found Gail?'

'Unfortunately, no. But Rog reckons it's the classic con job. He suspects Gail quizzed her mother before she died about the men she once dated, then tracked me down, stalked me for a bit, decided I was the perfect candidate, and used the information she found on me in a way to make me believe we could be related. Like the Italian ancestry. Gail must have seen the Facebook post where I announced my Italian genes, then the silly meme I posted on spreadsheets. She mentioned her love of spreadsheets to us once. I told Rog, it's like my mind has been hacked. He said that's how people like Gail work. They find your vulnerable spots and manipulate you to build trust. They're narcissistic, too. Rog said Gail would have convinced herself that she deserves the money I gave her and she's more than likely working on other gullible mugs, changing her story to suit theirs.'

'Oh, Len,' I said.

'Yeah.' He nodded.

'But what if she actually is your daughter?'

'That's the thing, Geri. I went over the dates again and when she said she was born and the times Anne and I saw each other don't add up. I also questioned one of my mates who was in our group at the time and whose parents were friends with her parents. He remembers bumping into Anne a few times after she and I broke up but never seeing her pregnant or ever hearing it talked about. I think Gail added a year to her age to make out she could have been my daughter. Anyway, even if it is true, I don't want to know.' He blew the party horn again in an effort to boost his spirits. 'Rog is going to keep sleuthing to see if he can track her down. Getting my money back might be another story but I'd hate for someone else to fall for her lies.'

'Thank goodness for Rog,' I said.

'Sue is having a field day as you can imagine. I'm fodder for Neighbourhood Watch, that's for sure.'

'You'll be doing a good deed for the community.'

He blew the party horn again, a little less enthusiastically, and that was when I thought I should give him his present. I fished out the envelope from my handbag and handed it to him.

'What's this for?' he asked.

'Open it.' I smiled.

He frowned and unsealed the flap. A wad of notes fluttered in the breeze. 'Woah, Geri, I'm not taking your money.'

'It's not *my* money. It's Jack's.'

'It's a thousand dollars!'

'Put it towards your next holiday.'

'I can't take this.'

'Yes, you can. That's why I gave you cash not a cheque so you couldn't rip it up.'

He rolled his eyes and looked as if he was about to give the money back.

'Please,' I said, stopping him. 'It's a gift. It'll make up for what you lost to Gail.'

'But . . .'

At that moment, Lottie's car announced her arrival, spluttering exhaust phlegm around the corner. 'And here's Lottie!'

We jammed into her small car.

'So how long will it take?' Len asked.

'About an hour,' Lottie said.

'An hour? This better be good.'

'Enjoy the suspense, Len.' Crystal squeezed his shoulder.

Lottie glanced at me in the rear-view mirror and smiled.

Fifty-five minutes later, we arrived. When Len saw the sign, he swivelled to look at me in the back seat and said, 'Oh my god, Geri, have you gone mad?'

'Not all, Len,' I replied. 'It's all perfectly logical. I was going to send Jack away in a helium balloon. I nearly bought one, too, until I found out that if you let helium balloons go, they will burst and shatter shards of latex everywhere, which is terrible for the environment and unsuspecting animals who could eat them. Jack would have hated that. Then I got some books out from the library for Lottie on skydiving. You see, Jack had not only requested an exotic ash-scattering experience but told me not to stop living when he did. As you know, I tried the barely living thing, which wasn't much fun, so I thought, what better way to feel alive than by jumping out of a plane! And even better, Jack could come with me. It would be his final send-off.'

Len's eyes looked like they were going to spring out and whack me in the temple.

'And why are you keen on skydiving, Lottie?' Crystal asked, sounding perplexed as to why anyone would trade designer sunglasses for wind-proof goggles.

'I'm getting over a break-up,' Lottie replied. 'It's meant to be symbolic. A way to move on from my old life and into a new one. I figured, if I can jump out of a plane, I can do anything.'

'I see,' Crystal said, although I don't think she did. 'But, Geri, aren't there other symbolic acts you could do – like turning Jack's old ties into a skirt? You could wear him against your thighs and think fondly of him instead of risking your life like this.'

'Actually,' Lottie added, 'it was Geri's desire to do it that made *me* want to do it even more. I thought, if she can leap from a plane, then so can I!'

'I also promised Lottie I wouldn't wear lip gloss, given the potential splashback of ash against our air velocity.'

I smiled but Len and Crystal looked horrified at the thought, which was probably fair enough as I'd had longer to get used to the idea than they had. Crystal frowned and bit her nails.

'There's little nutritional value in red nail polish,' I said, gently taking her hand away from her mouth. 'Save yourself for the special fruit cake I've got to celebrate the occasion.'

'Right. So. A skydive.' Len was still mulling it over. 'I suppose I *can* see how it would appeal to Jack's sense of adventure . . .'

'It does. And don't worry, I've checked it out. I'm fully informed. The instructors have made thousands of skydives and I'm not the oldest person to have ever done one. A one-hundred-and-two-year-old jumped last year. Plus, I've got extra layers to keep me warm, I'll be wearing a helmet and my doctor has given me the all-clear.'

Letting Go

The last time Jack and I had been in a small plane was when we treated ourselves to a seaplane flight over the city and up the coast for lunch at an exclusive restaurant for our fortieth wedding anniversary. We could have gone to our favourite Thai restaurant up the road, but the view left a lot to be desired. Looking out over rubbish bins in a car park didn't matter so much when it was winter, but on a spring evening it was better if you sat with your back to the window.

We held hands the whole flight, though, didn't we, Jack? We couldn't have done that at the Thai restaurant when we'd have been interrupted by the necessities of eating. His hand cupped mine. Mine cupped his. He squeezed. I squeezed. And we flew like a bird.

That's what I was thinking when Lottie and I climbed into a plane so small and toy-like that Sue would have questioned its safety. One side was a roll-up canvas door and there were no seats. I glanced at Lottie.

'Are you all right?' she asked.

'Yes. You?'

She nodded. 'Very soon, we're going to be new people.'

I reached over and squeezed her hand – something I could never have imagined doing a few months ago – and noted the same gratifying feeling I used to get from patting Jack when he was in the suitcase. I pressed the silver shell that was in my left trouser pocket against my leg. It was my new good luck charm. Then I touched my husband, who was, for now, safely nestled in my skydiving jumpsuit pocket until it was time to hand him over to my tandem instructor, Dan, who was going to look after the bags until the parachute was deployed. I felt acutely aware of every sensation in my body. My pulse was pounding, respiration pumping, temperature rising. I was not just one heart trying to stay alive; I was twenty hearts truly living. I could have offered to power up the plane had it been electric. As we took off, engine noise drowned out conversation and the view swallowed our attention. Fields became quilts, the ocean an enormous ink blot. Soon we were so high, perspective became skewed and details lost. The outside world, which I was once so fearful of, resembled a mere movie-set backdrop. I now had forty hearts powering my body and one had popped into my throat. Did Lottie feel like this, too?

At fourteen thousand feet, the plane plateaued and circled. Lottie's instructor unclipped the canvas wall. Cold air whooshed in as if we'd been unplugged.

'All right?' Dan asked, his mouth close to my ear.

I nodded.

'It's time for the bags.'

I drew in a deep breath and unzipped the pocket. Out came Jack, two bags leaden with the weight of my husband.

'Sorry, his last meal tipped the scales,' I tried to joke.

But the thought of his last meal, which wasn't a meal at all but a few sips of liquid to help with dehydration, made me gasp. I pushed the memory out of the plane and told myself to think only of the good things. Of the celebratory baked-bean lunch I shared with Lottie. The deliciously warm feeling I got from gifting Len some of the lottery win and paying for Lottie's skydive. The jubilation I felt donating money to the library, Neighbourhood Watch and Meals on Wheels. Of my friends on the ground who had stuck by me when I was suffering from every form of CGD – from Crotchety Geriatric Disorder to Common Garden-variety Disinterest. Of all the years I was married to Jack and how wonderful every second of it had been. How letting Jack go was about to set me free.

Then it was time. Our instructors clipped themselves to us. Lottie's life became Greg's; my life became Dan's. *This is it, Jack, this is nearly it.* Lottie and Greg sidled to the opening. Lottie gave me a thumbs up. One minute they were perched on the edge of the plane and seconds later, they were gone – an eight-legged beetle sucked into the atmosphere, limbs curling, a scream carried away on the slipstream.

Dan and I inched towards the opening. The canvas flapped. The air tugged. The earth waved at me from very far away. My bottom teetered, legs tucked; I was virtually in the lap of a young man I had only just met. Did I think this was how the start of my new life would begin? Not on your life. Not on Jack's life either. I laughed so hard I thought I might swallow the earth whole. Until a knee nudged my backside and we were out, too. The rush was dizzying, gravity exhilarating, the noise deafening. Oh, the release, the unburdening of the last seven months, the weeks freefalling away. Sixty seconds was all it took. Crazy Geri's Duty was almost complete. Arms out. Arms in. Parachute up. Whoosh. Pop. Legs swinging.

The calm.

The quiet.

The drifting.

The land below stretched far and wide like an elastic scene distended and taut. I was in the sky, of the sky, dangling precariously. There seemed to be no smell, no sound, no taste; just the sight of it all, bigger than I could ever have imagined, curved like a giant teapot in differing shades of green and brown. I dared to look down. There was Lottie, floating like a leaf. She saw me and waved. There was a cloud. I was above the cloud. I was beside the cloud. I reached out to touch the cloud, but it was as if it didn't exist. There were my feet, suspended, free. There was the parachute, a translucent rainbow keeping us afloat. I felt the morning fill my lungs and I had to smile to let it out. *We're doing it, Jackie-boy, we're skydiving.* Dan gently tugged the cord to change direction, right then left. Whoopee!

I was about to start humming to the tune of 'Top of the World' by the Carpenters when Dan tapped my shoulder and patted his pocket. *Here we go, Jack, are you ready?* I was ready. I had never felt more ready. I focused only on the handover, one bag at a time, slowly, measuredly. Then the careful unzipping. The breathing in, the breathing out. The tipping up of one bag, then the other. Both eyes welling. Tears streaming. My husband was flying, falling, dusting the earth like rainbow sprinkles on fairy cakes. Jack's final wish was complete. My new life had begun. I floated down in a glorious cloud of ash.

Later that day, when the celebrations were over and I felt as cooked as a burnt chop, I took out Jack's passport and turned to the very last page. His final trip had to be stamped. In the Butterfly Room I picked up a black pen and thought for a moment, before I slowly and carefully drew a picture of two stick figures dangling from a parachute. To finish it off, I added a sprinkling of little dots around them to resemble the faint freckles on my beloved husband's face.

Goodbye, Jack.

ACKNOWLEDGMENTS

A huge and heartfelt thanks to all the people who have helped make this book come alive: my wonderful agent, Ariella Feiner, and the team at United Agents; Sammia Hamer and the crew at Lake Union Publishing; editor Arzu Tahsin, copyeditor Gillian Holmes and proofreader Becca Allen. Plus, a shout-out to my family, Will, Hannah and Amy, who inspire me, encourage me and whom I could not live without.

ABOUT THE AUTHOR

Jane Riley began her career in public relations before moving into publishing and later launching an e-commerce business. She has freelanced as a writer and editor and wrote a design blog interviewing makers and creators. She volunteers as an English language tutor for the Adult Migrant English Program in Sydney. *Geraldine Verne's Red Suitcase* is her second novel.

You can find her on Twitter @JaneRileyAuthor.

Did you enjoy this book and would you like to be informed when Jane Riley publishes her next work? Just follow the author on Amazon!

1) Search for the book you were just reading on Amazon or in the Amazon App.

2) Go to the Author Page by clicking on the author's name.

3) Click the 'Follow' button.

If you enjoyed this book on a Kindle eReader or in the Kindle App, you will be automatically offered to follow the author when arriving at the last page.

LAKE UNION
PUBLISHING